MW00475063

THE DEVIL'S COURTHOUSE

Lawrence Thackston

PublishAmerica
Baltimore

© 2010 by Lawrence Thackston.
All rights reserved. No part of this book may be reproduced, stored in a retrieval system or transmitted in any form or by any means without the prior written permission of the publishers, except by a reviewer who may quote brief passages in a review to be printed in a newspaper, magazine or journal.

First printing

All characters in this book are fictitious, and any resemblance to real persons, living or dead, is coincidental.

PublishAmerica has allowed this work to remain exactly as the author intended, verbatim, without editorial input.

Hardcover 978-1-4512-1137-5
Softcover 978-1-4489-4783-6
PUBLISHED BY PUBLISHAMERICA, LLLP
www.publishamerica.com
Baltimore

Printed in the United States of America

For My Father

"…he taught me everything about these mountains…
the Cherokees and their legends…how to camp…climb….
He taught me…everything."

Mitchell County Weekly

The Voice of the Mountains

Today Cloud,   mid 70's   Ten Cents

----------------------------------- August 17th, 1953 -----------------------------------

LOCAL FARMER PUZZLED OVER SLAYING OF HORSES

Roan -- A ghastly scene was discovered at the homestead of Art and Iris Stone when six of the Stones' beautiful quarter horses were found mutilated last Friday morning.

According to Sheriff McClane's office, Art made the horrific discovery on his property off the Roan Mountain Road as he was making the morning feed rounds for his animals.

He had just retrieved the oats from his storage bin when he opened the barn and became sickened by the smell of the ravaged animals.

An immediate call to the Sheriff's office was made by Mrs. Iris Stone and deputies Wilkes and Zeigler were dispatched to the scene.

"I ain't never seen nothing like it," Zeigler said "It took me and Deputy Wilkes three hours just to clean the blood up from the floor and the walls It was everywhere."

No leads were immediately forthcoming in the case "We can't think of anyone who v

Mitchell County Weekly

The Voice of the Mountains

Today Sunny, High in 70's

··August 31st, 1953··

Ten Cents

TWN OFFICIALS AT A LOST TO EXPLAIN MUTILAED ANIMALS

Spruce Pine - Sheriff Red McClane and Ricky Daniels of the Carolina Agriculture Commission held a joint news conference this past Wednesday after the latest attacks on area domesticated animals had been discovered

After last weeks attack on the horses at the farm of Art and Ins Stone, two more copycat style killings were announced in the Kneesock Branch Community near Roan

"It's shocking just shocking," Sheriff McClane said "I can't for the life of me understand why someone would destroy defenseless animals in such a heinous way"

Horses, mules, cows even a dog belonging to the Kitchings family have been senselessly killed by someone or some people, the sheriff said.

Asked to speculate on the reasons behind the killings, the sheriff said "There have been all kinds of theories, from devil worshipers to who knows w

Ricky Daniels confirmed the highly aggravated nature of the attacks and suggested that all area farmers resort to round the clock watches of their property

"If I were a farmer here and had invested much in my li would make,

Mitchell County Weekly

The Voice of the Mountains

Today Cloudy. Colder Upper 60's   Ten Cents

·· September 15th, 1953 ·······································

MORE ANIMALS KILLED, SHERIFF VOWS TO CATCH 'MADMAN'

Spruce Pine – Sheriff Red McClane announced today that his department was stepping up their patrols in order to catch the person responsible for the series of attacks on local livestock.

"We believe this is one person acting alone," the sheriff said as he was leaving the Swaine Thomas Courthouse this past Tuesday evening. "And I promise will have him stopped before too long."

Asked to elaborate on the reasons why he felt it was a singular suspect, the sheriff declined further comment.

The series of brutalized attacks on domestic livestock has continued past the area's new livestock. Hogs and cattle seem to be favored by the perpetrator who has dispatched the animals in what the sheriff's office calls a "bizarre and twisted" manner.

The three week old case has been an unusual burden on the Roan Mountain Authority Sheriff's Department, stretched the of the in in all.

Mitchell County Weekly

The Voice of the Mountains

Today Sunny, Low in the 30's

-------------------- September 22nd, 1953 --------------------

Ten Cents

PLATT GIRL STILL MISSING, PARENTS FEAR THE WORST

Bakersville – For seventy-tw[...] youngest [...] Chester [...] Platt, E[...] has been [...] her home. [...] seen by her [...] Amos, 13, s[...] the two had re[...] home from Atwil[...] Middle School this past Tuesday

According to her brother, she was heading out to the barn to check on the family's cows around 4 15 and never [...]d

"She said she was going to check on the [...]hat's [...]ely," [...]idn't [...]way I [...]uch

[...]tt, an [...] for Tri-County Electric and Gas, returned home from work around 5 30 and immediately investigated He said he checked the barn and the property but could n[...] find her

After several hours of searching the [...] community w[...] help from the neighbors, a call was made to the sheriff's office

Local authorities found no trace of the young girl, but a disturbing piec[...] of evidence w[...]

Mitchell County W...

The Voice of the ...

Today Cloudy, High 50's

Septem...

Ten Cents

ROAN BUTCHER STRIKES AGAIN,
THREE FOUND SLAIN

Roan - Three family members were found murdered in their Roan Mountain home this past Wednesday The name of the family is being withheld due to the sensitive nature of the case, a spokesperson from Sheriff McClane's office said.

Sheriff McClane joined by North Carolina Law Enforcement Division detectives announced Thursday that they believe the killings are directly tied into the recent events that have haunted this community for the past several weeks.

"We have reason to believe that this is the work of the so-called Roan Mountain Butcher Evidence at the crime scene indicates that it is the same individual who has been attacking our livestock and perhaps the same one responsible for the missing Platt girl."

"This was perhaps th' worse crime scene I ...e ever seen in my ...three ...ars of

Mitchell County Weekly

The Voice of the Mountains

Today Cloudy, Colder Upper 40's

Ten Cents

--October 13th, 1953--

KILLER COMMITS SUICIDE, NIGHTMARE OVER

Roan - Our community can breathe easier now that the suspected killer also known as the Roan Mountain Butcher has been found dead of an apparent suicide

Authorities with the Sheriff's Department have confirmed that local resident John M Earley who is suspected to have committed several atrocious crimes over the past two months took his life this past Sunday at his residence off R Mou

An obviously relieved Sheriff Red McClane lead off with the announcement Monday at what has become his weekly press conference over recent events Having gained national attention with the bizarre case, McClane was ecstatic to put it behind him "All I can say at this time is that this has been pure hell for our little community these past few months, and I am just happy that

Edwin Whurter of the North Carolina Law Enforcement Division who has been spearheading the case in conjunction with the local sheriff's office addressed the possible reasons for the suspect's behavior "We're not sure of everything but apparent'

MAY 18, 1974

The blue-winged olive drifted across a turbulent stretch of the Oconaluftee River and came to rest in a quiet pool between two towering, cone-shaped rocks. Giant spruce pines and dew-soaked balsam firs on the far bank of the Great Smoky Mountain's central waterway were blocking the morning sun—the resulting shadows and silver mist created a dark tinge to the surface—perfect cover for spawning trout.

Self-appointed *king of the knee-deep*, Rayford Parker, had worked his fly into the coveted spot with ease. A westerly breeze, a southward flow and tactical experience were all working in the angler's favor.

At six feet four inches and two hundred and ninety pounds, the veteran fly fisher had, by default, earned the right to his nickname *Big Ray*—his hefty size being outweighed only by his ego as fisherman. To Rayford, fishing the Oconaluftee was a given—an almost certainty. He knew this river; he knew trout, and he damn well knew how to bring in his prey.

He wasted precious little time in nabbing the first catch. A bow of the rod here, a jig there, a quick pull on the backing and… *Gotcha*! Big Ray smiled to himself. It was a two-pounder. *Maybe two and a half*. He reeled in the slick rainbow and quickly unlipped him from the fly. He tossed his catch into the side-pouch of his snug hip waders.

"Now stay in thar while I gits another," he said aloud in his thick, eastern Tennessean drawl.

Rayford wrapped the wet line around his meaty fingers to brace for the next strike. He balanced the fly rod and reached with his free hand into the left pocket of his checkered flannel shirt digging out two pulls of Beechnut. He threw the chaw into his mouth and refocused on his footing. He knew trout fishing could be dicey at times and reminded himself to be patient. *Give 'em line… give 'em time*, he hummed over and over.

As it turned out not much patience was needed as he hooked three more of the colorful beauties, each one heavier than the last, in only twenty minutes. It was looking to be a banner day for the proud fisherman. Nothing was going to stop Big Ray now.

But on his very next casting attempt, Rayford did exactly that—he came to a complete stop. Something had stirred in the woods behind him breaking his concentration. It was a distinctive *rustling* sound. The kind of noise an animal makes as it moves through the brush or tall grass. At first, he ignored this as he was accustomed to the sudden and variant noises of the wilderness; however, when it quickly followed again, he turned and stole a glance at the embankment. Only the riverbank's jagged rocks and green-leaved rhododendron bushes stared back at him in return.

Crow takin' wing or a young buck on the move is all, the ace fisherman reasoned. And with a shrug and a quick spat, Rayford turned his attention back to his pattern bobbing against the current. He was satisfied—content to be fishing the *Luftee*—alone in the great outdoors.

But he was not alone.

Behind a clove of laurels on the river's edge, the *Judaculla* remained hidden from the fisherman's view. It had been watching Rayford from the moment he had emerged at the trail's head and descended into the river. And like all great predators, it had studied its target in an ominous silence. The Judaculla had gone quiet, motionless, invisible—daring not to blink or breathe. It had calculated its prey's weaknesses, noting all of the man's limitations—his sizable girth, his slow, deliberate movements, even his staccato breathing patterns. And through it all, it had remained patient. *Watching. Waiting.*

But then the moment came. A slow burn had been building inside the monster, and it now neared the critical point. Adrenaline was released into its bloodstream and was pumped throughout its giant body. Its pupils became dilated—a sudden wildness had enveloped its slanted eyes. It wanted to kill and kill quickly.

The Judaculla left its vantage point and using its clawed hands crawled serpent-like toward the river—ever mindful of its target. It had made its lone mistake as it tried to navigate through the twisting underbrush of the mountain laurel accidentally rattling the plant's thick leaves. But fortunately the fat man had paid no heed.

As it now inched closer, it felt the old hunger rising faster from deep within. Its heart began to quicken and excited beads of sweat formed on its forehead. The poisoned blood *swished* in its ears—drum beats leading its murderous procession. All the muscles of its body began to twitch in fiery anticipation—the kill, now, well within its grasp.

Rayford Parker turned upon hearing the water break behind him half-expecting to see that buck innocently stepping into the river for a drink. His mouth gaped open. Tobacco tumbled from his puffed cheeks and fell aimlessly into the moving water below. He felt his chest go tight as his pulse raced to dangerous levels.

"Jez-us!"

Rayford tumbled backward into the river unconcerned with the flashes of icy water breaching his waders and stinging at his corpulent skin. His trembling hands unwittingly dispatched his prized fly rod to the churns of the Oconaluftee.

"Y-y-you just stay away from me, ya hear?" Stay away from me, goddammit!" In an instant, fear had swallowed Rayford whole. He felt trapped as if in some bizarre nightmare. *This can't be happenin'. This ain't real…*

Rayford continued to back deeper into the river's flow. There was no doubt to the Judaculla's intentions. Its menacing glare had said it all. The big man leaned over and instinctively splashed at the water with his hands in an attempt to confuse it or slow it down.

It did not.

Judaculla kept even with its target, moving back and forth on the water's edge, mirroring his every move, getting closer.

Rayford suddenly lunged forward and took off running up river, but he quickly became ensnared by the forceful, rushing waters. His movements so precise and exact only moments before were now clownish and pitiful as he floundered to escape. He was finished—as helpless as the suffocating trout on his hip.

"Phil! Glenn!" he screamed in desperation to the wilderness.

He jerked his head up the river looking for last-minute help, but none would be forthcoming.

Exhausted, Big Ray finally turned and sank to his knees in the frigid water—the Judaculla moving in from behind for the kill. Rayford cowered like a child submitting to the will of his attacker. He felt his world slipping away. His once strong voice went breathless, soft, pathetic, "Please… Please don't do this…"

The Judaculla paused, hovering over Rayford in stony silence. For a moment only the tranquil sound of the moving waters of the Oconaluftee could be heard. Then like a sudden storm, the eyes of the beast rolled to white and with a high-pitched, *animalistic cry*, it viciously lashed out at Rayford's throat.

11:43 AM

The horror had passed—the deed was done, but the dying man's screams were still there—ringing in his ears—continuing to torment—reaching deep into his troubled soul.

Cole Whitman sat on the ground—his knees pulled in toward his chest. He had wrapped his arms around his legs and had his head hanging in between. Blurred images of blood and death came to him again and again. He fought it. Denied it. But in the end, he was helpless against it. His breathing had become labored like a man in the last throes of death. He had lost all emotional stability—sobbing uncontrollably.

Make it stop. I beg you. Please, God…make this go away. Stop this now.

His prayers went unanswered and he continued to suffer—an endless stream at this point. His tortured body was reaching its limit—his mind, its fragile breaking point. He had become a shuddering mass of twisted emotion and pain.

He now gripped even tighter around his legs, holding on for dear life. He knew this was his penitence—his cross to bear—yet he could not take much more.

But then, as he neared a point of no return, there was a sudden and unexpected reprieve. Somehow the sickness released its grip on Cole, and the inward storm began to subside. What he had come to understand as the *phasing episode* of his condition had finally begun to reverse itself.

Cole fell to his side and hacked the repressed air and spittle from his lungs. He rolled to his knees, arched his back and continued to cough as if having narrowly escaped a watery grave. Within a few minutes, he was able to process again—able to contain the eruptional forces in his mind.

And after a final few grueling bouts, the physical pain also began to wane away. He was coming around—gaining control.

Cole raised his head just a little. He rubbed his aching forehead and wiped the tears and mucus from about his face. He had begun to breathe normally again. It had been an especially excruciating one, but he was going to be okay. The last of the screams were now quickly fading into memory.

He got up and brushed the dirt and grit from his khaki uniform. He may have gotten up too quickly as he immediately became light-headed and had to swallow a sudden wave of nausea.

He managed to steady himself and then took a quick glance down at his watch. All sense of time and place had been lost on him. He could not remember where he had been or what he had done, but somehow, someway, he had made it to here.

But where exactly is here?

Cole did a quick scan of his surroundings. He saw that he was alone in an alcove of thin fir trees and sensed the cool air about him. *A ridge summit,* he logically reasoned. *Some high elevation...somewhere.*

He broke through to a clearing and scrambled across a flattened expanse of rock face—slick and grey-faced granite gneiss. The rocky slope extended several yards out in front of him and then opened up to a blue skyline.

He stood tall, looked to the horizon and got his bearings. Recognition came quickly. He was atop the Devil's Courthouse, one of the Balsam ridges near the Blue Ridge Parkway and only several miles from where he was stationed in the Great Smoky Mountain National Park.

Cole then hiked his way over to the observation platform which overlooked the unique multi-tiered precipice of the ridge. From this vantage point, it appeared the Courthouse's layered crest stuck out from the mountain like five, open-palmed hands—each one jutting out just a little further than the last.

The stone-lined viewing deck on the top tier was surprisingly empty of people, especially for this time of year. Cole knew that the Devil's Courthouse was a popular stop for the thousands of tourists who traveled the looping parkway through these Smoky Mountains of western North Carolina. With its steep but short climb, the Courthouse was easily accessible and provided excellent views of the rolling Pisgah forests below and the blue hills in the distance. But thankfully, for the moment, there was no one around to observe him now.

Cole eased out onto the edge and soaked in the gentle breezes allowing it to cool his still flushed skin. Standing there, leaning against the stone wall, he marveled at the dangerous, twelve hundred foot drop that befell the last ridge. The grey crags of the rocky bottom below shot up through the low-lying clouds like sharpened dragon teeth. Cole peered long and deep into its waiting abyss. He then closed his eyes and felt the lingering pangs of his nightmare.

For a moment, the lure of the dragon's jaws tempted him. But then almost immediately his eyes popped back opened—this time with staid conviction. *No...this will not end you. You're going to be alright. You're going to get over this.*

Cole began to make the covering transition as he had many times before. He methodically stretched his arms outward and rolled his neck as he continued to readjust. He looked down at his right hand and noticed blood dripping from open sores on his knuckles and a deep cut that drew a line from his inner wrist to his thumb. He licked the fingers of his left hand and tried to wipe some of the still oozing blood away. The tougher, coagulated spots he just tried rubbing deeper into his skin.

He dug a red bandanna out of his pants pocket and wrapped it around the wounds. It didn't immediately stop the bleeding of the sores, but it hid the damage well—a talent for which he had become quite skilled as of late.

He knew he had to refocus; he had to forget about this latest occurrence and move on. For some reason, the episodes were coming quicker now. But he dared not seek help for it. No one could know. *Ever*. He would do as he has always done: bury it deep within him. It was the only way. He quickly thought up an excuse—busting his hand while moving a fallen tree from across a secondary road in the park. That would work. That would fool them.

It always did.

3:33 PM

Cole raced around the curves of Big Cove Road. He was feeling much better now and he was enjoying taking his jeep hard into the twists and turns of the little mountain artery that ran from the parkway through the neighboring Qualla Boundary—the large proprietary lands of the Eastern Band of the Cherokee. The wind blew through his thick hair tussling it all about. The air was cool and brisk and felt familiarly comforting to Cole. He was relaxed. *Almost human again.*

He veered off Big Cove steering the jeep through a series of connected dirt roads. As the head of law enforcement at the Oconaluftee Station in the Great Smoky Mountain National Park, Cole could have used the modified Dodge Monaco cruiser driven by most park police, but he preferred this old '61 army-surplus Jeep CJ-3B. Years ago, it had been secured by the park as part of a government trade-off, and Cole had taken an immediate likening to it. He had the boys over in the maintenance division muscle up the engine a bit, slap it with a coat of the park's lime green paint and stick a blue bubblegum light on the back. Everyone joked that it was as ugly as sin, but it became a part of the official fleet and in a funny way—a bit of a park mascot.

Cole flew past Manny's General Store on the outskirts of the Qualla Tract signaling that he would be in downtown Cherokee in less than five minutes. The Qualla Tract was the communal section of the Cherokee reservation where the majority of the *Tsa-la-gi* actually lived. Its impoverished neighborhoods and rundown trailer camps were a far cry from what the tourists would see when they ventured onto the main drag of the city.

Despite its internal problems, Cole always felt at home there in the Cherokee's community. Even though his work as a ranger kept him busy in the nearby park, he could often be found in the Boundary working with local officials or visiting his close friend, Eddie Whitetree. At six-two Cole was taller than most Cherokee, but with his dark eyes, black hair and olive skin, it was not surprising that he was often mistaken as one of their own.

As he neared the town, Cole passed a few of the exploitive trappings the Cherokee used to lure the tourists on their way through the mountains. He drove past the Tomahawk Gift Shop with its buck-toothed caricature of a smiling Indian on the front door and then the Red Injun' Motel and its connected Bow and Arrow Restaurant where *the whole family tribe* was welcomed to *dine and recline.* Cole shook his head. Although he had gone through Cherokee thousands of times, it never failed to get to him. He saw it, wrongly or rightly, as a commercial raping of the Cherokee culture—a cheap sell-out. By nature it just seemed wrong, and it always pissed him off at how such a proud people had seemingly prostituted themselves for the almighty dollar. For a few bucks sightseers could have their picture taken with a *real redskin chieftain* and their children could crawl about a set of *authentic* plastic teepees as grandma panned for gold in the *lost mine* of the Cherokee. In Cole's mind it was a bit reactionary to the civil rights progress that the tribe, and in turn all Native Americans, had recently made. But his friend Eddie saw things differently always pointing out that the Boundary would not endure without their obvious pandering to white society and the lucrative tourist trade. And that in itself was a convincing argument. Besides if they were only pretending to be something they weren't in order to survive, then who the hell was *he* to argue with that?

Cole slowed as he entered the city limits. The summer tourist traffic was already heating up clogging the streets with vacationing rubber necks. He noted license plates from all over—Delaware, Ohio, Michigan. A tour bus from Charleston, West Virginia suddenly stopped in the middle of downtown letting its sightseers disembark near the museum.

Chief Thunder Eagle must be doing his thing, Cole figured.

As Cole wheeled the jeep down Tsali Boulevard, he could see that he had guessed correctly. An elaborate, outdoor stage had been erected in front of the Cherokee Museum of Natural History, and a small crowd was forming to watch Chief Thunder Eagle's show. Cole parked in the museum's lot and made his way over.

A Cherokee woman in a stark white tunic and calf-high moccasin boots was already seated center-stage; her legs were crossed with a double-sided elk skin drum braced between her bare knees and a makeshift tip jar within her reach. The tourists formed a crescent shape in front of her as she made single rhythmical strikes upon the drum—the yellow and turquoise beads in her long, jet-black hair rattled with each successive beat. To her left, a thin, elderly Cherokee dressed in his official curator's jacket stood very still in front of the museum's door awaiting his cue.

Cole noted the sightseers anticipating Thunder Eagle's arrival were a mixed bag of the usual suspects—those whom the locals had come to divide into four groups: *hawkers, gawkers, blue hairs* and *lollipops*. Hawkers were considered less obtrusive by the Cherokee than their gawker counterparts, and blue hairs and lollipops were just simple generational monikers. All were welcomed, of course, but there was still a quasi-love-hate relationship that existed between the locals and their guests.

Cole slowly ambled to the back of the pack. He was feeling more like himself again, but he still did not wish to draw any unwarranted attention.

As the drum beats grew faster, Cole focused in on Kina, the seated Cherokee woman. She was a striking woman with a round face, round eyes and soft, golden skin.

Cole watched her intently as she moved her body in rhythm to the beat. The sudden flashes of her skin and the casting of her long hair were beginning to work on him. Cole always did have a thing for Kina and had, over the years, a hard time not thinking about her *in that way*. He often imagined he might have ended up with her if not for certain *mitigating* circumstances.

With one last belt on the drum and a sudden shout from Kina, Chief Thunder Eagle made his swooping entrance amid small red flashes and a blast of smoke. "And now, ladies and gentlemen, the town of Cherokee and its Museum of Natural History proudly presents Chief Thunder Eagle and his deadly dance of the viper..." the old man barked into a bullhorn like a well-versed carnie.

As the smoke cleared, the spellbound tourists stared at Thunder Eagle who was already whirling about in his heavy ceremonial dress—a combination of bear claws, buck skins and an enormous eagle feather war bonnet. From the back of the headdress—his hair, also long and black like Kina's, was flowing with every cadence. He ghost-dipped and twirled with kinetic precision; the reds, blues and golds of his costume seemed to blend, hypnotically enthralling the on-lookers. His dance invoked the serious nature of an ancient religious ceremony—what the Cherokees called Ah-ni-ku-ta-ni—but with a little Hollywood flair thrown in to ensure a captive audience.

For her part, Kina continued supplying beats of her drum for Thunder Eagle's in-time steps, but her focus was less on the chief and more on the little Cherokee boy who was playing with toy trucks on the sidewalk just a few yards away. Cole caught her vision angle and zeroed in on Jonathon. He was amused by the boy's apparent lack of interest in his parents' occupation. *Welcome to showbiz, Jon-Jon.*

Cole refocused on the crowd when he felt them back up on their heels. Chief Thunder Eagle had pulled an angry eastern diamondback rattlesnake from a burlap sack, which had been conveniently hidden behind Kina, and was now holding its head precariously close to his face. The crowd appropriately *oohed* and *aahed* with each startled movement and feigned loose grip. The arm-thick snake wrapped itself around Thunder Eagle's bicep, its twelve-bullet rattle singing out.

Thunder Eagle danced with the writhing snake for several more minutes and then suddenly fell to one knee. Horrified gasps erupted throughout the crowd as the chief placed the snake's head within an inch of his opened mouth. Kina timed the last beat perfectly; and with a final series of maniacal *yelps* from Thunder Eagle, another blinding flash and puff of smoke sent the crowd retreating. Applause followed as they saw the chief appearing unscathed with only the snake's still vibrating rattles dangling from his lips. Cole found himself clapping along as well impressed with his old friend's showmanship.

As the spectators began to disperse, a little, blond-haired boy wearing a Miami Dolphins jersey with *Czonka* tattooed across the back became the center of attention as Thunder Eagle made him the benefactor of the snake's beads and button. His wide-eyed reaction seemed to delight the dance-weary chief.

"Don't forget to visit the museum while you're here, folks. Relive the history of the Ani-Yun-Wiya, the Great Spirit's principal people," the old curator said as he harkened after the crowd. "From the early clans to the Trail of Tears, come hear the legends of the Smoky Mountain Cherokees."

A few declined but most of those gathered followed the old man inside the museum. Cole remained in the back watching Thunder Eagle's interaction with a remaining tourist—a frail, aged woman with cat-eyed glasses who had sought out the chief's attention.

"Excuse me, Chief, but I was just wonderin'," the elderly tourist began. She hesitated for a moment and then asked, "You do speak English, don't you? *En-glish?*" Thunder Eagle twisted his brow as if momentarily confused but then confirmed with a solid nod. She smiled. "Good. Well, I wanted to know…how did the snake…?" She hesitated again and then continued in a stunted yet much more comprehensible speech for the *illiterate savage*, "How—you—make—snake—vanish? Oh, you know…*vavoom*?" She finished with a looping twist of her hand in the air.

As Thunder Eagle pondered the question, Cole caught sight of Kina who just shook her head and rolled her eyes. "Ahhh…" Thunder Eagle finally answered. "Ancient trick of shaman—Cherokee medicine man. Handed down—to Thunder Eagle—many moons have passed. No can tell secret—to outsider."

The old woman dug deep into her pocketbook and finally pulled out a dime. "Well, I guess I can understand that. And here then…this is for you." As she passed him the coin, she gave his hand a condescending little pat. "I really enjoyed your dancing, Chief. Thank you so much. Thank—you."

This time the stoic chief gave a profound nod and then watched her walk toward the museum. Kina stole the opportunity and quickly saddled in behind him. "The snake may have the forked tongue, but only Thunder Eagle knows how to *flick it*."

With his back to Kina, he held the dime up so she could see it. "And that's why I get the big bucks, sweetheart."

She smiled, leaned in and quickly passed the coin to the tip jar before giving him a hug around his big shoulders. "Every little bit helps."

He turned and gave her a wink. "If you're a good girl, later on I'll show you another use of the forked tongue," which he followed by flicking his tongue snake-like at her. Kina tossed her head back and laughed. She then gave him a glancing kiss before she hopped off the stage and headed for their son.

Cole now approached Thunder Eagle. He too was smiling—doing a slow clap of his hands. "That was some performance, Eddie. Do you think that lady would be surprised to find out that Thunder Eagle actually went to college? And graduated with an English degree, no less?"

Eddie gave Cole a twisted grin. "All part of the illusion, partner. The ol' moccasin shuffle."

"Still, you had every right to tell her what she could do with that dime," Cole added.

Eddie shrugged his big shoulders. "Aw, she's just some old blue hair who doesn't know any better. I swear, Cole, sometimes you take greater offense to our problems than we do."

Cole gave his own good-natured shrug. "Maybe you *should* take more offense, Eddie. Maybe the world will only get the message…"

Eddie held up his hand as a group of children flew out of the museum door. He then made a silent motion to Cole and the two men made a quick and discreet exit behind the stage curtain.

Eddie grabbed a wet towel from a hook on a large stand-up mirror that was leaning against the museum's outer wall. He began wiping the sweat and multi-colored clay marks from around his eyes. "Sorry to interrupt another of your bleeding rants out there, but I can't risk having any of the kiddies seeing their favorite injun' without his war paint—and I've got to get outta this stuff before I pass out."

Cole laughed. "Oh, come on, Eddie. Everybody in Cherokee knows how much you love wearing makeup."

Eddie shot Cole a look back in the mirror. "Smart ass."

Gentle laughter from both followed tacitly implying the end of the fraternal needling.

Eddie puffed out his cheeks and lifted his chin as he began applying cold cream to his face. "So, what's been going on, partner? We haven't seen you around the big town as of late."

"Oh, just keeping busy," Cole replied as he walked around back stage looking at the assorted dancing ritual props. "You know…park stuff."

"Yeah…." Eddie paused. "Well, if you don't mind me saying, you're looking fairly wiped out. You got the sagging shoulders going…big ol' sand bags under your eyes…you look like you're a batted eyelid away from sleepwalking."

Cole quickly nodded at the assessment. "Exhaustion. We're totally swamped this time of year. You of all people should know that." He rubbed his thumb and forefinger over his eyes. "And, of course, the past two days we've had to pull double shifts looking for those hikers over in Sevier County. It's just been rough."

"Oh, yeah, I heard about that. No word on them yet, huh?"

"No, and their families are sick with worry. Those two guys were apparently skilled outdoorsmen too. Sevier police said they hiked the Fork territory on a regular basis. Who the hell knows?"

Seeing Eddie struggle to remove his costume, Cole quickly changed the subject. "Can I give you a hand with that?" He reached up and untied the fastenings of the cumbersome war bonnet and then slowly removed it.

"Thanks. It's hot as hell under that thing," Eddie said. The hair on the crown of his head was sticky—saturated with heavy perspiration. He turned to the side and pulled off the heavy bear claw chains and silver-plated necklace.

The buckskin costume was soaked through, and Cole coiled back at the odd odor. "Damn, Eddie."

"Sorry about the smell. Wait until July, Kina won't even allow my ass in the house until after she hoses me down in the yard."

Cole laughed again as he studied the war bonnet. He ran his fingers along the soft, furry porcupine roach hair at the top of the headdress. He then looked back up at Eddie with a serious gaze. "So, as you can see, I got your message. I'm here…. What is it we needed to talk about?"

Eddie gave a disappointed look. "No reason, Cole—I just wanted to talk. Do I really need to have a reason?"

Cole carefully placed the headdress on the mirror's hook. "No, no…of course not…it's just…we're so busy. If you just wanted to chat, a phone call…"

"I hadn't heard from you lately," Eddie said firmly. He then went to a whisper, "I was concerned about you, okay?"

Cole nodded again fully understanding. "Don't worry. I'm fine."

Eddie stopped undressing and took a brief glance at Cole before returning to the mirror. "Then tell me what happened there to your hand?"

Cole lifted his wrapped right hand and gave a forced laugh. "Oh, man, just me being clumsy again, that's all. I was moving part of a fallen tree on the access road behind station…." He paused catching Eddie's hard stare in the mirror. "A limb splintered off and…the edge…caught my hand…ripped it real good as you can see."

Eddie turned from the mirror and pointed. "You've got blood stains on your shirt and there all down the bottom of your pants leg."

There was a long pause as both men stared at each other—a quiet and uncomfortable feeling developing between them. Cole then angled his eyes down his shirt and then to his pants. He looked back up at Eddie, "Yeah, I know."

Before anything further was said, Kina came back stage with Jonathon on her hip. Both men resumed an air of pleasantry as if the last moments of their conversation had never happened.

"Well, hey there, stranger. I thought I saw you out there with the hawks today," Kina said. She leaned over and kissed Cole on the cheek.

"Hey, Kina. Hi, Jon-Jon. How's my favorite little guy doing?"

Jonathon smiled at Cole but then buried his face in Kina's chest.

"Oh, he's fine…just shy as usual," Kina answered for him. She then turned to her husband. "Have you asked Cole about coming by tonight for dinner?"

"No, he's been too busy getting his jollies watching me undress," Eddie joked as he threw his large hands over his chest and his crotch.

Cole ignored the jab. "I can't tonight, Kina. We've got another meeting with the search unit from Sevier. I'll probably just grab something over at Manny's before I head back."

Kina made a sad puppy dog face. "You're always working. This weekend, maybe?"

Cole paused; he shoved his hands in his pockets and then shrugged. "I don't know. We'll see."

Eddie, looking a bit absurd standing there in his t-shirt and boxers, moved to Cole and gently grabbed his arm. "You know, partner, it's an open invitation—anytime you feel the need to stop by."

Cole gave an uncomfortable nod and then broke free from his grasp. "Yeah, thanks…I appreciate it. Listen, I need to be heading out. I've got that meeting and everything."

Eddie gave a pained look to Cole's quick words but then ultimately relented. "Alright, but do try to make it this weekend. We can sit out on the back porch and have a couple of cold ones. Maybe shoot at them damn squirrels across the fence."

Cole was already heading out from behind the stage when he threw his hand up with a wave. "Sounds good. See ya'll soon."

Kina adjusted Jonathon on her hip as she watched the curtain fall back. "Well, what do you think?"

Eddie frowned and then shrugged. "I don't know. He appears to be okay, but you can never tell with him." Kina knew that Eddie constantly worried about his friend, but he never shared with her the reason why and she never pressed him on it. She just accepted it as a part of their friendship—odd as it seemed.

Eddie stretched his arms and yawned. "All I know is that *I'm* dead-beat tired." He reached into his t-shirt and pulled out the limp rattlesnake which had been wrapped around his waist since the end of the show. He kissed it on its head. "I believe Earl is tuckered out too. He put on a hell of a show today."

4:35 PM

Manny's was an old-time general store straight out of southern Appalachian folklore. Its wooden frame was worn and dated, but that was a part of its overall charm. Despite the fact that the gas pumps had been removed years before, an orange and blue ESSO sign still hung loosely on the side of the building. Planting wheels, clay pots and stacks of feed cluttered beneath the large glass window and spilled into the store's small entrance. The front door to Manny's always seemed to greet the customers with an earthy, pleasant fragrance like a freshly mowed field in early summer.

Cole wheeled his jeep into the lot and parked among a ragged collection of trucks belonging to the locals. As he headed for the door, he waved at Tommie Chides, a slightly lumbering, dull-eyed young man, who was unloading a crate of early-harvested potatoes from the back of his parents' flatbed. Tommie just glanced up at the ranger and then continued his work.

At the entrance, Manny, the store's proprietor and namesake, was busy stacking heavy packs of grain against the wall. Manny was a bull of a woman who over her forty years had amassed close to 250 pounds around her otherwise smallish, five foot frame. She had short, mousy hair and a puffy face with cheeks that clipped in around her eyes. But Manny also had a heart as big as all outdoors and was thought of highly by everyone who knew her. And she managed the place well having inherited it from her father when she was only thirteen. Working at the general store was truly the only life Manny had ever known.

"Miss Manny, that ain't no job for a lady like yourself," Cole said.

Manny looked up and gave a toothless grin. Wiping the sweat from her forehead, she accidentally drug a dirt smear all the way across. "Glory be, if it ain't the high and mighty smoky ranger hisself."

Cole immediately began helping pull the fifty pound bags off the dolly. Manny remained on her knees and watched—grateful for the break.

"Well, where you been to, boy? We don't never see you round here no mo'. To what do we owe th' pleasure?" Her hillbilly accent was one typically found in these parts—a mishmash of Georgia smokehouse and Carolina pine.

"I've been stuck up in those hills for far too long, Manny. I was just itchin' to see a pretty face again." Cole smiled and gave her a wink.

Manny cackled wildly and slapped Cole on the back. "You a lyin' bastard, Cole Whitman. Ya know I looks like the hind end of an ol' sow." She paused and then added, "But it just so happens, I likes me a handsome liar."

Cole finished tossing the last bag and then he helped Manny to her feet. He offered her his arm and together they walked into the store.

Like the outside, the inside of Manny's had a distinctive old-world charm. A giant potbellied stove, which was lit all year long no matter the season, centered the room giving the store a slightly smoky haze. Rocking chairs, barrels and an odd, discarded couch were strategically placed around it and became the permanent hang-out for Manny's regulars. The wood-paneled walls were littered with various animal skins and deer racks; a gaping mouth black bear head was mounted near the back. The shelves were stocked with the daily essentials, and clear glass jars containing everything from sour candy to ten-penny nails were placed along the large oak counter.

"I've got a late night tonight, Manny; I'm gonna need a roast beef on onion roll to go."

Manny patted Cole on the arm. "I'll take care of ya directly, Cole, as soon as I finish up with Ralph and Emma over here."

Cole looked to the counter and saw Tommie's parents, Ralph and Emma Chides, two area dirt farmers who had brought their produce in to sell at Manny's. They both were lean and weathered—the result of leading the hard-luck life of the Appalachian farmer. Emma wore a wide brim straw hat with a turkey feather sticking out of the end hiding her unwashed hair. As he moved past the Chides, Cole casually peered into one of their baskets.

"Ralph, Emma…"

Ralph gave a subtle nod to the ranger as Emma continued to arrange the potatoes in her basket.

Manny went and stood behind the counter scribbling numbers on a piece of brown paper bag with a stubby, knife-sharpened pencil. "Alright, Ralph, let's see…fifteen bushels at 3.25, plus…" Manny began.

"A-hold on now Manny, it ain't a' fifteen; it's a' sixteen. Tommie is a-bringin' the last 'un in now."

Manny looked up as Tommie walked through the door with a large basket. He plopped it on the counter. He stepped back brushing a white powder from his shirt sleeves.

"That's good, boy. Now, go a-wait fer us out to the truck," Ralph said.

As Tommie left, Manny picked up one of the oddly-shaped potatoes and blew the kaolin mineral remnants from one end. "Honestly, Ralph, I don't know how ya'll grow such nice size taters this time a' year in all that chalky clay up to yer farm."

Emma piped up and proudly answered, "Lot a' rain, lot a' hard work and a lot a' help from the Lord." She looked at her husband. "Ain't that right, Ralph?"

Ralph lifted his cap and scratched his head. "Yup, and a lot a' cow shit too."

Manny joined Ralph in a good laugh as Emma meekly protested with a look of disgust.

Cole was attempting to muffle his own laugh when he turned his attention to the rear of the store. Milling around the stove were several of Manny's regulars—a collected group of stained overalls, worn bill caps, and work boots. They were men of various ages with smoky top names like Macon Eldridge, Zeb Tucker, and Daryl Gainey—those who lived and breathed the mountain lifestyle from the day they were born. They were true Appalachian folk which meant they could be a bit standoffish at first to outsiders—prone to keeping their talk, their business and their views tight to the vest. But once accepted into their community, they were known for lending a hand to their neighbor and weren't ever shy about giving their two cents in any discussion. Manny often referred to them as the *mountain mafia* saying that they met in her store to solve half the world's problems and then caused the other half the second they stepped back outside her door.

A few of them motioned to Cole. Even though it went against his better judgment, he decided it was best to keep up appearances and made his way over.

Sitting on one of the barrels and tearing into a green apple was another one of the regulars and a good friend of Cole's, Dr. Olin Hatcher, the local general practitioner who played up the role of the country doctor curmudgeon to perfection. Now in his upper sixties, Hatcher's practice had been whittled down to anything that could be cured with an aspirin or a shot of whiskey. He had moved to Cherokee from his home of Charlotte, North Carolina years ago when his wife, Lilly, passed away. He had set up shop outside the Qualla Boundary, but the locals were lucky if they ever could get an appointment with him. If he wasn't hanging out at Manny's, he usually could be found in the park hiking up Mount Le Cont or fishing in the Oconaluftee.

Hatcher smiled broadly as Cole approached—a piece of apple stuck between his two front teeth. "What am I jabberin' on about? Here's the man we need to talk to right now. Whatcha say there, Ranger Whitman?"

Cole nodded to the group and eased into their conversation with his own loosened dialect. "Gentlemen, from all that smoke comin' out your ears I assume Doc is holdin' court on a real sizzler today. Which is it this time? Huntin'? Fishin'?" He looked slyly at the old doctor. "Women?"

A man-of-the-world *chuckle* rung out from the group.

"Nope. Nothin' like that today," Hatcher answered.

"No, ol' Doc here is tellin' us what he thinks happened to them hikers over thar in Sevier," Macon added.

Cole muted a frustrated sigh having figured as much.

Wizened farmer Zeb Tucker leaned over in his rocking chair, "Yeah, he said you ain't gonna be able t' find them boys—cause they don't *wanna* be found. That they's hidin' out somewheres—like in a cave or sumptin'. Doc thinks they gonna wait awhile and then theys wives gonna throw 'em a big, fancy funeral with all the trimmin's. And once all the carry-ons is finished, they wives are gonna meet with 'em a fur piece down south wid all that insurance money."

"It's happened before. People do crazy things for money," Hatcher said with a wry grin.

"Unbelievable. Pretendin' to be dead to get money. Now that would be a pisser, wouldn't it?" Zeb laughed and stroked the white goatee on his chin.

Cole finally managed a weak smile. "Anything's possible, I suppose."

Daryl Gainey, an elderly farmer known for his constant, painful struggles with the gout as well as his annoying ability to repeat what had previously been said, cleared his throat of heavy phlegm before he weakly added, "Just ain't right. No sirree, ain't right at all. If theys hidin', they oughta be shot."

Hatcher shifted on the barrel and tried to get the conversation back on track, addressing Cole in a more serious tone. "What's the latest word, Cole? What's the scoop from the park?"

Cole shook his head. "Little scoop to go on, really. They found their truck abandoned near Roaring Fork—Tennessee side—and prints leading to the trail. That's about it. Sevier authorities have been doin' the police work—background checks on the hikers and all that—and they just asked us to hit the trails and look for signs."

Macon gave a sadistic smile. "I hear tell they found a bunch a' blood in th' cab of th' truck."

Cole shook his head while he adjusted the bandanna on his hand. "No, that's just a rumor. As far as I know, there ain't been nothing found."

"Well, ya'll better find sumptin' quick," Zeb added. "Otherwise them boys are gonners. Lost in them woods. No food…water. I mean, how long ya'll figure they can go it on their own like that anyways?"

Cole hesitated and caught Zeb's eye. There was something unsettling in the way the old farmer was staring him down. It was a hard look. One of judgment—perhaps even one of condemnation.

The phone behind the counter began ringing and got in Cole's ears. He turned to the counter and watched Manny shuffle over to answer it.

Still waiting for a reply, Macon followed up the question. "How 'bout it, Cole? Ya think ya'll find 'em soon?"

Sensing something, Cole ignored him and remained focused on Manny. His instincts proved right as she suddenly spun around and yelled over to him. "Cole, this here's Horace on the line. Says Nic's been lookin' for ya. Says theys some kinda trouble over t' Smokemont—needs ya thar quick-like."

6:50 PM

Smokemont was a strategically centralized campground that served the Great Smoky Mountain National Park's frequent hikers and fishermen. Popular for its intimacy and two dollar a night rate, it was also among rangers' favorites because upkeep was generally simple and requests for their services were always negligible.

The blue light on the back of Cole's jeep flashed across the north end as he entered the turn on the *tent-only* Loop C. Orange and red nylon tents randomly dotted a swiftly flowing stream along the otherwise abandoned retreat. Cole noticed commotion in one of the areas and pulled alongside into an adjacent campsite.

Nicholas Turner, a level-one grade ranger, was actively talking to two hazard-looking campers who wore mismatched fishing vests and waders. Nic was a big, athletic guy, and his buzz haircut and chiseled face reflected his no nonsense, kick-ass persona. Even though he was young, in his early twenties, he seemed to have a complete command of the situation. He had a pad and pen in hand—taking down everything that was being said.

Cole broke through some dividing brush and made his way over. Nic registered Cole's approach with a brief look but then continued his line of questioning. "So, you say he's about forty-five. Any medical problems that you are aware of?"

One of the campers, Phil Lawson, looked at his buddy and then back at Nic. "Naw, but I really ain't too sure. We only know him through my brother Jerry. They work together at Tyron's Tire in Elizabethton. Rayford was the one who brought us up here…was fixin' to put us on some fat rainbows."

The other camper, Glenn Harley, stuck out his bottom lip and nodded his agreement.

"Now, he *is* a big ol' hoss—they call him Big Ray, in fact—gotta be damn near three hundred. He might be diabetic or have heart problems; we just don't know," Phil added.

Cole stopped short and signaled Nic to join him.

"Excuse me, gentlemen," Nic said as he made his way to Cole.

Out of ear-shot of the campers, Nic was now face to face with Cole. Despite their obvious age differences, Nic and Cole made for an excellent tandem. Cole had the inside track on experience, but the can-do spirit definitely belonged to his partner.

Nicholas Ryan Turner had been newly sent in the summer of '73 for a four year stay in Vietnam as an enlisted man in the military police when he received a knife wound in his left shoulder blade, ironically from trying to break up a fight between a US airman and a shafted hooker at a local dive in the township of Bien Hoa. His wound became infected and he was sent back to the states for treatment. Two months later, he was medically discharged, and he went looking for work—signing up almost immediately with the ranger intern program. His background as an MP landed him with the law enforcement division of the park system, and he was assigned to Cole's unit at the Oconaluftee Station. Cole took Nic under his wing and they bonded early. Their chemistry made for a free and easy exchange between the two.

"Cole, glad to see you back." He motioned to the campers with his thumb and added, "Can you believe this shit?"

"Another one missing?" Cole asked wearily.

Nic nodded. "Yeah, I've just about given up on eating and sleeping around this place. Not what I had in mind when I signed up to police this park. I thought we'd just be citing litterbugs and running hippies out of the woods."

Cole gave a partial grin. "Never a dull moment." He quickly changed thought. "How long has he been missing?"

"Several hours at least. They split up early this morning—been fishing the Luftee all day. They were supposed to meet back here for lunch around one."

Distant thunder sent Cole's head leaning back searching the sky; he then refocused in on Nic. "They been drinking any?"

"Couple of empty PBR cans stowed in their trash, but not too much—nothing these ol' boys can't handle. I say he either went off in the woods to take a dump and got lost, or he slipped on the river rocks and busted his head somewhere."

Cole paused to think; his eyes shot skyward again upon the roll of more thunder. "This storm is going to eat up whatever daylight we have left and quick. Better make your way over to my jeep and put in a call to Horace—get some backup out here." Nic's eyes shifted to the nervous fishermen as Cole continued, "Then get those emergency kits and the extra flashlights out of my duffle…." He thought about it before adding, "Oh, and pull the tarp on the jeep for me while you're over there, will ya?"

31

Nic returned his gaze to the senior partner. He gave a brief nod and took off towards Cole's jeep. Cole rubbed his chin and then approached the two fishermen offering his bandaged hand. "I'm Ranger Whitman, a law enforcement supervisor here in the park. I understand ya'll have been up here doing some fishing. Any luck?"

"Couple a' rainbows and three browns...not nary a brook trout though," Harley muttered.

Cole smiled but ignored this as it was illegal for them to be fishing for brook trout in the park anyway. A cold rain began to settle in as he continued. "And where did you say you boys are from?"

"Elizabethton...all three of us. Me, Phil and Rayford—Rayford Parker, he's th' fella that's missin'."

"I see. Well, don't worry. We've had 'em wander off before; I'm sure we'll find Mr. Parker soon enough."

A crack of thunder suddenly exploded nearby startling the fishermen, but Cole remained unfazed. "Close, but no cigar," he called out to the heavens which brought a tepid smile back to the men.

Nic returned shortly handing out clear ponchos and water-proof flashlights to everyone. "Horace has a call in to Deep Creek Station and Cataloochee just in case. Buck and Lewis are on their way now."

Cole nodded and signaled for everyone to follow him. He walked them up the stream a bit and then stopped. The rain began a heavier downpour and Cole had to raise his voice to be heard. "Where about did you see him last?"

"Glen and I went out a little further up this cut towards the northern edge of the campground and worked this here stream down. We left Ray headin' the other way towards the main river not too far south of here."

"Toward the big rocks? Where the water slows?"

Phil and Glenn looked to each other for assurance and then gave tentative nods.

"Okay. You two continue through here 'til you get to the river. Look carefully through the brush along the way but don't stray from the path. If you see anything, holler out. Once you get to the riverbank stay there until Ranger Turner or I make it back to you. We've got other rangers on the way to search so don't do anything foolish—like getting yourselves lost. Understood?"

The miserable-looking fishermen quietly agreed—the rain water pouring off the bills of their caps. They slowly headed to the river with the beams of their flashlights striating through the dark.

"Nic, you head south and cross the river at Big Bend. That'll give us someone on the far side in case he went all the way across. I'll shoot through the gap north and work my way back to the rocks. We can regroup once S and R get here."

"Understood."

And with that, Nic took off across a split-log bridge and jogged down the stream levee. With the rain pounding the forest floor, footing was treacherous along the embankments now, but it was a mile and a half distance to Big Bend and the situation demanded a quicker-paced gait. Nic had been a multi-sport athlete throughout his high school years and his military training had kept him in top physical condition—an asset that proved valuable now.

Phil and Glen continued ambling towards the river. Tired, wet and hungry, the labored breathing of the two men exemplified their state of mind. They stopped periodically to catch their breath—flashes of lightning danced all around them.

"This ain't worth a shit," Glen finally said.

"I know it. That fat son of a bitch better not be in some bar huddled by a fire and sippin' on a beer. Phil added. "If he is, I'll personally take his golden fly rod and *shove it up his ass.*"

Further north Cole cut through the forest with ease. His ten years of experience hiking in the park's backcountry gave him a distinctive advantage. He contemplated the time, distance and range of an inexperienced hiker and reasoned out possible trouble spots.

He stopped for a moment in a patch of thick ferns under a giant red spruce to get his bearings. Rain continued to fall in heavy doses and he pulled his ranger cap tight around his head. The lightning continued to illuminate the landscape—the rocks and trees casting disjointed and macabre-shaped shadows.

As he tried to scan the forest, a foreboding feeling about the missing camper suddenly came to him. He saw an image of a man lying on the ground—bloody and cleaved.

He's dead...just like the others.

Cole felt a sudden chill at the center of his spine. For a brief moment he felt like he was starting to phase out again. But then the crackle of his walkie-talkie brought Cole back to the here and now. He staggered for a moment and batted the rain from his eyes. Hearing Nic's voice call out, he reached down and unclipped the walkie-talkie from his belt. "Yeah..." Cole said barely audible.

"Cole? Cole, it's Nic. Can you hear me? Over."

Cole cleared his throat and aggressively shook his head—clearing the cobwebs. "Yeah, Nic, I hear you. Whatcha got?"

"Fly rod...looks like an expensive one. Has to be our boy's."

"What's your twenty?" Cole was becoming increasingly more coherent.

"I only made it about three hundred yards south of the cut when I saw it."

"Any sign of its owner?"

"Negative. It's just here by a rock, sticking straight up out of the water."

"Alright, hold your position. I'll pick up the two others for confirmation and be there in a few minutes."

"Roger that," Nic said, hooking the walkie-talkie back to his belt. Using his flashlight, Nic ran the beam up and down the rod again. It was a G-1 Winston fiberglass rod in mint condition. *No way, this guy's just gonna drop this thing out here. Something has happened to him—big time.*

Nic carefully climbed up on the rock and perched himself on top. The rain continued to pour in buckets all around him, and he was now soaked to the bone. But he paid no attention to the conditions as the sense of urgency had seemingly multiplied.

He drew a steady wave from his flashlight across the dark embankment in front of him. The lightning flashes gave a static, blue glow to the thick forest across the way. For a moment, Nic thought his mind was playing tricks on him.

What the hell is that?

He almost dismissed the dark lump as the product of his exhaustion, but then he decided to check it out. Nic waded through the river—the freezing water jarring him with each step. As he neared the other side, another flash of lightning lit up the night and revealed a human form crumpled against the rock.

"Oh, shit!"

Nic tried to quicken his pace and became unbalanced submerging his entire body under the bitterly cold water. He resurfaced with a gasp and fought the sudden shock and numbness to his body. He managed to scramble his way to the other side, and he quickly knelt down next to the man.

"Mr. Parker, can you hear me, sir? Mr. Parker..."

As Nic rolled Rayford Parker away from the rock and onto his back, something wet and slimy flew out and stuck to his forearms. Puzzled, Nic stood and then cast the light down on the man's body. The flashlight jumped out of Nic's hands and dropped to the ground sinking into the muddy embankment.

"Cole!"

With the two other men now in tow behind him, Cole came to a sudden halt and immediately went to his walkie-talkie, "Nic...Nic, are you there? Nic, it's Cole." No answer. He looked back at Phil and Glen, "C'mon!"

Emerging from the trail head, Cole angled his light across the rushing river and onto the far bank. He saw Nic standing there on the opposite side of the river staring down at a mass at his feet.

"Nic...?"

Nic slowly turned in Cole's direction but did not say anything. Cole told the other men not to follow and made his way across.

As he approached Nic, he could tell that the young ranger was staggering. He cast his flashlight upon his partner's face—remnants of vomit still hung there on his chin. He passed Nic without saying a word and knelt to inspect the body.

He studied the pallid face of the late Rayford Parker. His eyes were wide—in shock of what he had faced in his final moments. Cole focused in on Parker's mouth which remained gaped open in horror. His tongue was curled and pushed to one side—thin lines of blood seeped between his teeth. Cole reached out with a trembling hand and gently pushed the dead man's mouth closed. He stared at him for a moment.

Doesn't matter...I can still hear you screaming.

MAY 19, 1974

2:00 AM

Flashing lights of blue, orange and red from the gathered emergency vehicles permeated the night at Smokemont. The rain had ceased; the storm had passed on and outlines of emergency and park personnel flashed through the darkness in chaotic fashion. And at the center of it all, zipped up in a black bag, lay the body of Rayford J. Parker. It was all too surreal—dream-like, nightmare-like.

Nic stood with a doleful look as he took it all in—his adrenaline rush had long since faded away. He had been trained to expect the unexpected; he had dealt with death before; he had seen horrors in his brief tour of Vietnam that would chill the strongest man, yet he had never been quite as affected by anything like the ravaged body of Rayford Parker.

Parker's throat had been torn wide open, his spinal cord barely keeping his head attached. The white-ringed trachea stuck out of the wound like a bony finger. Parker's right arm had been savagely ripped off—hanging meat of the deltoid muscle, blood and the jagged edge of the humerus bone were all that remained. But it was the gouges to Parker's midsection that had gotten to Nic. When he had turned the body on its back, Parker's ruptured intestines had sloshed out all over the young ranger's arms. He had managed to jump back and call out to Cole, but the sick smell of bile had been sucked deep within his lungs causing him to become violently ill.

He wanted to make amends somehow, to do right by this, but he had no idea what to do or how to do it. He slowly trudged to the back of a waiting ambulance—the oscillating lights reflecting in his eyes. He had been cleared by the paramedics, but he was not himself. His head hurt—he was exhausted—and ashamed. But he was determined not to make this about him; he just wanted to make sure the two fishermen were okay.

Phil and Glen were huddled under blankets—their vital signs were being checked. Nic wanted to reach out to them, to say something meaningful and reassuring, but the words were impossible at this point. Phil caught a glimpse of Nic but just lowered his head. The door of the ambulance was then coldly slammed shut.

Confused, tired, drained of his emotions, Cole sat on the hood of his jeep watching Nic and the others. He rubbed his hands compulsively wishing it would just all go away. He would talk to his young partner later, but now he had his own issues. He tried to piece everything together in his mind, but the more he thought, the less he wanted to know. He was afraid of those thoughts, those memories...he dared not go too deep.

Upon hearing a familiar voice, Cole turned his attention to Doc Hatcher and watched him interact with Melvin Smoak, the coroner from neighboring Buncombe County. They stood near the body of Rayford Parker as it awaited shipment in the coroner's hearse. They laughed and joked with that seemingly callous attitude most old medical men possess.

Hatcher slapped the coroner on the back and made his way over to Cole. He quickly changed to a more serious demeanor as he took note of Cole's despondency. Hatcher fumbled for his words, "Hell, Cole, I really don't know what to say. It's just awful. Goddamn awful."

Cole remained silent.

"That's the worst attack I've ever seen. In all my thirty-five years of practice nothin' comes close. Some of those claw marks must have reached four to five inches along his torso. Tic-tac-toe lacerations along his back...half his scalp gone...I mean to tell ya, that thing ravaged that poor son of a bitch. And Melvin said his boys still haven't found the right appendage. It just gives me the willies to think of some bear out beyond those trees chewing on that guy's arm."

This comment pricked Cole's ears. "Pretty sure it's a blackie?"

"Well, yes...what the hell else could it have been? I suppose a cougar of some kind, what my grandpappy's people would've called a mountain panther maybe, but more than likely it was a bear. Probably a strong male, three to four years old." Hatcher laughed. "I'm sure you boys would know more about that than me."

Cole nodded in agreement and even offered a weak smile.

Lewis Boyd and Buck Matthews, the head search and rescue specialists for the entire park system, wandered up to join the conversation.

Lewis was a wiry, taut man of forty who was experienced in all forms of mountain and river rescue. Like most of the rangers, he had served in the military and learned his trade from those experiences. Cole always found Lewis to be a bit too impressed with his own skills, but he was definitely the man to go to if someone needed rescuing. Cole had lost count of the number times Lewis had risked life and limb to go after a park visitor who had exceeded beyond his limits.

His partner Buck was the more laid back one and much easier to like. A native of Louisiana, Buck's country boy charm and deep-fried sense of humor was the antithesis to his partner's by-the-book personality. Buck's appearance was always disheveled—like he had just roll out of bed after only three hours of sleep, and for this night at least it was no doubt an accurate description.

"Cole, everybody's checked back in," Lewis began. "The campsites have been emptied and I've sealed the perimeter around the campground. I'll stay on the search tonight. Buck and some other rangers can relieve me in the morning."

"A search? Tonight?" Hatcher asked.

"Of course, it'll have to be caught as soon as possible. In order to be destroyed."

"Any tracks? Blood trail?" Cole followed.

"Not much of nothing yet. No blood, no tracks, no disturbed grass. I guess the rain helped wash away its escape route. Once things fair up a bit and we get some morning light will have us a clearer picture."

"It sure is strange behavior if it is one of our blackies. I ain't never seen one do this kind of damage," Buck offered in his slow Louisianan twang. "Grizzly or brown maybe, but not one of our blackies."

Cole agreed and then looked directly at Buck. "How about give Nic a ride back to the station for me, will ya? I'll be along directly. We'll rejoin your crew in the morning for the search."

"Alrighty then—'til tomorrow," Buck said ambling Nic's way.

"I may pull Smitty's reserves at Deep Creek if you think we'll need them tomorrow," Cole said to Lewis.

"The more manpower the better." Lewis slung a pack on his back and turned and faced the river. "I'll cover the bank west-side tonight; see if I can't get us a lead for the morning run."

Cole held up his walkie-talkie and shook it back and forth. "Keep in contact, Lewis. I'll be at the station working on the field report."

Lewis threw up his hand and then quickly disappeared into the night.

Clipping the walkie-talkie back onto his belt, Cole massaged his pulsating temples and then pinched the bridge of his nose.

"Still gettin' them goddamn headaches, huh?" Hatcher asked. Cole nodded his head. "Well, at least you got a reason for 'em tonight."

"Got anything in that bag of tricks of yours?"

"No, but follow me back to my office, I might be able to get ya whatcha need."

As Hatcher headed for his car, Cole slid off the hood of his jeep and took one last look around the campsite. He slipped his hand under his ranger cap and slicked his hair back. He stood tall trying to summon an inner strength that he knew he would need in dealing with all of this.

But as he watched Melvin Smoak's men shove the body bag into the back of the hearse, he felt a new emotion creeping in. But this felt different than anything he had sensed before. Fear and guilt were no longer the culprits—something else was now at work. He tried to deny it at first, but he could not. *Is this even possible?*

Right or wrong, he now felt *envy* for Rayford Parker—a man who was stone-cold dead and whose remains had now been tossed into a waiting hearse. In Cole's mind, Parker had been set free. No longer did he have to deal with the problems in his life—nothing consumed him anymore—he had to answer to no one. The peace and serenity in the man's death appealed to Cole above all else. Yes, Rayford Parker was truly free— unpolluted of thoughts of any kind racing through his mind.

Lucky bastard.

3:15 AM

Doctor Hatcher's private office was small, dark and plain. A black iron stove, worn and outdated furniture and medical oddities cluttered the room. His graying diploma, a 1964 farming calendar and an anatomical chart of the digestive system hung upon the dingy walls as the few decorations.

Hatcher was seated atop his desk tipping an Old Crow whiskey bottle into two coffee mugs which he held with one hand. He handed one of the mugs to Cole who was seated in a patient's folding chair in front of him. They both took a quick sip.

"Omophagia," Hatcher finally said.

"Come again?" Cole asked for clarity.

"Omophagia. It's Greek. It means the eatin' of raw flesh. It's what our animal friend had on its mind this evenin' when it found your fisherman out to its feedin' grounds."

Cole popped two blue pills and took a bigger swig from the mug.

"A bit unnervin'—ain't it," Hatcher continued with a coarse laugh. "A man comes out here to relax, do a little fishin', breathe some of our mountain air, and then wham! When he least expects it…"

Hatcher bent his fingers like a bear claw to simulate the attack. "Can you imagine what that was like for him? Those last seconds of life knowin' that a four hundred pound blackie was about to tear him apart? Jesus, there can't be a much worse way to go."

Cole remained silent looking at the remnants in his mug. Hatcher reached for the bottle to offer a second round, but Cole just waved him off. Hatcher took another draw for himself and then pulled his eye glasses down on his nose to peer directly at his friend.

"You know, Cole, I appreciate you callin' me out to the scene tonight for my *expert* opinion," Hatcher said exaggerating the word. "But I get the feelin' that I wasn't there for the victim…now was I?"

Again Cole said nothing.

"Is there something we need to discuss maybe? Friend to friend…." He leaned forward. "Or patient—doctor maybe?"

Hatcher continued after Cole with an uncomfortable stare. Cole just diverted his eyes. Part of him wanted to talk about it—just blurt it out and get some help. But he knew better; he knew that wasn't possible. In the end he just shook his head. "No, I appreciate your concern, but this ain't about me. I just thought you could help with the medical side of things— that's all."

Disappointed, Hatcher gave a half-hearted smile. "Cole…." Hatcher stopped—interrupted by a door opening up front.

"Cole! Doc!" a voice bellowed from the waiting room down the hall.

"Back here, Tully," Hatcher responded.

Tully Lawton, the superintendent of the entire Great Smoky Mountain National Park, plodded down the small hallway to Hatcher's office.

Lawton was a big man in both stature and sense—a true success story of the local boy who made good. Raised on a farm in the shadow of the Smokies, the popular superintendent graduated from nearby UT in Knoxville and quickly jumped into the park's management system. With his folksy mannerisms and virulent love for the park, he quickly ascended the hierarchy to the eventual top spot. Once there, he was well-received and enjoyed the support of just about all those who worked for him. And everyone who *did* work for him eventually believed his credo, what came to be known as *Lawton's Law*: the park first; *everything else*—second.

As Lawton framed himself in the door to Hatcher's office, Cole noticed his silver hair was sticking on end and that under his open coat he wore an un-tucked pajama shirt that barely covered his ample belly. Cole actually smiled at this—unaccustomed as he was to seeing his superior in such a manner. Tully did have his trademark *Smokin' Joe's* cigar hanging from his puffed lips. It was always there no matter what the circumstances. Cole imagined taking the cigar out of his mouth was the last conscious act Tully performed before falling asleep and its return to his mouth was always his first morning ritual—save opening his eyes.

"What in hell happened tonight?" Tully asked. "I was out at the farm when I got the call—liked t' broke my neck trying to get back out here. I just can't believe this." He looked directly at Cole. "One of our guests attacked? Attacked right there in the river?"

"Yeah, and it's a pretty bad one, boss," Cole replied.

Tully slid into a metal chair next to Cole. "They radioed me that you guys had finished the investigation a little while ago. Horace told me I might find ya here."

Hatcher picked up the bottle and held it out to Tully. "Can I offer you…?"

"No thank ya, Doc. I better keep my wits about me. My morning's getting off to a rough enough start as it is."

Tully looked to his head ranger. "Horace said it took the poor man apart. That we've never seen anything like it."

"It's the first fatality for the park that I know of," Cole began. "We've had several attacks, but none of the guys can remember this kind of damage on a human. The closest I can compare it to is when ol' Papa Jake got hold of that Arkansas man's dog three years ago…same kind of bloody mess."

"Yeah, and we had to put a bullet through Papa's brain that day, too, if you recall. All over some goddamn dog." Tully grunted and flicked his ashes on the floor. "What's the word on this one? We got it bagged?"

"No, sir, not yet. But Lewis is still out there now, and we'll head back tomorrow when the sun rises."

Tully took a big drag on the Smokin' Joe's. "Of all the shitty luck…No chance it's something other than one of our bears? I mean, it couldn't be anything else, could it?"

Cole just frowned and pent up his shoulders. Hatcher, who had hopped off the desk, was walking behind Tully stretching his old bones. "We talked about it, Tully. But even as infrequently as bear attacks occur, they still do occur. With the lacerations as deep as they were and with the appendage missing, it sure as hell looked like a bear attack to me—just a particularly savage one." Hatcher leaned against a metal file cabinet. "Melvin and his group can tell for certain after the autopsy tomorrow."

Cole was rubbing his still pained face as Hatcher explained. He then jumped back in. "Besides what else can we say we've got roaming the park that's gonna make any difference?"

Tully crossed his arms. "Good point. Bear, cougar, whatever…and with those hikers still missing over there in Sevier County, this ain't exactly the best time for this kind of news."

Cole stood up and looked point blank at Tully. "Give me and my men twenty-four hours. If the rain holds off, I'll have it for you by tomorrow evening."

"You'd better. I don't have to remind you that the Green Corn Festival starts this weekend followed by the Qualla Arts Expo and then the Rhododendron Festival next week. This ain't gonna sit too well with the folks in Cherokee or the heads at the Department of the Interior."

Cole was already making his move to the door. "With all due respect, sir, if you handle the people; we'll take care of the bear."

8:31 AM

Atop the Oconaluftee Ranger Station, the American flag flapped against the blue, Appalachian sky. The rain had pushed on through, and the new day brought hope that the sun might shed pivotal light on the previous night's violence.

Cole sat at his desk in his cramped office poring over the incident report. He had not slept a wink and he looked it. He rubbed his bleary eyes and drained another cup of Horace's hickory coffee trying to focus. It wasn't easy.

Next to him on a small green cot was Nic, who after a couple of fitful moves, suddenly shot up to attention. He threw his legs over the side of the cot and leaned over squinting at Cole. "What time is it?"

"Half past eight," Cole replied without looking up. "Horace has the black magic brewing if you're ready."

Nic ignored this with a morning smack of his lips. "Any word from the field?"

"It's all negative. Lewis radioed a little while ago he hadn't found as much as a broken leaf. We need to head back soon, meet up with Buck and the Deep Creek guys."

Nic shook his head, but he did not speak. He rubbed his right arm trying to get the blood circulating. He finally looked up at Cole rather sheepishly. "Sorry about last night. I can't believe I let it get to me like that."

Cole leaned back in his chair, tapping a pencil on his desk. "It got to everybody, Nic. We're just not use to this. None of us are."

"Still..."

"Just forget it, Nic. You don't have to apologize...to anyone."

Nic nodded a thankful confirmation and decided to move on. "I remember my first day on the job you said the black bear was one of the most easy-goin' creatures in these mountains. What the hell got into this one?"

"I don't know to be honest. Attacks on humans *are* rare. Especially considering how hard it can be to provoke a bear sometimes. The blackies in the camping areas are addicted to the handout, but they aren't looking for a fight. I'm thinking it must be a new kid on the block—an aggressive one. The kind that needs to be taken out as soon as possible. That is, if we can track it."

"The daylight should help us some," Nic said.

"Agreed. Maybe Lady Luck will cut us some slack today."

"Yeah, the ol' bitch owes us."

Cole laughed. He reached in his desk drawer and flipped a key to Nic. "Here. Go get the rifles, the darts, and the M-99 vials out of the gun bin and secure 'em with our packs. If we do run into our target, we may have to get a shot off from a good piece away."

Nic lumbered out the office and down the back hallway toward the gun bin.

Cole got up as well but headed out the opposite way into the connected visitor center where the coffee brewer had its permanent home. Although the law enforcement office was no more than a cramped four wall police station, the visitors' center was much more aesthetically pleasing. It was constructed of oak wood floors and had huge rafters of heavy wood beams that greeted tourists with that certain rustic allure most expected in their visit to the Smoky Mountains. Small plant and animal exhibits dominated the foyer and a huge stone fireplace centered the room—effectively blending ambiance and information. Cole and his crew could often be found milling around there whether coffee was needed or not.

Getting his fifth cup, Cole noticed Peggy Timmons, the visitor center's graying secretary. Peggy was a skilled office worker, but filled in as part-time housekeeper, money changer, ticket collector, or whatever else was needed around the center. She and Cole were not close, but they were always cordial to one another.

"Morning, Peggy."

Peggy, who was getting the cash box ready, looked up from her desk "Good morning, Cole." She paused and then, despite not another soul in the center, went to a whisper, "I hear we had a fairly rough night last night."

Cole nodded. "Yeah, I'm afraid so."

Peggy shook her head and put her hand over her heart. "I am so sorry."

Cole agreed, but what could he say to that? "Peggy, have you seen Horace?"

She pointed to the window. "Yes, he's already taken the early birds out to the village this morning. Should be back shortly."

Peering through the large plate glass window that fronted the visitors' center, Cole saw that the parking lot was filling up—a tour bus was also parked along the side. To his right, Cole could see his friend, Ranger Horace Beal, the resident historian. He was leading a small touring group back from the adjacent Pioneer Village, an 1800's replica of a typical Appalachian frontier home and farm.

Horace was a tall, lanky red head with matching moustache. He wore the wide brimmed "Eisner" ranger hat which led to his overall goofy appearance. But Horace knew his stuff; and with his unobtrusive manner, no one was better suited to running the visitors' center than Horace.

The center's door swung open.

"...and they used the ash from their fireplaces to mix in with their gardens as fertilizer—nothing was ever wasted—ever. They had to be very resourceful during this primitive time," Horace said as he held the door for the group of smiling tourists.

Horace backed the rest of the way in, leading them with a wave of his arms. "Now if you folks'll just follow me to our map over here...." Horace looked over and noticed Cole. There was so much he wanted to say but he knowingly stuck to his routine, only shooting Cole a look of concern.

"Now this shows the Old Indian Gap Road, which many of our pioneers used to pass through the Smokies—quite a treacherous road even for this period. In eighteen thirty-nine the gap was widened for farmers and merchants. But they had to pay a toll for its use, if you can believe that," Horace said to polite laughter.

"How much did they charge?" a large woman in a floral print dress asked.

"Three cents for your wagon and your party. Five cents extra for any head of cattle or sheep you might be towing. Farmers often took their herd back and forth through the pass to find seasonal pastures."

The tourists nodded and smiled, their heads twisting about the room.

"So, that about wraps it up. Are there any further questions about the pioneers...or about our park in general? Anyone?"

An auburn-haired woman who was hidden in the back of the group broke forward with her hand raised. "Yes, I have a question."

Horace put his hands behind his back, rocked to the back of his heels and simply raised his eyebrows inviting the query.

"I understand there was an animal attack of some kind at one of your camping facilities last night which resulted in a fatality. Just what is the park service doing about this situation? And is there a possible connection between this man's death and the still missing hikers over in Sevier County?"

Cole's eyes lit up as he almost choked on his coffee. He mumbled under his breath, "Son of a bitch...."

Peggy sat at her desk with her back straight, her face in a frozen stare. The tourists alternated between looking at the woman and whispering amongst themselves.

Horace appeared stunned by the woman's question. "I…uh…believe that the park is doing all that it can at the moment…I hardly think that the incidents are related…but I'm not sure of the…uh…."

Intuitively, Cole moved across the room and stepped in right beside Horace. "That's right. The incidents are definitely not related, and the situations are being normalized even as we speak. So there really is no need to pursue this matter any further. Okay?" Cole said it with a half-smile, but daggers were shooting out of his eyes.

The woman moved from the back of the group to an open area in front of Cole. Almost immediately there was a sense that she did not belong with the others. She wasn't dressed like a tourist. She had on a dark blue suit jacket and matching high-hemmed mini skirt which had the double-benefit of showing off her determined, business-like attitude as well as her athletically-toned legs. Despite Cole's dismissal, she was unfazed and pressed on. "Yes, but what exactly is being done? I mean surely you have taken security measures to guarantee your visitors' safety?"

Cole contorted his face trying to keep his smile—clenched teeth and all. "Visitors to this park are in no danger as long as they follow our simple guidelines…Ma 'am."

"Oh, and which guideline did Mr. Parker break before he was so brutalized yesterday?"

She said it in such a bitchy way that the blood vessels in Cole's neck bulged out. He felt the crowd's eyes intently upon him and realized he was losing it.

"Come with me, please." Cole forcefully grabbed the woman by the arm and made a beeline for his office.

Shoving her in, Cole slammed the door behind him. "Alright, lady, what the hell do you think you're doing?"

"My name is Amanda Rivers. I'm a reporter for *The Asheville Chronicle*. And what the hell I'm doing is my job."

"Your job? Well, Miss Rivers…"

"*Ms.* Rivers," she corrected him.

"Well, *Ms.* Rivers, I'm the head ranger here, and it's *my job* to keep you from stirring up a goddamn hornets' nest. How dare you come ask those kinds of questions here—in front of a group of tourists like that."

"Those people, *especially* those people, have a right to know what happened here last night."

"The hell they do!"

Cole put up his hands to stop and backed off realizing that his words had gone too far. He settled down; his voice became more subdued. "What I mean is…they deserve to know, but not like that. Believe me, Ms. Rivers, we want to deal with this issue as fast as possible, but your questioning couldn't have come at a more inappropriate time. We don't want to start a panic based on any wild rumors…."

Amanda's eyes went tight. "Rumors? Sir, I don't go after stories based on rumor. I saw the body this morning myself—the lacerations, the missing arm. Mr. Parker was completely mauled—no rumor or speculation there."

"No, but…"

"This incident took place at Smokemont one of the park's campgrounds that this station serves, correct?"

"Yes…"

"I was only hoping somebody here could verify the information I received at the morgue this morning—that's all."

"Proper channels," Cole blurted out. "If you had gone through the proper channels—that's all I'm saying. The superintendent's office…Dalton Clary our public relations…"

Amanda shook her head and interrupted. "No, Ranger Whitman, I've dealt with PR dipshits before. I was just looking for a little honest feedback from those who were there. That's not too much to ask for, now is it?" Amanda took an up-and-down-look at Cole's uniform. "After all, they do still teach honesty in the Boy Scouts, don't they?"

With his hands on his hips, Cole let the comment slide only retorting with an eat-shit grin. After all it was not the first time someone had used that line as an insult. He was a big boy, he could handle it. For her part, Amanda just waited, returning the insincere smile. She was obviously skilled in handling hot heads.

"Ms. Rivers, if its information you want, perhaps you should use a little tact and diplomacy. Our superintendent's office…"

Amanda shook her head and blew past Cole towards the door. "My God…I should have known this would be a waste of my time. Maybe I will go to your superintendent. I imagine he's the only one who can talk without having to get his thoughts pre-approved through public relations." She swung around to face Cole. "In the meantime, maybe you could practice a little diplomacy of your own, Ranger Whitman. Things like: how not to jerk people by the arm or yell at them in public places. You know, the kind of mannerisms a park official, who doesn't want to appear in the papers as a total ass, should be made aware of. And who knows, if you're a real good scout, there may even be a merit badge in it for you."

Amanda turned and was out of the door before Cole could even think of a reply. He stood their dumbstruck as if he'd just been run over by an out of control semi.

Nic's head suddenly popped in the door frame. "And just who the hell was *that*?"

Cole finally blinked and shook his head. "Reporter…from Asheville. Found out about the attack last night…came here all full of piss and vinegar.'

Nic made his way in the office carrying the hunting packs and rifles. "How'd she find out about it so quickly?"

"A contact at the morgue, no doubt. Someone knew a good story when he saw it—called her up."

"Quite the firecracker. I heard her all the way down the hall."

"Yeah."

"Not bad looking either," Nic said with a grin.

Cole shrugged. "Really? I hadn't noticed. Must be getting old."

"Like hell. A man would have to be dead not to notice her."

Cole laughed. The truth of the matter was that Cole *had* noticed her, and what's more, he agreed with his partner's assessment. For all her fury and determination, there was no doubt that Amanda was also a very attractive woman. Cole figured her to be about 5' 6" with her thin, athletic build. She had an overall feminine quality to her yet she was anything but soft—the kind of woman that could command a delicate touch and then turn it around and kick some serious ass. She wore her fiery hair in a sporty ponytail that swung back and forth like a pendulum as she argued with him. But Cole's most lasting vision of Amanda was her eyes. They were a deep steel blue—intoxicating even when they were burning holes in a man's skull.

"Forget her, Nic. Let's get moving," Cole finally said. He reached down and grabbed the packs stuffing one into Nic's waiting arms. "Apparently, we've got merit badges to earn."

10:00 AM

The morgue at the Mission Hospital in Asheville was appropriately cold and sterile. The lime green floor tiles and the metallic cabinets and doors added to the morbid hue of the basement level pathology department and its connected examination rooms. The low-lit rooms were filled with enough of that harsh antiseptic smell to choke twenty morticians.

Coroner Melvin Smoak, decked out in a stained white lab smock and apron, was seated next to an exam table up to his arms in blood. A large magnifying glass was angled over Rayford Parker's nude body and Smoak gingerly prodded through the man's exposed bowels. Two others, Smoak's deputy coroner, a black woman named Etta Darby and Charlie Gleaton, a wide-eyed young intern, stood directly behind him peering over his shoulder writing notes and waiting to assist.

"The dominate laceration to his abdomen measures thirty-four centimeters across and reaches thirteen centimeters at its deepest point. A portion of his large intestine, his liver and his spleen have all been compromised." He poked around some more. "And his descending aorta was completely severed here. That thing sure took a helluva swipe out of him."

Gleaton pushed up on the bridge of his glasses. "Cause of death...major disruptions to his abdomen then?"

"Hmmm. Not necessarily. Might have bled out from the tear to the brachial artery after the removal of the right arm. That would be my guess. The animal may have attacked this area after the fact—kind of as a follow-up...dessert maybe."

Gleaton smiled under his mask but Darby just rolled her eyes.

Smoak pushed his high-seated metal chair on its rollers and it squeaked toward the head of the table. He began to inspect the throat area.

"The cut exposing his hypopharnyx measures twelve centimeters with a depth line of…" Smoak paused in his assessment as he caught a glimpse of something under the glass. "Hello there…"

"What is it?" Darby asked.

Smoak held out his arm. "Forceps, please, Etta."

With a delicate touch, Smoak extracted a yellowish fragment of a claw from underneath the wall of the aryepiglottic fold. He held it under the glass looking at it from various angles—a single drop of blood curled off the tip end and fell to the table.

"And there, ladies and gentlemen, is your smoking gun." He reached over to Gleaton who held out a Petri dish to catch the prize.

"Smoking gun of…Smokey the Bear?" Darby asked.

The coroner nodded his head. "Yep. I'm afraid so."

"Couldn't be a bobcat or some kind of wolf then?" Gleaton followed.

"No. See that smaller curve line on the thicker, upper portion there? That's inherent to the black bear—makes 'em good climbers and diggers. My mother had one on a pendant just like it. It was a wedding present from Dad."

Darby and Gleaton shot looks at one another. Smoak noticed and laughed. "Dad wasn't exactly the most romantic guy."

"So what's our next step?" Gleaton asked.

"We'll need to finish up with our subject here of course and then run some more tests on the claw in the lab. And then I guess I'll have to call our findings in to the park."

"They're not going to want to hear that it was one of their bears," Darby offered. "My God, the black bear is the poster child for that park."

Smoak got out of his chair and looked back on Parker's body. "Yeah, well, this is one child that doesn't play well with others and needs to be taken out A-S-A-P."

11:17 AM

Buck's morning search crew was fanning out through the forest beyond the west side of the Oconaluftee. They remained in steady contact with one another as they sought out any signs of the *killer bear*. Breaks and squelches from walkie-talkies could be heard echoing throughout the dense wooded area.

Nic and Cole decided to stick closer to the riverbank to see if anything had been overlooked. As they searched the river south, they catalogued several tracks of deer, elk and raccoon, but bear signs remained painfully elusive.

With his legs aching and his old shoulder wound throbbing, Nic was almost glad when they arrived at the turn of the river. Cole stopped in his tracks and looked out to the Oconaluftee as it spread out into a massive river. The sun was reflecting off the surface like so many diamonds.

"End of the line," Nic said. "Bears can swim pretty good, but no way would one have crossed at this point, huh?"

Cole gave a reluctant nod. He began thinking of what he would have to say to Tully. How he would have to explain his failure to the superintendent. *And* to the press. He offered up a silent prayer and then went to his walkie-talkie once more. "Buck, this is Cole. Any word on the target?"

"*I think we got us a Houdini, Cole,*" Buck's voice fired back. "*No leads whatsoever. We've started to double-back toward the cut but it ain't looking good.*"

"Roger that. We'll regroup at Smokemont in two hours." Cole's words were empty, emotionally flat.

"*Understood.*" Buck replied.

Nic went to his knees and cupped a handful of the river's cool water taking a tiny sip. He cast an eye up at Cole. "So, what do we do now?"

Cole hesitated at first but then gave a widening grin. "We get some advice."

"Advice? From who?"

"Selu...the corn mother."

Nic hopped to his feet. "The corn mother?"

Cole indicated beyond the bend in the river. Nic looked out and saw several elderly members of the Cherokee tribe standing ankles deep in the sparkling river. They were intermittently bending over and splashing the water onto their arms and faces. Some dipped towels and rags in the river letting the water stream down their heads.

"What are they doing? And why are they way out here for Christ's sake?"

Cole slapped Nic on his good shoulder. "C'mon."

They walked down the embankment to the river's edge. A stout, one-armed Cherokee with graying black hair was standing on the side overlooking the others. As Nic and Cole approached, he turned in their direction. Cole gave him a broad smile. "Chief Sanooke, forgive our intrusion," he said. "It's good to see you again."

Sanooke turned and nodded his greeting to both, but his eyes stayed on Cole.

"I see you've brought the tribal elders with you today," Cole said.

"Yes, I brought them out for *the cleansing*—today marks the beginning of Green Corn."

Cole nodded that he understood, but Nic furled his brow. "The cleansing? What's that?"

Sanooke looked back at his people as he slowly answered. "It is a ceremonial washing away of the past year's sins. A cleansing of the soul. It is Green Corn—a special time for our tribe. It is a time for our renewal and a time to honor Mother Selu."

"Cole was just saying something about this Selu. Who is she?" Nic asked.

Sanooke looked at Nic and gave him just a hint of a forced smile—his arm sleeve flapping in the breeze. "Selu is mother to all of our people. She provides us with life's bounty. She takes care of us. The Cherokee are her di-ni-yo-tli, her children."

Nic was still confused; but Cole admonished him with a look not to ask any more questions. He knew from his years of dealing with the old chief that Sanooke could be a bit standoffish with outsiders. In fact, it was Cole who was one of the first white people to ever have gained the chief's trust and was allowed inside his inner circle.

Years before, Edami Sanooke had been a card-carrying member of AIM, the radical American Indian Movement, and had quickly moved up the ladder of the tribal council solely based on his platform of Cherokee separation from privileged society. At the time, he butted heads with many of the conservatives of the council, but he had quite the following with the youth, including a young Eddie Whitetree.

However, a hunting accident in 1968 proved to be a turning point for Sanooke and in turn all of Cherokee. While out scouting for deer on the reservation's section of the Pisgah Forest, he had climbed a massive boulder to get his bearings. He slipped on the lichen-stained edge of the rock and lost his balance. His Winchester M70 rifle fell to the ground butt first and was accidentally discharged, blasting a gaping hole in his right arm. He tended to the wound as best he could and valiantly tried to stagger back home; but the loss of blood soon led to shock, and he eventually passed out somewhere on the forest floor.

Eddie had been called in by Sanooke's wife, Nan-yehi, after Sanooke had failed to come home on time. Eddie, in response, called for assistance from his new ranger friend, Cole, who organized the entire search effort. And it was Cole himself who found the dying man and was able to get him to the hospital in time. But more importantly, Cole treated the whole rescue with such decorum and gave Sanooke such respect that day that it truly touched the old man.

Sanooke softened his views and began a slow acceptance of Cole and the park in general. Tensions throughout the sixties and early seventies between Native Americans and whites had been high in other parts of the country; but because of Cole's friendship with Eddie and to a lesser degree Sanooke, those who passed through the Blue Ridge Parkway never saw evidence of that kind of animosity.

At least not to this point.

"How long have you've been out here, Chief?" Cole asked.

"Not long. We've only just begun our ritual."

"Have you seen anything unusual out here? Specifically, have any of you come across any bears or bear tracks…any signs, maybe?"

Sanooke paused and then, seeing through the odd question, responded silently with a negative shake of his head.

"I see. Well, we don't want to take up any more of your time, Chief Sanooke. We wish you success with the festival this year. Please let us know if the park can be of service to you," Cole stated. Sanooke gave another simple nod back to the rangers.

Cole turned to go but caught Nic's worried look. He spun back around. "Oh, I guess I should have warned you—the reason we were asking in the first place is because we did have a bad accident out here last night involving one of our guests and perhaps…"

Sanooke interrupted, "We know of the *accident*, Ranger Whitman. It is most unfortunate. But do not worry about us. We are well-protected."

Nic was about to protest, but Cole silenced him again this time by grabbing his arm.

"Of course, Chief. We understand. We'll leave you to your ceremony now. Do-na-da-go-hv-i."

"Do-*da*-da-go-hv-i," Sanooke replied.

Cole and Nic started to make their way back up the cut toward Smokemont. Now out of earshot of Sanooke, Nic stopped. "Hold up a second, Cole." Cole turned and faced his young partner. "I don't get it. I mean, how can you just leave a group of elderly people out in the wilderness like that? Especially knowing what has just occurred a mile upstream."

Cole shook his head. "The bear didn't come this way. I feel positive about that. And I don't think they'll have any trouble as long as they're in a large group. Besides, you heard the chief, they're *well-protected.*"

"How? And don't tell me it's because of some supernatural Cherokee lore bullshit like the bear is their brother and it's not gonna harm a fellow family member. Or that the Great Spirit will keep some kind of protective cloud around 'em. Please tell me you don't swallow all their mumbo-jumbo."

Cole laughed. "Nic, if you're gonna be a ranger in these mountains for very long, you've gotta learn one thing."

"What's that?"

Cole put his hand on his shoulder and leaned into him. "Never underestimate the power of Cherokee mumbo-jumbo."

Cole laughed again and took off up the trail. Nic fell in behind shaking his head.

3:46 PM

On the outskirts of Pigeon Forge, Tennessee, Amanda shifted her '66 red Mustang convertible into high gear as she careened through the green, picturesque valley. With her ragtop down, the ride was pleasant enough—beautiful scenery, fresh mountain air, clear skies—but Amanda was unable to focus on the drive. Her mind was replete with random thoughts—the various angles for her story, the mauled body of Rayford Parker, her editor, the deadlines, and the infinite details that went along with her recent move—new job, new apartment, new town. *Plus* the face of that son of a bitch ranger she had to dress down just hours before kept popping back into her head.

Amanda Rivers didn't mind a fight—of that there was no question—she actually sought out confrontation. Daughter of defense attorney Dan Rivers, captain of her debate team at Blacksburg High School in Virginia, political radical in college, establishment nose-puncher during her reporting days in D.C., champion of the underdog, activist—her resume on confrontation was rather lengthy. And this certainly wasn't the first or the last squabble she would have with an interviewee in some manner. She just wasn't sure if she handled it correctly. *Was I out of line? Did I push him too far? Could I have been a bit more diplomatic?* Amanda thought for a moment and then laughed out loud. *Nah, he had it coming to him—the prick.*

From Highway 441, Amanda turned by the landing at the Little Pigeon River and took the second dirt road on the left. She passed several nondescript barns and farmhouses until she reached Bear Lake Farm, the home of Superintendent Lawton. She didn't know the superintendent, but she was a bit surprised to find out he was not just another office-dwelling, pencil-pushing bureaucrat. But then again perhaps he was the kind of politician that preferred staying away from his office and letting his subordinates run the show. She had known both types while covering the nation's capital, and she really wasn't sure which one was worse.

She ran the Mustang through the gate and pulled past the simple, wooden house to where she saw several men gathered in front of an old, red-door barn. Tully Lawton stood with his foot propped up on the bottom rail of a wooden fence—a Smokin' Joe's clenched between his teeth. He was directing two farmhands who were dragging a pinkish-brown hog to the barn doors.

"Luke, Kyle—now make sure he doesn't reel back when you put that knife to his throat. Plunge it right through his *goozle-ere*—take it to him quick," Tully said.

The two men struggled pulling the prize hog into the barn. Luke pushed it on its head while Kyle dragged it clutching its hind legs. The hog squealed and groaned putting up a hell of a fight.

"And for God's sake, don't let him slip away from you like the last time." Both men chuckled and managed to point fingers at one another as they continued on into the barn.

Amanda had parked and was now quickly approaching Tully—her walk possessing a hint of indignation. "Superintendent Lawton?" Amanda asked.

Tully turned. "Yes, Ma'am. Who wants to know?"

"My name is Amanda Rivers. I'm a reporter…" Amanda began. Her opening to Lawton was greeted with the *sordid sounds* of the butchering emanating from inside the barn. "I'm a reporter for the…*Asheville…Chronicle…*" Her eyes darted back and forth between the superintendent and the open barn. "…I was going…." She stopped and indicated with her head. "I'm sorry, but just what is going on in there?"

Tully pointed a finger to the barn. "Oh that? That's nothing. Just some of my boys preparing one of our hogs for the smokehouse. This is a working farm, ya know." Amanda barely nodded her head as she stared transfixed upon the barn. The desperate *squeals* continued for a moment but soon came to a merciful end. "Is there something I can help you with, Miss…Rivers is it?"

"What? Oh, yes. Sorry. I just…came here to see…" She said pulling herself together. "…to see if you wanted to voice an opinion about last night's attack."

Tully frowned. "I thought as much. Ma'am, my secretary will be releasing my official comments this afternoon after we finish contacting the victim's family, and a press conference with our park's public relations director has been set up for tomorrow. I'm afraid you're gonna have to wait 'til then."

"Superintendent Lawton, it is not my intention to come all the way out here just to be blown off with a *no comment*. I've already met up with some of your less than courteous staff and have gotten very little from any of them. Now, whether you want to admit it or not, this *is* a big story for our area—it could, in fact, hit the wire and go national. And I would think that you, of all people, would want to come out in the papers on the side of being rational, decisive and emotionally supportive." She paused then added, "What do *you* think?"

Realizing what he was up against; Tully gave a slight grin and blew out a heavy puff of smoke. "Alright, Ma'am. Don't get me wrong…I am not trying to dismiss this at all. I can tell you, officially, that we are all saddened by this tragedy, and we, of course, wish to extend our deepest sympathies to the family of Mr. Parker. We hope they know our special prayers go out to them during their hour of need. And we especially want all of our visitors planning to come to the Great Smoky Mountains to know that everything now is back to normal—as it should be."

"And the animal, Mr. Lawton?"

"As far as the bear is concerned, I have my top rangers tracking it down this very minute. It will be caught and eliminated, rest assured."

Amanda looked up from her note pad. "That simple?"

Tully locked eyes with the doubting reporter. "That simple. Now, any other specific questions you might have will have to wait until the press conference, Ma'am. There are rules and legalities involved in these types of situations."

With knife in hand and blood smeared on his clothes and face, Kyle emerged from the barn interrupting their brief stand-off. "Got him fer ya, Mr. Lawton. All done."

"Good job, Kyle. Let him bleed a little longer, then drag him to the pot and give him his bath." Tully said. He looked back at Amanda and grinned. "You wouldn't want to stick around would you, Ma'am? It's a fascinatin' thing to witness."

Amanda shot back a confident smile and began walking away. "Some other time perhaps, Superintendent." She held up her note pad. "Deadlines and all."

Amanda stomped back to her Mustang—the dirt from the driveway flying up from her heels.

Pricks. Unbelievable. The whole fucking park department is nothing but pricks.

8:22 PM

With the lot full, Cole and Nic parked their jeep on the side curb opposite of Manny's. Exhausted and frustrated, they shuffled across the road toward the entrance. Approaching the store front, they heard rousing chatter coming from inside.

"Big crowd tonight," Nic said. "It looks like *the incident* has brought out the gossips."

"We'll have to face them sooner or later. Let's just stay long enough to grab a bite to eat—keep the talk to a minimum—then we'll get the hell outta here."

Their entrance into the store immediately grabbed everyone's attention as the crowd's collective voices went silent. Nic looked around and smiled. He noticed mostly familiar faces, but none were looking too friendly. "Evening." The curious crowd just continued to eyeball them in silence. Nic leaned over to Cole. "Maybe this wasn't such a good idea after all."

Cole motioned him toward the counter.

Manny was wiping down the counter with one rag and had another draped over her left shoulder. Her smile she greeted them with was half-hearted at best and she had a hard time looking them in the eye.

"How do, boys? Any luck so far?"

Cole looked at those gathered at the counter and measured his words fully knowing the significance of what he had to say. "No. We've still got a team out there looking, but nothing's turned up yet." Cole's comments brought back the low murmurs of the crowd.

He looked back at Manny. "We could use a little hot food, Manny." Manny nodded and popped the counter with the rag turning to the kitchen door.

Zeb Tucker was leaning against the counter stroking his white beard. He cleared his throat. "Cole, hope yeh don't mind me askin' but how do ya'll figure sumptin' like this coulda happened?"

Cole turned and smiled at Zeb realizing now that the old farmer had been the one chosen to speak for the group. "I don't know, Zeb. He got too close. He got careless. He just screwed up—I guess."

Zeb nodded affirmatively. "Yeah, yeah, he probably did screw up—anybody gettin' that close. But what about the blackie?"

"It was an isolated incident. A onetime thing. It was probably startled and reacted out of instinct. We won't have to deal with that bear anymore. End of story."

Zeb lifted his chin to have a scratch at his prickly beard. "Yep. End of story—I reckon that's possible. On the other hand, we might have us a more serious problem than ya think."

"How so, Zeb?" Cole asked—genuinely curious.

"Well, anytime an animal loses his fright a' man ya can 'spect the attacks to continue. And they'll keep a-comin' 'til somebody puts a stop to it. Hell, when I was a boy, I remember mountain cats use to come outta the hills and attack our farm, a-killin' our cattle night after night. Blackies too—a-chasin' Daddy's hogs all the time, makin' a helluva racket. And we'd have to put an end to it. We'd load up and go after 'em—no question 'bout it."

Cole noticed that the crowd had pushed forward to hear the conversation and was adamantly agreeing with the old farmer. "Point is, Cole, you gotta force the animal to make a decision…leave ya alone or *die*." It was the way Zeb said *die* that brought an increased intensity back to the rest of those gathered. Cole and Nic glanced at one another, fully aware of what Zeb was hinting.

Macon Eldridge broke forward to put in his two cents. "Zeb's right. If this blackie ain't nailed soon, it might attack again. And who's to say it ain't done this kinda thing a'fore?"

Another man, whom Cole did not recognize, also came forward. "Hey, hold on a dang minute. Them two hikers from over in Sevier ain't been found yet neither. They mighta met up wid this same blackie—ya'll think of that?"

Cole shook his head as the crowd's voices rumbled excitedly. "Impossible. Bears don't travel that far that quickly. It's not in their nature…"

"How the hell do you know?" the man smarted back quickly.

Cole tapped the badge on his chest. "I think I know a little something about it, sir."

"Oh, yeah? Well, if *I* had been a-trackin' this bear, I'd have *his head* on a stick by now."

Nic smirked and turned to the counter. "More like the bear would have *your ass* in his mouth by now."

The man's face went flush with anger. "Th' hell with you two! I know somethin' 'bout trackin' too, goddammit! I wasn't born yesterday! I been a-huntin' all my goddamn life!"

Neither Cole nor Nic responded to the man but watched the crowd as they began to talk over one another in a frenzy of excited voices.

Another of the locals joined in. "I'd have it by now too, dammit!"

"The bigger the huntin' party, the sooner we'll get it!" called a voice from the back.

"We'll get it if y'all ain't up to it!" another voice rung out.

"I'll kill it in no time!" said yet another.

"We can all go! Let's do it tonight!"

Yelling and cursing, the gathered men had worked themselves to the point of a violent boil. Cole found his muscles tightening—his eyes darting about. He could not believe that he lost control of the situation so quickly. There was an angry movement forward by the crowd, Cole braced his legs underneath him and then…a gunshot *rung out* overhead.

Cole was about to reach for his side arm but then realized what had happened. He looked back and saw his partner holding his smoking .38 caliber hand gun toward the ceiling of the store—smoke and dust swirling about his head. Nic had frozen the crowd into dead silence.

Manny emerged from the kitchen door, two steaming bowls of bean soup teetering in her hands—her mouth opened and eyes wide. She looked at Nic, the ceiling and then back to Nic. "Gawd damn, boy!"

Nic lowered the weapon and secured it in his holster. He gave a weak smile to Manny. "Sorry." He then turned to the crowd. "I'm sorry if I startled you, but there are a few things we need to make abundantly clear to you…*gentlemen*. Number one, this bear that you are all so fired up about killing is on federal property, which means it's protected by the law *and you're not*. Two—if there is gonna be any handling of park animals then it is going to be handled by park rangers—that's our job. And three— you know me and Cole. We know what we're doing. We ain't gonna let this thing slip away; I promise. But you gotta trust us…alright?"

The store gossips looked around and gave simple nods—peacefully moving about the store. They seemed to have gotten the point for the moment.

Nic looked over at Cole apprehensively. "Saw it in an old cowboy movie once. Worked for John Wayne." Cole just shook his head and emitted a laugh of disbelief.

Nic then turned to the counter and the hot soup that awaited him. He was about to dig in when he looked up at Manny who stood with her hands on her hips still giving him the evil eye. Nic shrugged. "Said I was sorry."

Cole watched the crowd disperse around him and noticed in the back of the store that Doc Hatcher was seated on his favorite barrel near the stove. He grabbed his soup, went to the back and pulled up a box next to his friend.

"Hey, Doc, I didn't realize you were back here," Cole said.

Hatcher just nodded but remained tight-lipped.

"Everything alright, Doc? You know, we could've used your voice of reason just now," he said as he choked down a dollop of the bean soup.

Hatcher turned down the corners of his mouth. "Well, it ain't like I totally disagree with what they had to say, Cole." The old man searched Cole's eyes. "This animal…I've never seen an attack on a human like that before. They're right about wantin' this thing stopped."

Cole drew back—a bit affronted. "We know that, Doc. We'll stop it soon enough."

"Yeah, I know. It's just I don't envy you having to deal with all this."

"What do you mean?"

"I believe your young friend may have the right idea—speakin' through the barrel of a gun, that is," Hatcher said.

"People get jittery when an attack like this occurs. You saw how easily they can get worked up about it."

"That's what I'm sayin'." Hatcher stopped and then leaned over to counsel Cole in a hushed tone. "Let me give you some advice, my friend. Go out and kill the ugliest bear you can find and hang it from the station's flagpole. Say, this is the bastard that done it. Only, go and do it, *now*. Get this thing over with. Get it over with before you really have to deal with these…jokers." Hatcher stood, looked around the room and then back down at Cole. "Or be prepared to buy your partner some more bullets."

May 20, 1974

6:26 AM

The sun began a blind rise over the Oconaluftee Station. Cole's jeep was parked upfront, but it was hidden by a heavy fog. On typical May mornings like this one, it sometimes took hours for the mountain haze to totally burn away. Mountain folk called it *blue morn*.

Cole was already at his desk sifting through a mound of papers and maps—a cup of coffee at his side. He was convinced that they had overlooked something about the attack. The coroner's office confirmed that it was indeed a bear attack, but they found no tracks, no other indicators. *How could that be? What am I missing? So brutal...* His mind began to drift....

A solitary rap on the office door jamb broke Cole's concentration. He looked up and saw his boss, Tully Lawton. Circumstances of the past twenty-four hours seemed to have contorted Tully's face into a permanent scowl—an unlit Smokin' Joe's hung from his mouth. He took *The Asheville Chronicle* from under his arm and plopped the rag on Cole's desk. The screaming headline jumped out at Cole:

CAMPER MAULED TO DEATH IN ATTACK IN PARK

Cole read through the headline but nothing further and looked back up.

"The worst part is she goes on to try and connect it with the missing hikers. Like we got some kinda killer bear on the loose, targeting our park, plotting against its victims," Tully said dishearteningly.

"The same shit we were hearing down at Manny's last night. I can almost understand it coming from some clueless reporter, but from our own people...people that have dealt with wild animals all their lives."

"Yeah, they should know better, but *this* ain't gonna do nothing but fan those flames," Tully said pointing back to the paper. "I guess people like it when they can lump story one in with story two."

Cole leaned back in his chair. "So, what do we do about it?"

Tully picked up a painted woodcarving of a black bear off Cole's desk. "The D.I. put in a call to me last night. They were highly pissed but reasonable. I'm to go in front of the cameras with my pretty face and claim all is right in our little world. That our bear friends here are minding their *p's* and *q's*." He patted the model on its head before placing back on the desk.

"What about us?"

"They want the park to do a toe dance with some of our friendlier bears—the ones that we know have been hunting around the picnic areas or have a reputation for being a general pain in the ass. They want us to tag 'em and watch 'em for a few days until things get back to normal."

"That shouldn't be too difficult," Cole said. "It's either that or we close off that section of the park. And at this time of the year…"

"And at this time of the year, that would be economically crippling," Tully finished for Cole.

"And I know no one wants that."

"Exactly. Cherokee, Pigeon Forge, Maggie Valley…I've heard from all of them already. Every cabin rental from Asheville to Knoxville would be affected. We've got to do everything to keep our corner of the world running as smoothly as possible."

"Sounds like the way to go to me," Cole said.

"Right. And I'm glad to hear you are in agreement, my friend, because I'm putting *you* in charge of this little operation."

Cole leaned forward again. "Me? Why me?"

"Because you're the best qualified. You have the top rating in backcountry certification, you're a good tracker, you're in law enforcement and you know these people and these parts better than anybody. Besides…" Tully leaned over, struck a match on Cole's desk and brought his Smokin' Joe's to life. "…of all my rangers, you're the only one I can trust to get this job done."

Cole gave a nervous grin. "Why's that?"

Tully blew out a rise of blue smoke. "This one pains you, Cole. I could tell it right away. The other night in Doc's office, I could sense you felt personally responsible. And I know you're gonna do whatever it takes to clear this thing up."

Tully's words echoed in his ears…*trust…pains…personally responsible*. Cole just nodded at the old man.

You have no idea.

7:53 AM

Amanda crawled under the simple wooden crossbar that sealed the entrance to Smokemont. A *Closed for Winter* sign hung on the ranger cubicle just beyond the gate. Easing onto the loops, Amanda saw that the campground was empty—void of any human activity. She was cautious anyway and stealthily approached the camping areas keeping an eye out for patrolling rangers. She had even kept on her morning sweat pants and running shoes in case the need arose for her to run like hell.

She really didn't know why she had returned except for the fact that she knew there had to be a follow-up story here somewhere and she sure as hell wasn't going to be well-received by the park staff anytime soon. She had her Nikon F2 35 mm slung around her shoulder in case she came across anything of interest.

Despite the still foggy conditions, she found the campsite on Loop C without any problems. It was strangely quiet and Amanda was struck at how beautiful the entire area was. As her eyes followed a meandering stream that cut through the loop, she suddenly found herself understanding why so many from all over the country might bypass the amenities of four star hotels just to pitch a tent amongst these mountains.

Amanda soon caught herself and the news reporter in her abruptly returned. She turned to the target area and visualized what the scene must have looked like two nights ago. She studied the inordinate amount of tire tracks that led away from the campsite and even discovered some discarded bloody gauze. She had covered gruesome deaths before, but that was in D.C. where some of the neighborhoods seemed ripe to spawn such horrors. But here it was different. This was an oasis—a place where these kinds of incidents should never occur.

She then ventured behind the site and headed down the trail toward the river. There was a light breeze and the tops of the giant firs and evergreens that lined the trail waved back and forth. The forest floor was damp and cool, and Amanda felt goose bumps rising on her skin.

She scanned the tributary as best she could trying to figure out where the actual attack took place. She crossed the stream and walked the path to the large rocks in the river—taking pictures along the way. A *boomer squirrel* crawled atop one of the rocks and seemingly posed for Amanda's camera. Amanda watched the squirrel in her viewfinder as it played about the rock. Suddenly it froze and focused on an area behind Amanda. Then it quickly darted from the rock and scurried into the forest. Amanda became unsettled by the animal's actions and turned to look behind her. There was nothing there, but...*Something's not right.*

Amanda peered past the rocks and trees and looked deep into the heart of the forest. "Hello?" she called out. There was no answer. The wind picked up again and some remaining fog rolled down the top of the river. For some reason, the image of Rayford Parker's body on the slab suddenly popped into her head. Her stomach went tight, and she felt her heart beginning to race. The hairs on her neck were standing on end. *Time to get out of here.*

Amanda followed her instincts and began a quick-pace walk back up the trail. She was having a hard time wiping out that image of Parker from her mind. When her contact at the morgue, Etta Darby, her new friend and roommate, had snuck her in to view the body yesterday morning, it really didn't make that much of an impression; but now out here, alone, images of the mutilated body began to weaken her resolve.

Amanda kept looking back behind her as she climbed the embankment. Justified paranoia or not, she felt that something was now following her and she suddenly broke into a light jog. As she crossed the tributary, her fears grew into a full blown panic. She secured the camera over her shoulder and began to hit full stride up the trail.

She flew back through the campsite and followed the loops out to the main road. She didn't stop running until she made it back to her Mustang outside the gate. She stood by the hood of her car for a moment catching her breath. She blew out hard and even managed to emit a sarcastic laugh at herself. *Very brave, Amanda. Sam would be so proud.* She opened the car door and slid inside. "You're such a chicken shit sometimes," she said aloud to herself. She cranked up the Mustang and drove off.

Back on the campground road, only a hundred yards away, *it* stood there...watching her drive away.

11:33 AM

A number of rangers were gathered in the small auditorium housed in the Sugarlands Park Headquarters near Gatlinburg. A tired but determined group, they were sprawled about the auditorium seats like junior-high students awaiting a lecture. Some sipped at black coffee from Styrofoam cups, but most were just using the cups as spit receptacles for their Copenhagen or their preferred Kodiak.

Having just made the hour drive from Oconaluftee, Cole now loomed on the stage with his back to the rangers. He was reading the latest sightings report, gathering his thoughts. A raised wall map of the park was hanging in the back with colored pins dotting certain areas.

Cole finally turned and looked up from the paper. "Gentlemen, if I can have your attention for a moment...I think everybody here knows what's goin' on, so I won't bother you with a recap. The bottom line is the Department of the Interior wants us to step up our watch of our friends in the woods to measure any *unusual* behavior patterns. The hope here is that the problem bear will resurface, and we will be able to identify it and have it eliminated."

The rangers just nodded and continued their sipping or spitting.

"Those of you assigned to the backcountry should be particularly mindful that our country bears aren't used to seeing man and may be quick to act on their defensive instincts. Those of you assigned to the camping areas...well, you know your panhandlers—just take all basic precautions. Play it safe. Just this morning we have had confirmed sightings from Abrams Falls trail, Trillium Gap, and Crooked Arm Ridge. Keep up your warnings to any guests in those areas."

"We got us a timetable, Cole?" The question came from Lewis Boyd, the search and rescue expert, who was seated in the back.

"The order sounds like a formality to me, Lewis," Cole answered. "Let's give it two weeks and see how things shake out. Hopefully we'll be done with all this sooner than that."

Lewis shook his head in agreement and leaned back in his seat.

Another veteran ranger and the only Native-American of the group, Keye Williams, piped up. "How are we suppose to have time to do this bear watch when we're already behind in our normal routines from pulling double duty on the hikers search? They think we're a bunch a' supermen?"

"I know…I know. Your plate is full. I can appreciate that, but there is little we can do it about it right now, Keye. Hopefully we will continue off duty rotation so those of you here in the western part of the park can catch a break."

Cole's comments were met with near unanimous groans.

"I know it's not gonna be easy, but we've gotta do what we gotta do. Now, your coverage areas are in your boxes. We'll go with split teams around Smokemont since that was the problem bear's last known whereabouts. And we'll reroute any plan changes through my office at Luftee." He paused and then finalized. "Right now we're about public relations, gentlemen. There's a bear out there that's lost his fear of man; we need to get him…and soon. Are there any other questions?"

Sitting next to Lewis, Buck Matthews slowly rose from his seat and equally slowly raised his hand.

Cole knew it was coming and even emitted a slight grin. "Yes, Buck, you have a question?"

"Yes sir, jes one," Buck said. "How are we all suppose to know which un is that mean, ol' *nasty* bear?" His question was met with soft laughter throughout the auditorium. "What I mean to say is—does he have any distinguishin' marks that can help a feller to spot 'im among our good, Christian bears? A scar on his cheek, perhaps? Beady eyes? Or maybe he's one of them kind that walks round the woods with a limp?" The laughter steadily grew as Buck imitated all that he described including the limp. He even walked up to a few of his fellow rangers and growled at them using his hands like bear claws.

Cole just smiled and waited for him to finish his performance. "Sorry, Buck, I'm afraid this bear doesn't even have the courtesy to wear a black hat. But come to think of it, there is something…I understand his penis bone is exactly four and a half inches long, so when you're out in the field don't forget your gloves and your ruler."

The rangers exploded into laughter at Buck's expense. Having been one-upped, Buck could only smile and tipped his hat to Cole.

With the meeting over, Cole exited the building to the parking area—a small hiking pack strapped to his shoulder. He began to slow down as he saw Tully who was standing a few feet in front of Amanda. She had changed from her running apparel into khaki shorts and hiking boots and was arrogantly leaning against Cole's jeep. Cole's look of disdain sent Tully scurrying over to greet him.

"What the hell is this?" he asked his boss—not caring if Amanda could hear him.

"Some things have changed since we met this morning, Cole. I got another call from the national office. The D.I. wants the press to be on our side in an official capacity as we try to clear up *our problem*—you know, instead of reporting against us? So I invited her to tag along with you...."

"Tully, you gotta be kiddin' me!"

"No sir. I'm as serious as my last heart attack." Tully put his hands on Cole's shoulders. "Cole, we need you to show her how we're handlin' the situation. It's the best way to indicate we're still on top of things." He turned to look at Amanda and then back to Cole. "Look, I had to kiss a lot of ass just to get *her* to go along with this."

"Yeah, but why couldn't you put her with Smitty or Lewis for God's sake?"

"Because her editor knows you are in charge and they want to get the story straight from the horse's mouth—as it were. It ain't gotta be for long, Cole. Just one or two days—tops." He looked again briefly at Amanda and then went to a whisper. "Besides, if you play your cards right, you might end up havin' a little fun out there." Tully raised his eyebrows up and down in a playful manner.

Cole looked past Tully and watched Amanda who appeared equally pissed to be saddled with him.

"You realize when I get back I'm gonna kill you."

Tully nodded and bit his lip, suppressing a laugh.

Cole walked to the jeep and hopped in without saying another word. Amanda climbed aboard as well, and the jeep unceremoniously sped out of the parking lot.

Tully put his hands together in mock prayer and cast his eyes heavenward. He then popped another Smokin' Joe's into his mouth and headed into the building.

2:56 PM

An hour into the drive and Cole and Amanda still had not yet made eye contact. Cole focused in on the turns as he flew down the Newfound Gap

Road cutting through the middle of the Great Smoky Mountain National Park. For her part, Amanda kept her vision to the sights on the right side of the road. She was grateful to her editor for setting up the assignment, and she kept reminding herself that at least she was getting her follow-up even if it did mean having to ride with the son-of-a-bitch.

Cole pulled into the Alum Cave Bluffs parking area and came to a stop. This was the headway to a popular trail that led would-be travelers on a scenic hike through dense forest, towering overlooks and was the gateway to the tree-barren tops of Mt. Le Cont. It was also a popular crossing for the black bears and one that was high on the rangers' list for observation.

Amanda hopped out of the jeep quickly and did a brief stretch. Cole pulled out a map from his bag and circled the area with a red pen. Then after attaching his jeep's canopy, he abruptly grabbed his gear and without saying a word, headed for the trail entrance. Amanda also grabbed her stuff out the back and followed him without missing a beat.

Cole kept a five pace lead as they followed the trail that looped under a canopy of impressive oaks. Amanda readied her camera and even managed to fire off an ironic first shot as she passed the warning sign about *dangerous bears*.

Deeper into the forest they came across a small wooden bridge. As they crossed, it amazed Amanda that all the surrounding sounds of the forest including the high-pitched chirping of a several goldfinches swarming overhead were drowned out by the splashing of the rushing stream which flowed beneath it.

Cole's lead increased as he remained focused on the task at hand. Amanda kept him in her view but lingered just a bit as she took pictures of the forest's natural beauty. She gazed up at the array of giant tree tops as if she were marveling at the ceiling of the Sistine Chapel. She was struck by the utter vastness of the forest—its twisting vines and moss covered rocks. The floor of the forest was seemingly covered with centuries old fallen timbers hidden by ferns and hemlocks left over from some prehistoric era. She noted with gratitude how the darkness of the shrouding forest had dropped the temperature by several degrees and continued to do so as they progressed.

After a few moments, Cole began to wander off the human cut pathway and into that lush, green forest. He had his reasons for doing so, but he had no intention of sharing them with *that woman* behind him. Perplexed,

Amanda stopped. She twisted her head in all directions and finally *cleared her throat* to gain Cole's attention.

"Excuse me," she began. "I hope you don't mind me asking, but where exactly are we going?"

Cole kept his back to her and reluctantly held up his arm, pointing ahead. "This way."

Amanda gave a biting grin. "Yes, I can see that. But why exactly?"

Cole finally turned and faced her. "Well, this may come as a shock to you, *Ms.* Rivers, but bears seldom stick to the trails like people do."

"Oh, no kidding," she returned in her best sarcasm.

"That's right. And you're perfectly welcome to stay here while I go in and try to flush him out."

Amanda just closed her eyes and shook her head in a condescending manner. She wasn't about to let him know that her morning's trek into Smokemont had freaked her out and the idea of being left alone in these woods still terrified her.

"No, I wanna go. But why pick this section of the forest to search? Why not over there?" She pointed behind her. "Or up that little knoll? What makes you think a bear has gone this way?"

"Because his scat is right there." He pointed near a fallen cedar.

"Scat?"

"Yes, Ms. Rivers, you know…droppings. Large, fresh, shiny, blue-black droppings—bear scat. Now, why don't you take your little camera over there and see if you can't get yourself a front page close-up. Make it tomorrow's headline. You know: Ace—Reporter—Finds—*Shit*!"

Enjoying his little moment, Cole smiled and then stomped off into the woods. Amanda begrudgingly followed—hating every fiber of the man's being.

2:15 PM

The observation tower at Clingman's Dome always felt out of place to Nic. The stone structure was built in 1959 to give the public an easy, accessible way to look at the spectacular views from the top of this high elevation, but Nic believed its saucer-like design and finished texture made it contrast too greatly with its natural surroundings. *A better fit for Paris* was Nic's way of thinking about it.

Nonetheless, Nic rapidly climbed its stairs and walked out to the observation deck. Frankie Abrams a young man around the same age as Nic was waiting for him by the outer railing. Frankie was a thin man with glasses and bookish type features. He was casually dressed in jeans and a powder blue Tar Heel sweatshirt.

"Well, well, Nicholas Turner, look at you."

"Hey, Frankie." They shook hands. "Thanks for coming all this way to meet me."

"Actually I was in the neighborhood. Besides what wouldn't I do for a fellow Alpha Tau?"

Nic kind of shook his head quickly—the college frat-scene-speak always made him a little uneasy. He had had a few classes with Frankie his freshman year at UNC and let him talk him into rushing the fraternity his sophomore year. Nic figured Frankie felt a little more strongly about their *brotherhood* than he ever did. In fact, he wondered if Frankie would have even be talking to him now if he had known that during that sophomore year Nic had been out banging Frankie's cute little girlfriend while Frankie was holed up studying in the library. It was all part and parcel to the disillusionment that Nic felt about his time on the quiet campus. He came to realize he needed a little more action in his life than what a few frat parties could provide so that's when he decided to drop out of college and up it to Vietnam.

"Besides, any reason to get out here to the park is good enough for me," Frankie continued.

"You're still into animal research, right?" Nic asked—anxious to get this over with.

"Yeah. Received my B.S. in animal sciences a few weeks ago and have already been accepted into the grad program. I think it's going to be a relatively interesting ride. In fact, one of my professors pulled some strings and got me into a work-study program with National Geographic starting next week. We're gonna fly into the Serengeti and study their big cats for a couple of months."

Nic pulled down the corners of his mouth and gave an impressed nod. "Sounds cool."

"Yeah. We're supposed to document their every waking hour. We'll probably be living in their habitat with them for most of the time. They say if we don't get eaten then the mission will be a success," Frankie said with a nasally laugh.

Nic paused. "Yeah, well, that's kind of what I wanna talk to you about."

Frankie was momentarily confused but then put two and two together. "Oh right. Yeah, I read about your bear attack this morning. Any luck nabbing the culprit?"

"No, not yet. Thing is, Frankie, I'd just like to know what you think. I remember when I first met you, you were writing some behavioral science paper about the conflicting aggressive nature in animals or some shit like that."

Frankie laughed. "Yes, I seem to recall..."

Nic jumped the conversation. "You wrote about a particular case...about a series of bear attacks on people in Maine, I think. The attacks were committed by the same bear."

Frankie adjusted his glasses and nodded his head. "Yes, that's right. But it was in Vermont and I believe it was recorded in the early 1800's."

"But it occurred, right? Some mean ass black bear attacked and killed three or four people over a span of several days?"

"Well, that was the story. But remember records weren't exactly confirmed during those days. Sometimes fact and fiction blended quite a bit. Are you asking me if that is a possibility in your case?"

"You saw the paper yourself, Frankie. That bitch from *The Chronicle* and a whole bunch of other people are saying exactly that."

Frankie shook his head and leaned against the railing. "I don't know, Nic. You've got one confirmed bear attack and a couple of missing hikers..."

"Is it possible?"

"Nic, for me, as I'm sure it is for you guys, it's hard to believe a black bear would attack a person at all. In fact, I was just over at the bear reserve at Grandfather Mountain yesterday looking at Mildred and her cubs when I got your message to meet you here. They are hardly frightful beasts."

"You're not telling me anything, Frankie..."

Frankie gave a surprised laugh. "Look, Nic, bears are wild animals. They're unpredictable and can be aggressive. Could this bear have killed more than once? Yes. Could it kill again? Yes. Is either scenario likely? No. I don't know what else to tell you."

Nic paused for a moment and furled his brow. "In the case in Vermont, how did they know it was the same bear making the attacks?"

Frankie gave a ghoulish smile. "Well, according to the records, it attacked and killed some woman who was doing the family laundry in a stream behind her cabin. Her husband heard the screams and came out firing. They apparently strung the bear up and then they gutted it...."

"And...?"

"And then...now remember this is according to some ancient record...the decomposing head of an infant that the bear had attacked days before came rolling out and hit the ground. Followed by the hand of another one of its earlier victims. In some versions it was his whole arm."

Nic squinted his eyes. "That's bullshit, Frankie."

Frankie shrugged his shoulders. "Might be. Like I said it's just an old story."

The conversation died and an awkward pause hovered between them. Frankie moved off the railing. "Well, look, if there's nothing else, I guess I should get on back."

"Sure. Oh, and thanks for the info."

"My pleasure. I'm just glad I was in the neighborhood so I could see you again."

"Yeah. Same here." Nic shook his hand and watched him walk toward the stairs. "And good luck in the Serengeti."

"Thanks."

Nic called out as Frankie was heading down the stairs. "Hey, Frank, maybe you should take some infant heads with you, just in case."

The smile on Frankie's face evaporated as he disappeared down the stairwell.

Now it was Nic's time to smile.

3:34 PM

After several hours of a fruitless search, Cole and Amanda emerged from the forest and reengaged the Alum Cave Trail. Amanda was now struggling. They had hiked the incline the past few hours without the benefit of a cleared path and she was exhausted. She had soaked through her clothes and her leg muscles were beginning a slow, torturous burn. Her lower back felt cramped like her spine was being sadistically twisted into some kind of knotted rope. But she dared not protest in front of Cole. *Show no weaknesses—no weaknesses.*

For his part, Cole was barely fazed. Spots of sweat had formed on the back of his khaki shirt, but he felt no pain otherwise. The joy he had taken from ramping up his hike for the benefit of his *guest* was beginning to diminish however. And his lack of success with finding a roaming black bear was truly beginning to piss him off.

He took furtive glances behind him now and he could see that Amanda was wearing down. She was keeping her head down watching her own progress step by step. He noticed that under her Virginia Tech baseball cap her ponytail swung back and forth with each cadence as it had done the day before when they were arguing. He knew she was not going to complain about anything though. She was much too fiery for that. Actually he was beginning to respect that in her—her toughness. And with those killer legs and toned body damn if she wasn't something to look at as well.

Up the trail, they neared a misshapen, grey boulder that was beaded with droplets of water. Small streams and rain runaways were common on just about every trail in the park. They usually came along on the trail when they were needed most—a kind of mini-oasis for the weary hiker. As Amanda passed, she ran her hand over the smooth rock and pressed the cool water to her face. She cupped her hand and placed it in a small fissure bringing precious ounces of water to her lips. It restored her and gave her a much needed boost.

But as she moved forward to catch up with Cole, Amanda slipped on the slick rocks that cut through the runaway. She fell hard to the trail path busting her right knee and scraping the palms of both hands.

Cole heard her fall and quickly returned. Amanda was still on all fours cursing under her breath.

"You alright?" Cole asked in as sincere a tone as he could muster.

Amanda jerked her head up quickly—her blue eyes firing at Cole. Cole wasn't quite sure what to do next. He picked up her pack and then nonchalantly offered his hand, but Amanda refused it—getting up under her own power. They locked eyes briefly like two prize fighters. Amanda snatched the pack out of his hand and quickly hobbled past him.

For the next two hours they climbed the trail in silence. Amanda had again fallen behind Cole and she was now using a huge stick to help her keep her balance. Her body ached and the burns in her hands made it hard for her to maintain a grip on the walking stick. She felt next to dead, but her ego refused to let her give up.

Dark clouds soon rolled in and a heavy rain began to fall. Cole stopped and went to his pack and pulled out a green rain slicker. As he pulled it over it his head, he looked back at Amanda. She was just standing to the side catching her breath. The rain was doing a fair job of finishing her off for the day.

"You got rain cover?" Cole called back to her.

She began digging into her pack. "Yes, of course," she said tersely. She pulled out a yellow vinyl cover-up and slung it on. "I was just enjoying the rain for a bit."

Cole nodded. He could tell she was about done, but he didn't want to confront her about it.

"There's a cave about fifteen more minutes up this trail. We can hang out in there until this passes and rest for awhile."

Amanda shrugged. "If that's what *you* want to do…"

Cole just grinned and shook his head. "Unbelievable," he mumbled under his breath. He then turned and began the hike upward.

Arch Rock jutted out from the side of the bluff like a twisted hornet's nest. A geological phenomenon, it had been carved out naturally by centuries of water erosion. Years before, park personnel had chiseled out a block of stairs so that one could easily climb right through it. And even though technically it was not a cave, it was still a unique part of the mountain trail.

"Is that it?" Amanda called out.

"Yeah. It will offer some protection. C'mon."

"Is it safe to climb?"

Cole nodded and signaled for her to come with his hand. "Yes. There's even a wire tethered to the wall in here to help you keep your footing."

Cole eased into the dark entrance and began to climb the stairs. The sound of the heavy rains dimmed to sporadic drops hitting at the top of the arch.

Amanda peered in. "Are you sure it's safe?"

Cole was already half way up the stairs, his flashlight reflecting off the interior walls. "It's safe; I promise. I just hope all the bats have had time to clear out. It's mating season, you know."

Amanda entered cautiously, scanning for the flying creatures. She was unable to see the large grin waxing across Cole's face.

4:15 PM

Chief Edami Sanooke drove his black Lincoln Town Car down a dirt road on the outskirts of Big Cove—the windshield wipers working overtime. Seated next to him was Amadahy, a teen-aged Cherokee boy. He was sitting quietly with his hands folded in his lap.

"How much further?" Sanooke asked the boy.

Amadahy looked up. "Not much longer. Just around this curve, I think."

Within seconds they arrived at the designated point and Sanooke pulled the Lincoln to the far side of the road and stopped. Despite the rain, both left the car without protection. They climbed a steep embankment off the road and made their way into a wooded area—Amadahy leading the way.

Fifteen minutes later, the young boy came to a stop. He held out his arm and pointed to a mass between two natural rows of pine trees. Sanooke followed the indicated line and lead the rest of the way. Once there, he went to one knee to inspect the remains in front of him.

"When did you discover this?" Sanooke asked.

"Yesterday. I was hunting squirrels out here when I found it."

"Who else knows about it?"

"Just my older brother. He was the one who told me to tell you. He said that since it was on Cherokee land, you should be the first to know."

Sanooke nodded that he made the right decision.

"Should we call the police now? Or the park rangers maybe?"

This time Sanooke shook his head *no*. "No one else must know. *No one*. This must be our secret." He turned and looked at the boy. "Understood?"

Amadahy aggressively shook his head in agreement. "Yes. But what do we do with it? Just leave it?"

"Take my keys. Go back to my car and look in the trunk. You will find a small spade next to the spare tire. Bring it here and we will bury it," Sanooke said.

The young boy took off and made his way back through the woods. Sanooke in turn got closer to inspect the dead black bear. It was a medium sized female bear weighing in around 250. It had been mutilated and was drenched in its own filth and blood. Someone had stabbed it repeatedly and then gouged out its eyes and cut the teeth from its head.

Sanooke paused turning to see if the boy was now out of sight. He then reached up under the bear and pulled out its front leg. He slowly ran his index finger over the bloody stump where the bear's powerful paw had once been.

5:58 PM

The rains gone, Cole and Amanda were back on the trail. The time spent in Arch Rock was awkward at best, a brief time in purgatory at worst. Although the animosity had died down between them, a slight tension still existed there. Beyond that, Cole was an admitted failure when it came to making small talk and Amanda saw very little possibility in engaging in a conversation with a man whom she considered a Neanderthal. And although Amanda was grateful for the time out allowing her muscles to rest, most of the two hours were spent listening to the *tap, tap, tap* of rain spiraling through the top of the arch.

Cole had made radio calls back into the station and Horace had informed him of a few random bear sightings at Henwallow Falls and Cades Cove, but nothing of great interest. They decided to press on and make camp somewhere further along the Le Cont Trail.

Not too far from Arch Rock they passed a wide opening along the Alum walls. With the clouds gone, Amanda got her first view of the scenery from the high-pointed elevation. She was able to look down at the dense forest they had traversed and it underscored the sense of wonder and scope that she was beginning to feel about the entire park.

"My God, it's so beautiful up here." she said.

Cole stopped and gathered in the view. "Yes, it is very impressive. I never tire of it."

Amanda looked at the sloping pink and brown granite wall behind her. "What's this place called?"

"Some call it Inspiration Point," Cole answered. He quickly added, "You wouldn't want to make out, would ya?" He immediately winced—regretting the words the moment they left his lips.

For whatever reason, Amanda did not return his intended humor with one of her barbed salvos—perhaps too exhausted to engage him now. Cole gratefully and quickly changed the direction of the conversation.

"We could camp here tonight. The Alum wall will give us protection from the wind and there's water nearby. Or we could head on up to the lodge. It's a couple of more miles from here."

Amanda dropped her pack and sank to her knees. "As pleasing as a lodge sounds to me, not having to hike another step makes more sense to my feet and legs right now."

Cole threw down his pack. "Just as well. The lodge ain't much more than wire fence in front of about eight bare cots that we use to roll our bags out on anyway. Can also be a haven for mice during this time of the year."

"Then we're definitely making the right move," Amanda added.

"I'll get the lean-to's set up and then we can concentrate on supper."

"Sounds good," Amanda replied. As she watched Cole go to work on the lean-to's she was actually grateful to have him along at this point. *The moron may have some value after all.*

Amanda reached into her pack and slipped on a hooded Washington Redskins sweatshirt under her yellow rain parker as the temperature began its nightly spiral downward.

Cole set up camp within fifteen minutes; a roaring fire included, and was now busy opening cans and pouring them into a pot. Amanda was huddled on the opposite side of the fire tearing into some jerky that she bought for her supper. She had unrolled her goose down sleeping bag and was using it as a buffer from the cold ground.

"What are you making?" Amanda asked in a fairly civil tone.

"Canadis."

Amanda drew in her brow. "Canadis? What's that?"

"Oh, you know, a can of dis, a can of dat," he said with a laugh.

Amanda rolled her eyes.

"It's actually called climber's stew. You just take a pot and throw whatever cans you got in your pack into it. I know it sounds awful, but most times it turns out okay." He lifted the ladle out of the pot. "Wanna try some?"

"No thanks. I think I'm good with this," she answered tearing off another piece of jerky.

Cole shrugged. "Suit yourself." He leaned over and stuck his tongue to the steaming soup in the ladle. He made a pretend look of disgust that actually drew a smile out of Amanda. He then filled a yellow plastic bowl and sat down with his legs crossed. They ate in silence for a few minutes.

"How cold will it get tonight?" Amanda finally asked.

"Low thirties, I imagine. The wind might make it feel colder though."

"Well, I may just sleep by the fire tonight then," She said holding her hands out to the flames. "I have to admit, you do make a great fire."

"It's something we *Boy Scouts* have to know how to do from time to time," Cole said with a half grin. "I think we might even get a merit badge for it."

Amanda could only muster a guilt-ridden half-smile in response. It was said in jest, but both knew there was a measure of salt to it as well.

Neither spoke much after that. Amanda simply stretched out in her sleeping bag and turned her back on the long day, the fire and ultimately to Cole as well.

Cole finished his stew and watched the fire for a few more minutes. He cleaned up and then went to the lean-to against the wall. He slipped into his bag and tried to get as comfortable as possible. He laid there thinking about what he had said and then about Amanda herself. He liked thinking about her actually. It was much more pleasant than thinking about…about…*other things.*

Suddenly he felt cold.

May 21, 1974

5:47 AM

Amanda's eyes shot open. She felt a bit disoriented. Cold. Sleeping bag. Smell of smoke. Throbbing muscles. *Oh, yeah, the scenic tour*. She sat up—keeping the opening of her sleeping bag held high insulating her from the neck down. Cole was there. He was crouched next to the fire blowing on his hands to get them warm.

"Good morning, Ms. Rivers. Did you sleep well?"

"As well as can be expected, I guess," she said groggily.

Cole tended to a pot on the fire. "Care for some breakfast?"

"What's on the menu? Not more climber's stew?"

"No, a little less gourmet this morning: a cup of freeze dried coffee and that all-American favorite…" He went to his pack and produced a small silver covered package. "…a grape Pop-Tart."

Amanda reached for the uncooked pastry. "Thanks." She took a small bite as Cole poured some hot water into an orange, collapsible hiker's cup. He passed the coffee over as well. She blew on it and then took a brave sip. "Mmmm…terrible."

Cole laughed. "Yeah, well, so much for being good to the last drop, huh?"

Amanda smiled. She couldn't believe it. The morning cobwebs were still there, but was she actually having a pleasant conversation with this man? "So, what's our agenda for the day? Are we to stay on Le Cont?"

Cole eased into a sitting position blowing on his own cup. "That was the original plan. I was to cover the in's and out's of this trail for two days before heading back to Oconaluftee."

"A lot of sightings on this trail?"

Cole shrugged. "Yeah, a few. It's part of the overall strategy. The DI wants us to secure the areas where the hikers and campers go first. Tag any wanderers or troublemakers and just be on the look-out for problems."

"Think it will work?"

Cole hesitated. "Is this *on the record*?"

Amanda took another sip—the warmth and caffeine if not the taste hitting the right spot. "Of course."

"Honestly, I think we're just pissing in the wind. Being preemptive where wildlife is concerned is a bit absurd, don't you think?"

"So you don't think it will happen again? The bear attacking, I mean."

Cole shook his head 'no.'

"And you don't think it has anything to do with the missing hikers?"

"Of course not. And that is exactly where we *should be* concentrating our manpower—looking for those guys over in Sevier. Not chasing after some poor bear."

Amanda crawled out of her sleeping bag and began pulling on her hiking boots. "I thought it would have been easy for you rangers to track down the bear that killed Rayford Parker."

Cole nodded in agreement. "It should have been."

"So you think the rain washed away all the tracks...all the possible evidence?"

Cole took a big swig of the coffee. "Not likely."

Amanda turned up the right corner of her mouth. "So what's the answer then, Ranger Whitman?"

Cole hesitated and then looked hard into those daunting blue eyes. "I have no idea."

8:43 AM

Manny held the broom tightly as she dug at the dirty wooden floor boards near the store's front door. She gave swift, stabbing brushes trying to fling the muck from between the varying widths of floor cracks. It almost always happened after a hard rain. Customers would track mud in all day and she'd spend the better half of the next day trying to get rid of it.

But there was something more to the angry swipes she was giving the floor than a need for cleanliness. She was upset, but she just wouldn't admit it to herself. The truth was the past several days had gotten to her. She was Cole's friend and yet she had to listen to the almost constant barrage of negative chatter that came from those who thought Cole and the entire park for that matter had blown it. It wasn't Cole's fault that the bear had somehow escaped she kept telling herself, but hear tell it from the store regulars and that's exactly who they blamed. And Manny felt caught in between—*just like the damn mud in these cracks.*

*And speaking of mud...*Manny thought as she looked to the rear of the store. Old man Zeb Tucker, and fellow farmers Marston Williams and Daryl Gainey were seated near the stove. All three had sections of newspaper in their hands and all three were ready to pounce on anything to do with *the story.*

"Says here they gonna bury that Parker feller Wednesday up t' Elizabethton," Tucker said aloud. "Leaves behind a wife, Bertha and two sons, Benjamin and Rayford Junior. Pity. And it says he was only forty-four. Damn shame."

"Damn shame," Gainey repeated.

Williams nodded. "Yeah, and I hope they ain't gonna find them hikers dead the same way. We won't never live that down, ya know it? Public'll stop comin' to our lil' injun' town all together."

"Damn straight," Tucker said.

"Uh-huh...right, right." Gainey agreed. "Stop comin' here all together."

Williams shifted in his chair. "I just wish the park hired fellers that knew what the hell they was doin', ya know it? It's just embarrassin'. This shoulda been over and done with by now."

Manny just shook her head in silent protest as she went about her cleaning. But her attention soon turned to other matters.

Through the door window she saw a beige VW van pull into the lot and squeeze into a space next to Tucker's Chevy truck.

"Who's this jasper?" she asked of no one.

She eyed the strange van as best she could, but all she could determine was that it wasn't from around here. It was beat-up looking and severely weathered. The same kind of van she'd see the young college crowds come barreling down the parkway in time after time.

The windshield was plastered with remnants of dirt and the wheels, at least the front two, were covered in bright red clay.

A man of some size climbed out of the driver's side door and headed for the store. Manny wasn't a great judge of height, but she figured him to be well over six feet. He had dark wavy hair and a thick moustache. Most of his bulk was covered by an olive army-style raincoat that reached down to his hiking boots.

Manny stepped back as the man entered the store. She got a better look at him now. He had a big bulbous nose that was somewhat muted by the mustache, and his face was leathery as if he had spent a great deal of time out in the sun.

Manny gave to him her big, crooked smile. "How do, sir? Can I help ya with anything?"

The man barely glanced at Manny and shook his head. He began walking up the aisle near the counter and started looking at her inventory. As he passed, Manny could see that he had a silver cross earring in his left ear. *This one is unusual.*

The man picked up some fishing line and studied it carefully. Manny saw her opportunity.

"Up here doin' some fishin', is ya?"

No response.

"We got the bestest rainbow trout fishin' in the state. That is, if that's whatin' yer after?" she continued. "Brown trout, too."

Again the man said nothing not even turning to acknowledge her. By this time the three farmers had taken notice of the peculiar man and had put their papers down.

Manny angled over to face him. "Ya know, it gets kinda cool up here at night. Ya might wanna pick ya up some extra firewood before ya head out. I mean, ya is campin' out, ain't ya?"

The man responded with an unenthusiastic nod of the head and brushed past her. Manny gave up with a slight *what the hell* tilt of her shoulders and moved back behind the counter.

He finished his brief shopping spree by picking up two cans of Vienna sausages, a pouch of Red Man, and tin of lighter fluid. He paid for the items in cash and then quickly headed for the door.

"Thank ya. Come again," Manny called out.

The man said nothing and was out of the door in a flash.

Manny looked over to the farmers. "Talkative sumbitch, ain't he?"

All three men laughed and then went back to their papers.

10:45 AM

Amanda walked out from behind a clump of flowering Catawba rhododendron sticking in her shirt tail and buttoning her shorts. She fastened them quickly—agitated as hell.

Brilliant, Amanda. You buy out a whole camping store for this assignment, but you forgot to bring a single roll of toilet paper. Absolutely brilliant.

She scanned ahead for Cole, but saw him nowhere. The last thing she wanted at this point was to be hip-deep in some forest left alone again. She was about to call out to Cole when she spied him thirty meters left of the trail crouched behind a slightly tilting mountain maple. The deliberateness in which he was moving his body indicated that he was in observation mode and did not wish to attract attention to himself. Amanda took the not so subtle hint and carefully made her own quiet approach, whipping out the camera just in case.

Now with only a few meters separating them, Cole cautiously turned to Amanda and signaled her to join him by his side and then pointed his index finger straight ahead. Amanda followed the lead of his hand and looked through the thick brush until she saw the movement.

It appeared as only a black blur to her at first, but then the outline of the bear became quite clear. Amanda's Nikon *whirred* as she fetched a series of incredibly close action shots. It seemed to be pacing back and forth, keeping a tight line of three or four yards in either direction.

"What's it doing?" she asked in a whispered voice. "Why is it pacing like that?"

Cole tilted his head back as if he were pointing with his chin. "Beyond her…there about ten yards to her left. See that uprooted sycamore?"

Using the camera lens Amanda focused in on the area per Cole's direction. Her lens soon found two bear cubs rooting about a soft section of the decayed tree.

"Tiny grub worms…the little ones love 'em," he continued in his own soft voice.

"So she's just keeping an eye out—to make sure they get enough…grub time?"

Cole just shook his head in the affirmative as Amanda took several more shots. The two playful cubs intermittently fought with their food and with one another as they rolled about the sycamore.

After several more shots, Amanda pulled the camera away from her and looked over at Cole. Her face was a study in mixed emotions—her enjoyment of the cubs and their over-protective mother was tempered by the events of the past few days and Cole picked right up on it.

"Not quite the killer bear you were expecting, is it?"

Amanda remained silent—her eyes finding the ground.

"This is how the park sees our bears. This is how we want the public...anybody who comes here to see our bears. What we had at Smokemont was...." He stopped lost for the right word.

"An aberration?" Amanda offered.

"Yeah. Things like that just don't happen around here."

Amanda now looked him in the eye—her determination had rebounded. "But it did happen, Ranger Whitman. One of your bears attacked and killed a man. Maybe not this bear, but it was certainly one of them. And until you can show me otherwise, anyone who comes to the Smokies may be putting themselves in harm's way."

Cole bit his lip and shook his head. He disagreed, but at this point he did not want to be contentious about it.

Amanda backed off too, not wanting to destroy any of the goodwill that had been established between them. "Still...I appreciate you showing me this. It certainly helps to balance *my* perspective."

Cole grinned. "Good, at least that's something." He slowly stood up. "C'mon. We should check on some more areas. Balance that perspective of yours some more."

As Cole and Amanda backed away from the area, the black bears continued with their morning meal, unaware of how their world was about to drastically change.

1:11 PM

Within a few hours, Cole and Amanda had made a careful check zigzagging back down the trail and had arrived at the Alum Cave trail head. They had come across several signs of bear activity which Cole had pointed out along the way including overturned logs, scooped ant mounds, several paw prints and rubbed trees, but there had been no other visual sightings.

Amanda had hoped for more up-close encounters, but for now she was just glad being at the bottom of the hill. Despite having angled down the slope for the past few hours, Amanda found her muscles stressing as much as the day before. The pain, however, had now moved from her thighs and lower back to her ankles and knee joints. But the sight of Cole's jeep in the parking area gave her a brief surge of healing power.

"I never thought I'd be glad to see your jeep again so quickly," she said in an honest tone. "My legs are threatening to snap in half."

"You did fine," Cole replied, marching quickly to his jeep. "We've got rangers who aren't in half as good a shape as you."

Amanda managed to laugh. "I run five miles every day, lift weights, calisthenics…but one crazy bear hike through these mountains and my ass is whipped. I don't know how you guys do it."

Cole just smiled as he lowered the canopy and emptied their gear into the back of his jeep. It didn't pay for him to think about Amanda's ass—whipped or not.

Amanda went to the passenger's side and eased down into her seat letting out a relaxed breath as if she were slipping into a hot bath.

As Cole hopped in and cranked up the jeep, his walkie-talkie gave off a series of signaling *beeps* and Horace's distinctive voice followed.

"Bear Cave to Mobile one, do ya copy? Come in One. Cole, ya got your ears on?"

Cole gave a half-smile at Horace's attempt at the CB jargon. It wasn't official call for the park rangers, but Cole knew Horace was into it and what harm did it cause?

"This is One, Bear Cave. I read ya, Horace. What's the good word?"

"Pretty routine stuff in the park, Cole. I've heard from most of the teams. We've already tagged about half of our known panhandlers, and I've got reports in on several sightings at Cades Cove, Roaring Fork and Cataloochee—nothing out of the ordinary though—over."

"What about Smokemont?"

"Quiet as a church cemetery—both teams reporting in—sorry."

Cole held the walkie-talkie against his chest and he gave Amanda a look of disappointment. She merely returned his half-frown with her own contrite look.

Horace cut back in. *"Oh, yeah, Cole...we did get a report from over on the Blue Ridge Parkway. Let me see...I put it round here...Here it is. It's from Black Balsam Ridge. Seems a maintenance worker from over there found a deer carcass on a frontage road near the 441 marker. Said it been mutilated real bad—probable bear attack. They said they would wait to move it if we wanted to investigate."*

Cole turned down his lower lip. "Naw, that's way too far away. Our bear still has to be in this vicinity. Besides that's not our jurisdiction."

"You're right. You want me to call 'em back? Tell 'em to toss the thing?"

Cole hesitated and looked over at Amanda. She raised her eyebrows.

"An animal attack is more than anything we've had here in the park, maybe we should investigate," Amanda said. "Of course, I'm just along for the ride," she added respectfully.

Cole thought for a moment and then pressed the talk switch. "Horace, I've changed my mind. We're gonna check it out after all. Call the forest ranger over at Pisgah, uh, Lem Astin is his name—I think—tell him to have one of his guys meet us there around three.

"Consider it arranged, buddy. Good luck...Bear Cave out."

Cole tossed the walkie-talkie on the middle console and began pulling the jeep out of the parking lot.

"You think we're off on another wild goose chase, don't you?" Amanda said, the cool wind whipping her auburn hair about her face.

"Perhaps," he said and then added with a smile. "Or maybe this time I just need to balance *my* perspective."

3:23 PM

The white-tailed deer's carcass was grotesquely splattered about a bed of dark pink Oswego Tea flowers. Amanda kept her left hand about her nose and mouth as she walked around it capturing the sight on film while simultaneously trying to prevent a bout of nausea. And though she didn't think of it at the time, when she later looked at the photographs, the ravaged animal atop those stunning flowers, she would be intrigued at how well the image captured the wild's dichotomous nature of beauty and brutality.

The animal had been lacerated into three sections. The head and throat of the large buck remained partially hidden as it had sunk beneath the blooming flora—only the tip of its pink ears and its charcoal-black nose rose into view. The midsection was so mangled that no one could tell if represented the top or the bottom of the animal's body. Hundreds of blue bottle flies had horned in on the open tears performing their dirty but necessary work. The rear legs of the deer were found several meters away beneath a group of spruce pines.

Cole stood there beneath those pines inspecting the animal's hind quarter. To his right was Forest Ranger Lem Astin. Lem was a short, balding man who wore steel-toed cowboy boots and a long black tie with his forest ranger uniform. He had a bad facial tic—making it look like he was blinking his left eye when he talked.

"Our man was moving a tree which had fallen across that road over yander and just happened to come back here when he found it. From what I can tell the buck must have been here for at least two or three days—just rottin' away," Lem said. "Goddamn the smell, huh?" he added.

Cole ignored this as he surveyed the grass and the surrounding hills. "The attack happened there near the top of that rise," Cole said pointing twenty meters passed their position. "The blood trail leads to and from the target area. It grabbed the deer *there,* wounded or already dead, and then dragged the carcass to the flower bed where it tore into the body."

Lem Astin gave a one shoulder shrug to Cole's theory—indifferent to it all. Amanda, however, moved closer to hear what he had to say.

"It may have been feasting on the carrion when someone drove up the road," Cole finalized. "Scared it away."

"Which direction?" Amanda was now in full reporter mode.

"The second blood trail...see there?" Cole said pointing a line away from the carcass. "Over that mound toward Black Balsam."

Amanda looked to the ridge and then back to Cole. "Do we follow?"

Cole nodded. "Might not be a bad idea to look around here for awhile. If the bear is keeping to its normal circular path, we should catch sight of it in a day or two." Cole then turned to the forest ranger. "That is, if you don't mind us hanging out around here?"

Lem shrugged again. "Do what ya want. But I sure as hell hope ya'll don't think that the bear that did *this* is the same one that got yer feller over in the campground. It just ain't possible," he said—his facial tics working overtime.

"No, but it may be about confirming actions at this point. If we can get a bead on this bear so soon after its recent kill, follow it, watch it closely, it may give us a clue as to how *our* bear left undetected," Cole said.

"Makes sense," Lem followed.

Cole couldn't tell if Lem was truly agreeing with him or just trying to humor him, but he reached over and shook Lem's hand anyway. "Thanks for giving us a call and meeting us out here."

Lem slid his left hand down his thin black tie. "No problem. We weren't too busy no how."

As Lem waved goodbye and walked back to his truck, Amanda moved to where Cole was standing. "So we're going to need our packs again?"

"Yeah, let's go back to the jeep and get our stuff. I actually use to camp out here a lot when I was a kid. I think you'll find it…interesting. And don't worry; the hiking will be a lot less stressful than Le Cont."

Amanda nodded with a smile and then took a quick look back at the deer. "What about the carcass? Will they come back and clear it?"

"Probably. Of course, nature has its own way of dealing with such things."

As Cole moved toward the jeep, Amanda focused back on the remains and noticed the hundreds of flies swarming about. And as she took some last minute photos she became increasingly aware of the *buzzing* sound that the flies made. It was a noise that Amanda never liked. She had bad associations with it that went all the way back to her childhood.

To her it was the sound of death.

4:33 PM

An old Cherokee woman hobbled alone down an unmarked, red clay road somewhere in the vast expanse of the reservation's Qualla Tract. Her footsteps were heavy but she moved with a definite sense of purpose. She may have appeared lost to anyone who might have passed her by, but she knew exactly where she was going.

She wore a red traditional *Mother Hubbard* wrap that looked more akin to a night gown than an actual dress. Her long gray hair was fastened in braided loop that reached long down her back. She was adorned with several silver and turquoise necklaces that pulled on her already weakened back, and she struggled to carry a heavy, twisted burlap sack that she held clenched in her right hand.

At a certain point in the road she took several glances in front and then behind her. She backed her way down an embankment into the forest and then made her way down a tiny trail. The path was so overgrown that it would have been missed by any unknowing passersby.

Several hundred meters deep into the woods, she eventually emerged into an open grassy area. In the center was a ring of large stones which encircled a fire pit filled with kindling and several branches. The place had been prepped properly by those who had come before and now it was her turn.

She reverently went to her knees and then pulled from the sack several knife-like prongs each one a different shamanistic color. The blue prong she stabbed in the ground to the north of the fire pit. A black prong went in the ground to the west, the white one south and the red one next to her on the east side of the fire.

A quick break of flint on stone and the fire soon came to life. The old woman raised her back a little but remained on her knees. She began mumbling and then chanting in the lipless language of the Cherokee. Smoke blew into her face and she breathed it in deeply.

As the fire in the pit grew in intensity so did the fire in her eyes. Her chanting became louder and sweat began to form around her brow. She placed her left hand on the small mummified bear paw that was attached to one of the silver necklaces. She began to rub it between her thumb and forefinger.

The elderly woman then reached deep into the sack and pulled out an object bound tightly in white bandages—stained through with crimson blood. She slowly unwrapped the casing from the object and threw the bandages into the fire. It felt cold and wet to her touch. She raised it up to eye level. She looked at it from several different angles appreciating its texture, its strong muscle lines as well as its value for her purpose.

Completely entranced, she leaned forward and bit into the meaty organ. Blood poured from the ruptured mass and ran down onto her chin. She took another bite and then wiped the blood from the organ on her forehead.

Afterward she closed her eyes and swayed back and forth as if following some unheard music. Her body began to convulse with a series of oddly shaped movements. Suddenly, she became very still—scarcely breathing at all. She held in that position for several minutes and then finally broke free batting her eyelids in rapidity. She sat for a moment letting the vision sink in. She drew down the corners of her mouth in concern. It was going to be more than she could handle, she thought to herself.

Much more.

She stood and began to rid the area of the ceremonial evidence. She used her sleeve to wipe the blood from around her mouth. She then collected the shaman tools and did her best to bury the fire with surrounding dirt. She threw the rocks from around the fire pit into the woods and covered her tracks as best as she could. She scanned the area one final time and then confident that she was leaving the *e-ti-ka-i-e-le na-nah-i* as undisturbed as possible it, she disappeared into the woods.

5:49 PM

After two hours of following the bear's trail, Cole and Amanda found themselves on top of the first ridge of Black Balsam. Also known as the balds, these ancient hills were covered with brown and gold bear grass but were mysteriously barren of trees.

Amanda called out to Cole. "Are we still on the right track?"

Cole nodded. "Caught a half print in the mud a few yards back. We're getting warmer."

Amanda stopped and looked about the top of the ridge. "What happened up here? It seems the trees just stopped growing past this point."

Cole also came to a stop and took a look around as he adjusted the pack on his back. "There are many scientific explanations for it: erosion, pollution, westerly winds—all are possible, but the Cherokees provide the most...*satisfying* answer."

Amanda turned an inquisitive ear to Cole. He in return gave a weak grin. "Well, they say that long ago a monstrous bird known as the *Tlanuwa* wreaked havoc up in these parts. It was an enormous, majestic hawk that the Cherokee revered, but it had an unfortunate thirst for human blood. They say it would often swoop down from the sky and grab the children as they played among these hills. The adults ran after it...yelling...cursing...chasing it with sticks...."

Amanda smiled as Cole became animated in describing their reactions.

"Anyway, they never could catch it and they lost many children over the years."

"That's terrible."

"Yeah, so you can imagine how their parents felt about it. Anyway, one night the elders gathered around the council fire and prayed to the Great Spirit to come and smite the giant bird out of existence. And the next time it flew through the air looking for the children, the Great Spirit came down from the heavens and hurled his lightning bolts toward it. And those that missed..."

"And those that missed," Amanda finished, "hit these hilltops rendering them treeless for all eternity."

Cole smiled and nodded. "Yeah—something like that."

Amanda also smiled and fell in next to Cole as they began walking again. "And what about the monster bird...the *Tlanuwa, was it?* Did the Great Spirit rid the skies of the horrible thing?"

Cole shrugged and scratched the back of his head. "Well, I dunno, but it has been quite awhile since anyone reported a Tlanuwa sighting."

Amanda cast her eyes over at Cole in appreciation. "You're right. I can't imagine a better explanation than that."

"The Cherokees explained everything spiritually. They saw no dividing line between nature and their god. They believed that everything is connected somehow. And the formations of the Smoky Mountains held this special, supernatural sense for them."

Cole stopped again and moved behind Amanda—his hands delicately touching her shoulders. "Looking Glass Rock—way over there—was niv' do—a rock filled with living spirits. And that's Graveyard Fields below us—there...see where the Prong River flows? It's where hundreds of invisible warriors helped the Cherokees chase a bitter enemy to their deaths. And back here—that multi-tiered ridge over there, near the tunnel we passed through on the parkway to get here—that's the Devil's Courthouse, which the Cherokee claimed was the dancing chamber and dwelling for their legendary monster—the Judaculla."

Amanda's head turned in the various directions soaking it all in. "Graveyard Fields...Devil's Courthouse...monsters...as grand as they are, there does seem to be a hint of evil about these mountains."

Cole hesitated at her words, and she swung around and caught his serious glare. He then smiled at Amanda. "No, there's nothing evil here."

8:53 PM

Cole had picked out a camping area on top of the bald between two rock formations as to dissuade the elements, a whipping wind and heavy moisture, which were forecasted to come in the night. He reinforced the lean-to with extra rope and ties and he dug deep into the earth with his hand spade to forge a pit for the fire.

With the nighttime meal complete and the fire now giving off a heavy glow and much needed warmth, Cole and Amanda sat across from one another unsure of what was to come. There was already a different feeling from the night before. The antagonism that so clearly defined their relationship in the beginning had certainly softened, but neither wanted to appear too open or too vulnerable to the other. Their conversation had remained somewhat one-sided with Amanda feeding Cole questions about the mountains, the Cherokees, and of course bears.

"Be honest with me," Amanda said. "What's the real reason why we're tracking this bear? I mean I have to agree with that strange, little forest ranger from before, there can be no possible connection to the bear that killed Rayford Parker."

Cole dug at the fire with a stick. "I guess I was hoping it would be harder."

Amanda leaned forward—her arms embracing her legs. "What do you mean?"

"To track it," Cole said. "This bear we're following has practically left his calling card every few yards or so. Prints. Brushed grass. A broken tree limb. I can picture his every move since we started on his trail. I can see him. I understand him. It's that simple really. I just wanted to know *if I could* track a bear. Any bear. I think I was beginning to doubt myself."

"And you couldn't *sense* the other one? The one that got Parker."

Cole nodded pushing embers back into the fire with his stick. "None of us could. And that's a helluva problem if you're a ranger in a park full of bears."

Amanda could see that it was bothering him and decided not to push it any further. She broke from the conversation and took a look around into the creeping blue-blackness that had enveloped the ridge. She could still make out the lines of the different balds and the odd rock formations. She turned back to Cole.

"You seem to know this area fairly well, Ranger Whitman. You talk about it as if you were talking about an old girlfriend."

Cole smiled. "Yeah, I guess you could say that." He added softly, "Oh…and you can call me Cole, by the way."

Now Amanda smiled. "Alright…Cole. I noticed it earlier when you were telling me about Graveyard Fields and Looking Glass Rock. You kind of get this gleam in your eye."

"It's been a part of me for as long as I can remember," he said. "Actually, I grew up in a little town not too far from here. Dad used to take us camping up here every summer." He added wistfully, "God, the times we had."

Cole pulled out a short blade from a sheath tied to the ankle of his boot. "See this. On the weekend of my eleventh birthday, my dad took me camping on Shining Rock—a ridge very close to this one—and gave this to me. It's rusty…not much good for anything, but I've kept it with me ever since."

He passed the small knife to Amanda. "I know that's kinda weird, isn't it?"

Amanda shook her head in a non-condemning fashion as she studied the knife.

"You're close to him…your dad?"

"Yeah, he taught me everything about these mountains…the Cherokees and their legends…how to camp…climb. He taught me…everything."

Amanda looked back at Cole and noticed his faraway look. "I imagine he's proud of you…having become a park ranger and all. Up here in the Smokies."

"Yes, I think he is," Cole began. "All good fathers are in a way, don't you think? Proud of their sons? No matter…what we've done…or didn't do."

Amanda gave a perplexed look to Cole. "I'm sure yours is. I can't imagine why he wouldn't be."

Cole simply shrugged and threw the stick into the fire.

Amanda leaned back over and handed him the small knife. "By the way, what do the initials C T M mean?"

"What?" Cole glanced at the knife and then looked back at Amanda— his eyes flashing uneasiness.

"C T M...there on the handle. What do they stand for?"

Cole hesitated and then frowned. "I'm not...I mean, I don't really..."

Amanda gave a confused laugh. "It's okay, Cole, I just thought since it was your knife that you've been keeping all these years..."

Cole paused for a few moments looking at the knife again. The firelight threw wildly striated shadows on his face. Amanda wasn't sure but she could almost swear she saw his lower lip tremble. Cole finally looked back up at her. "I think it belonged...to a friend of my dad's. I can't remember really."

Amanda granted Cole a brief smile trying to put the awkward moment behind them. She figured Cole knew more than what he was saying, but she decided to be gracious and let it pass.

Cole slid the small knife back into its sheath on his boot. He gave it a quick pat and then flashed Amanda his own forced smile.

Cole then began acting nervous—agitated. He started breaking twigs and throwing them in the fire with quick, short throws—like he was extremely pissed about something. Amanda just watched unsure of what to say or do. He followed this by unexpectedly feigning a yawn. "It's getting late," he said. "Maybe we should get some sleep."

"Yes, of course, whatever you say," Amanda said standing up to stretch.

Cole scrambled from the security of the fire without saying anything further. He found his space and quickly disappeared into his sleeping bag.

"Goodnight," he called out abruptly.

"Goodnight," Amanda responded still standing near the fire. She eyed him for just a moment—more than a little perplexed by his behavior.

One minute you're all smiles and charming talking about the Cherokees and the mountains, and then you're angry as hell, and then silent and distant hightailing it to your sleeping bag. You're one hard man to figure out, Ranger Whitman.

The wind picked up behind her and Amanda turned from Cole and the fire to look out in the vast inky black sky around her. Several hundred feet below her position she could make out the wave pattern of thousands of synchronous fireflies that were hugging the tree line of Black Balsam. And with the stars sparkling white above her, she felt as if she were standing dead center in the middle of a cosmic fireworks show.

"So beautiful," she whispered to the night.

Thirty feet away, Cole was lying on his left side positioned away from the fire. He was trembling trying to control himself. His eyes were wide opened—inflamed.

No! Please don't do this. Not now. Control it! Control it!

The night screams came anyway flooding his thoughts, castrating his mind. He was losing himself again.

And hell was sure to follow.

May 22, 1974

6:08 AM

Amanda's eyes were wide open, but she thought perhaps she was still dreaming. She had awoken to a radically different environment than the one from the night before. The predicted storm had failed to materialize, but a cool, heavy fog had rolled in during the early hours blanketing the entire hillside. As she tried to focus, she could see no more than five feet around her in any one direction. Last night she was one with the stars, but now she felt closed in—claustrophobic on top of an open ridge.

She checked her watch and then slowly rose from her sleeping bag. Everything was wet, her bag, her clothes, everything. It wasn't as cold as it had been the morning before on Le Cont, but the dampness brought a chill to her bones anyway. She vigorously rubbed her arms through her heavy pullover trying to get the blood moving.

She made her way over in the direction of the fire hoping to hear Cole rustling up some of his depraved coffee, but she was greeted only with silence. And as she came to the fire pit only glowing embers remained from the previous night's blaze. She crossed her arms and kind of hopped around unsure of what to do next. She decided to call out to Cole to see if he was awake.

"Cole…" she said barely above a whisper. "Cole…"

There was no response so she moved several steps closer to where she thought he had fallen asleep. "Cole…" she said a little louder.

She finally made out his rumpled sleeping bag in the fog. "Cole…? Ranger Whitman?" She bent down to wake him but found the bag empty. She stood up. Her eyes darted about—propelled by an increasing sense of dread.

"Cole…" she called again in a loud steady voice. There was no reply.

Probably out answering nature's call. Amanda thought trying to humor herself. *I'm sure he'll be right back.*

And then Amanda heard something she was totally unprepared for. It was a low, pacing noise brushing against the tall grass—the sound of something heavy traveling through the mountain reeds. And it was close by—only a few yards from where she was standing.

"Cole...?"

The sound stopped when she called out. Then it started again.

But this time heading back towards her.

Amanda swallowed hard; she could feel her heart pounding in her chest. She took a cautious step back and went to her knees. She frantically searched the ground about her for some kind of weapon. She latched hold of a three pound rock and then gripped it with both hands. Then she remembered something that Cole had told her. If a bear ever decided to attack, it was best to assume an aggressive pose in hopes that the animal would turn and run. Playing dead or running away often made things worse.

I'll run at it...scream at the top of my lungs...and hit it with the rock. That should scare the hell out of it...I hope.

Amanda got in a set position to lunge out at the animal. She put the rock in her right hand and raised it to shoulder height determined to hit it square on the nose if need be. As she tried to summon up the courage, she heard the movement again in the tall grass. It was close—very close. Only seconds away now. She thought of Cole....

You'd better be right about this.

Amanda was about to run but then the approaching noise seemed to stop—causing her to hesitate. She still felt a presence close by, but the fog was too thick and she couldn't make out anything. She waited for a moment—her pulse rate skyrocketing. Then inexplicably the presence, whatever it was, seemed to withdraw. It disappeared altogether.

Amanda waited for a few moments—still frozen—her heart in her throat. She then saw an outline through the fog coming from the opposite direction. It was moving directly toward the fire. But this wasn't a bear at all. It was a man, and he was cradling something in his arms.

"Cole?" Amanda cried out.

"Yeah, right here," he said as he dropped the kindling and broken limbs onto the fire.

He walked over to Amanda who was still clutching the rock.

"Only problem with camping way up here is you have to make a trip down the hill every now and then when you run out of fuel," he said with a half-smile. He then furled his brow at Amanda's startled expression. "What's the matter?"

7:45 AM

Amanda had relayed her experience to Cole over breakfast and even admitted to him being quite frightened by the whole ordeal. Cole was attentive and showed a proper amount of concern without being patronizing which Amanda appreciated. They even found humor in the situation when they considered what Amanda might have done with that rock to Cole as he unwittingly came back to the campsite.

A bit of uneasiness stayed with Amanda when a sweep of their campsite had shown no signs of a crossing bear. But as Cole pointed out, in that deep grass it would have been almost impossible to uncover its prints. The good news would be that it could not have traveled far and hopefully they could track it within an hour.

They packed their gear and continued with their hunt following the ridge line over the grassy knolls toward the area known as Shining Wilderness. And within minutes of beginning their hike, gusts of wind began to blow the fog from around them allowing blue sky to pop through. Visibility increased dramatically.

Almost immediately Cole threw up his hand to signal a stop. He walked back to Amanda—his finger pointing in a far off direction.

"Cold Mountain. Kind of hard to see at the moment but its right over there," he stated. "On an extremely clear day you can make out Mount Mitchell, the tallest peak this side of the Mississippi. But today...? Eh...maybe later."

Amanda only nodded at the bumps and crags on the horizon. She wouldn't know Cold Mountain or Mount Mitchell from a volcano, but she appreciated Cole's interest in the area and appreciated more the fact that he seemed to care that she know all about it as well.

Three *beeps* from Cole's walkie-talkie sang out before they had a chance to continue.

"It's the station. I forgot to report in this morning. They're probably just checkin' up on us," Cole said.

Cole pulled off his pack and rested it at his feet as he went to the radio. Amanda just stood patiently drumming her fingers on the straps of her pack.

"Oconaluftee—this is Cole. That you, Horace? Over."

"*Cole, it's Nic. We've got a problem.*" The young ranger's voice was staid yet somewhat weak sounding.

Cole frowned and instinctively turned away from Amanda. "What is it, Nic?"

"*We got another one, Cole. Another attack...last night or early this morning.*"

The blood seemed to drain out of Cole's face and he temporarily closed his eyes to the news. Having overheard, Amanda walked around to face Cole—emanating her own concerned look.

Cole opened his eyes and stared right into Amanda's. He decided he would no longer try to hide any of this news from her. At this point he knew she was in this as much as the park was.

"Where? Not near Smokemont?" Cole pleaded.

"*No, Cole, it wasn't even in the park. It was off the parkway, near where ya'll are now. In Graveyard Fields.*"

Amanda overheard Nic's static-filtered voice and went numb. She felt sick to her stomach. She tried to speak but couldn't. Her morning experience on top of this sudden news had her head spinning.

Cole took a quick glance at the path behind them as if had the power to stare right down into Graveyard Fields itself. He gripped the walkie-talkie a little tighter.

"Nic, listen to me. Get Lewis and Buck outta the woods now and meet me down there as soon as possible. Got it?"

"*Understood. Oconaluftee—out.*"

Cole let the walkie-talkie slip from his hand and fall on top of his pack. He stood there for a moment trying to gather it all in. As much for him as for herself, Amanda moved forward and grabbed his hand. Cole looked up at her. And then he pulled her close, gently placing her head on his shoulder.

"What's happening, Cole?" Amanda asked in a far-away voice.

Cole did not reply. He just held Amanda lost in his own thoughts.

My God...not again.

10:23 AM

Graveyard Fields, a valley in the Pisgah National Forest, had been aptly named twice before. During the early pioneer days many of her large spruce pines were blown over in a wicked storm and the uprooted trees looked like forgotten graves to those traveling past. Later in the 1900's it also achieved similar notoriety during Pisgah's extreme logging period. It was said that many of the trees in the valley had been chopped down and a certain moss grew on the stumps giving them a grayish tinge. From high above, these stumps looked like headstones. But now by virtue of this latest development, the tiny valley's name had immediately taken on a more sinister connotation.

The parking lot at Graveyard Fields looked to be almost a carbon copy of the campsite after the first attack at Smokemont with all the emergency vehicles jammed together, their lights flashing wildly. Cole and Amanda wheeled in and came to a sliding halt near the wooden stairs that led down an embankment to the trail entrance. It had taken them over an hour of high speed hiking to make it down Black Balsam to get to the jeep and they had barely enough time to catch their breath before they were out again heading down the laurel covered path of Graveyard Fields.

As they proceeded down the trail, Cole was in the lead but he kept Amanda close as he helped her leap across several washed out areas and navigate the slippery split log bridges that crisscrossed the valley's Yellowstone Prong River. They encountered several groups of hikers and campers who were being led out of the valley by resource officers and emergency personal. The officers knew Cole, and they let him continue to the scene unimpeded with Amanda in tow.

They eventually came to an area that opened up along the south end of the river. A team of rangers and medics were spread out doing their investigation including Nic and others from the park.

As Cole broke away to talk to the rangers, Amanda decided to size up the area herself. She took note of the victim's small two-man tent, an empty clothesline, fishing gear and several packs and containers near the water's edge. And as she moved beyond the tent she also noticed that lying beneath a green blanket was the unmistakable shape of a human body. She immediately began taking pictures of the area knowing from experience that the officials might soon insist that she stop.

Cole walked up to Nic and Lewis near a small waterfall that fronted this section of the river. Both men had their hands on their hips as if they were out of patience and out of answers. Nic's jaw was tight and his eyes smoldered with anger. He didn't even wait for Cole to ask him a question.

"We don't know what this is, but it sure as hell ain't like any animal that *we've* ever crossed."

"What's the situation?" Cole asked. His voice was dispassionate almost callous.

"Same as before, Cole. Same type of attack. Just ripped out the guy's insides," Nic fired back hardly believing the words that were coming out of his mouth.

Lewis joined in. "And before you ask, no, there are no discernable tracks near the victim or in this general area. It was the first thing the forest rangers looked for when they came on the scene. I found some prints dried in a clay bank up that rise over there but they look old—at least a week or two. Buck's still out in the field looking in that laurel mess behind us."

Nic moved closer for a face to face with Cole.

"No tracks, no blood trail and nobody else that was camping in the valley claimed to have heard a damn thing. What the hell is going on?"

Cole dropped his head and kicked at a little stone that flew into the waterfall's splash pool. He looked back up and gathered in Nic and Lewis with his eyes.

"I don't know." He paused and then repeated in a whisper, "I don't know."

"Ranger Whitman," a voice called out.

Cole turned recognizing it to be that of Lem Astin, the forest ranger, who was now approaching—his eye twitching away.

"Just had to bring that bear with ya, huh? What are these bears of yours—members of the Manson family?" Lem asked. He said it as a joke but none of the park rangers even cracked a smile.

"As you said yourself, it couldn't possibly be the same bear," Cole retorted. "But it does look like we've got the same problem now, doesn't it?"

Lem just grabbed his thin tie. He didn't quite know what to say to that.

"Has your crew had any luck tracking it?" Lewis asked.

Lem shook his head. "Nope. That's what I done come over to tell ya. We couldn't find nothing. This thing beats all, don't it? It don't act like no bear neither. None of the camper's food coolers were touched. Hell, there was even a stack of bacon waiting to go in a fry pan that didn't get touched. It just went after that man like nobody's business. I'm telling ya, there's something screwy going on in our little corner of the wild kingdom."

Across the way, Amanda continued taking pictures of the area. For the most part, the rangers had left her alone mainly because she had arrived at the scene with Cole. And despite the horrid nature of the incident, Amanda couldn't help but feel excited—realizing that she was now piecing together a story of such an explosive nature.

She had made her way over to the body and took a lingering look down. Despite the dark green coloring of the blanket she could make out the heavy blood stains that had soaked through—mainly in the abdomen area. *Just like with Parker.*

Amanda went to her knees and quickly looked up at the rangers just to see if she was being watched. She then carefully drew back the blanket from the head of the victim. She noticed his eyes—they were opened as in a state of shock—blood had streaked like tears from the corners and ran down into his ears. Amanda then closed her own eyes. The realization that this could have been her lying here suddenly hit her like a ton of bricks. She reopened her eyes and forced herself to do her job. This was no time to get weak-kneed—she had to be disciplined. She knew not to take a picture of the man—that would have been crossing the line—but she studied his face. She didn't recognize him, but he did seem a bit unusual with his dark hair, thick moustache…and a silver cross on his left ear.

1:22 PM

In Gatlinburg, Tennessee, Tully Lawton opened the door to the reception office at park headquarters and rushed inside. He was under great duress and it showed. His face was beet red and he had heavy sweat stains under the arms and around the collar of his white shirt. His red and blue striped tie was twisted like a hangman's noose around his swollen neck. And despite missing his ever-present cigar, he still looked like he was only one more crisis away from a massive coronary.

His secretary, Mary Blevins, a petit but tenacious woman, the one he secretly called his little bulldog, jumped up from behind her desk with the intent of blocking him from entering his private office.

"Superintendent Lawton, I'm sorry, but you really need to call these people," she urged.

Tully stopped momentarily but cocked his head and waved her off. "Mary, I ain't got time to return anymore goddamn messages today. Now enough is enough—I've had 'em up to my eyeballs." His hand angled at eyelevel.

But, Superintendent, Senator Ervin's office..." she began in vain.

Tully stepped aside of her and headed for his door. "Not now, Mary!"

He slammed the door to his private office behind him and then froze as he turned and saw Cole, Amanda and Nic standing around his desk. They looked totally out of place in Tully's manicured office.

"What the hell ya'll doin' here?" Tully asked—unable to hide his thick southern accent. The question was for them all, but his eyes zeroed in on Cole.

No one answered as Tully made his way around to his side of a large, oak desk.

Amanda then reached over and confidently put her fingertips on the rail of his desk to address him. "Superintendent Lawton, as the official liaison for the press, I need to know how you're going to handle this latest...incident."

Tully pulled up on the waist of his pants as if he were getting ready to fight. "How am *I* gonna handle it? Well, I ain't exactly sure, Ma'am, but I'm certain large quantities of alcohol will somehow be involved."

Amanda persisted. "Look, I understand what an ordeal this must be for you. But I need to know..."

"We're shutting it down, Miss Rivers," he interrupted. "The whole goddamn park."

He looked over at Cole. "How's that for handling it?" He then plopped down in his red leather-back chair and rubbed the brass-studded arms. He reached into a pull drawer and produced a Smokin' Joe's which he quickly lit with a desk lighter and threw into his mouth.

"You want the official word? I got it right here," he said blowing the blue smoke to the office ceiling. He dug about his shirt pocket and unfolded the memo. "Secretary of the Interior, Rogers C.B. Morton..." he started. He then noticed everyone was still standing. "Look, why don't ya'll sit down before ya'll fall down, for Christ's sake."

Cole and Nic wearily moved to the office's wingback chairs as Amanda found a semi-seated position leaning on Tully's desk.

Tully continued with the memo, "...Morton has officially declared the Smoky Mountain National Park to be closed until further notice. All park services will be withheld until such time the park has been declared reasonably safe and free from all...*incorrigible* elements." Tully then gave a sarcastic laugh. "Incorrigible elements my ass."

"What about the parkway?" Amanda followed—now fully in reporter mode.

"It's been closed too. From here to the Shenandoah Valley, everything's down and out." Tully leaned forward to address Cole. "Oh, and get a load of this...we have also been ordered to round up *and* remove all black bears that are found within a thirty mile radius of all of our camping and picnic areas."

Now Cole leaned forward with his own puzzled look. "They can't be serious. That could be over five hundred of 'em. How are we supposed to do that?"

Tully drummed his hands on his desk. "Cages...traps...any way we can. We've got to smoke 'em out and send 'em packin'. And you can bet your ass Wildlife Services will be called in to *help us out* on this one."

Amanda gave Cole a confused look.

Cole explained as bluntly as possible. "Wildlife Services...government paid coyote assassins. They always bring 'em in whenever animals need to be taken out."

"Sir..." Nic joined in. "don't you think we may be jumpin' the gun a bit on this one. We haven't even determined if the victim this morning was attacked by a bear or wolf or whatever. Shouldn't we at least wait for the investigation results before we condemn *all* of our black bears?"

"It's public opinion now," Tully said throwing a quick glance at Amanda. "There's not a whole helluva lot we can do about it."

"But two similar attacks in three days and less than forty miles apart? And we haven't found as much as one damn bear track in either case? Doesn't anybody else find that the least bit troublesome?" Nic fired back.

A single, loud knock diffused the conversation as everyone turned to see who was at the office door. Anson Thurmond, the sheriff of Swain County, stuck his bald head around the open door to make himself visible to Tully.

"I'm sorry to bust in on ya like this Superintendent, but I wanted to give you our outline while I was still in the area," Thurmond said in his deep, baritone voice.

He moved in through the door and walked towards Tully's desk. Thurmond was big, meaty guy with swollen arms and thick waistline. His body seemed strangled by his tight-fitting lawman's uniform. His shaved head effectively highlighted the black goatee he wore on his bubbled chin.

He bumped right past Cole's chair and then nodded toward Amanda who backed off the desk as he handed the file over to Tully. "I went over the plan with Larry Hawkins in the governor's office—it only needs your approval now."

Tully flipped through the papers quickly. "Oh…yes, thank you, Sheriff. I'll get right on this…soon as possible."

Cole rose from his chair and stood right next to Thurmond but looked only at Tully. "Did he say a plan? A plan for what?"

Knowing their shared animosity for one another, Tully rose quickly and forced Cole to look in his direction.

"Sheriff Thurmond thought we could benefit from using his department as a kinda border patrol for the park. You know, to keep the bears in and possible poachers out," Tully explained. "Now that all this hell has cut loose."

"Yes, I've already heard several rumors that some of the locals were gonna go after the bears—since they feel *ya'll* can't seem to get a hold of 'em," Thurmond added.

Cole didn't say a word. He just stood there fuming—his eyes slowly locked onto the sheriff's.

Thurmond flashed Cole a bit of his graying, tobacco-stained teeth and then turned to Tully. "Well, I've taken up enough of your time, Superintendent Lawton. Let me know what you think about it," he said. "We're just waitin' for you to give the word."

"Will do, and thanks again Sheriff."

Thurmond nodded at Tully with a smile and then retracted it as he turned past Cole.

Cole waited for the door to shut behind the Sheriff and then he leaned into Tully's desk. "You put me in charge of this operation…remember? The next time there's a *fucking* command decision around here, *I better be a part of it!*"

Cole bolted out of the office and was quickly followed by Nic.

Tully took a hard drag on the cigar and then blew out in relief as much as anything else.

"Good God…what was that all about?" Amanda asked.

"Oh…a lot of water under the bridge, I guess you could say," Tully said condemning the moment with a shake of his head. He then lowered his voice. "This is all I need."

"I'm guessing there is some existing bad blood between those two, huh?"

Tully made two fists and then jammed them together. "Egos, Miss Rivers. They're both good men, but to be honest, I wouldn't want to cross either one of 'em."

Amanda nodded figuring she would find out about it later and headed for the office door. She then made a quick turn to Tully. "Superintendent…I'll be contacting you later. Give you a chance to gather your thoughts. I know you'll want to address all of this. This situation, I should think, is far from over."

Tully only gave an accepting nod as Amanda walked out the door. He then crossed over in front of his desk and went over to a large wall map of the Great Smoky Mountain National Park on an adjacent wall. He ran his large hand tenderly over the representation of the vast acreage. For him, the park was like his own child. He thought about how all of this could have happened under his own watch and what was still yet to come. Amanda's parting words hung over him like a sharpened guillotine.

"Yes, Ma'am, far from over indeed," he whispered.

3:11 PM

The Qualla Civic Center was built for the Cherokee people by the Bureau of Indian Affairs in 1966. Conveniently located in the middle of downtown, the center became the designated meeting place for the Tribal Council and the Cherokee's Executive Department and became home to the day to day operations of the reservation.

The building itself was lavishly designed by Native American artists who creatively interwove traditional motifs from ceiling to floor. Many historical artifacts that weren't kept in the nearby museum such as *The Talking Leaves*, the original Cherokee alphabet created by Sequoyah, were also found in the civic center encased in glass boxes.

But most visitors who came to the center were drawn to the over-sized masks representing the seven clans of the Cherokees which were placed prominently throughout the building against its interior walls. These demonic looking masks were over four feet long and hung hauntingly from the ceiling at an angle as to be imposing to would-be visitors. Each tribe member was a descendant of one of the clans and took pride in being represented by the wolf, the red tail hawk, the blue holly, the deer, the long hair, the paint, or the wild potato. Each clan was significant to the first Cherokees and each was still represented by the modern tribal council.

Using his good shoulder, Sanooke pushed through the front glass doors of the center and hurried right through the busy central office to get to the conference room where the emergency meeting was being held. The tribal council, including Eddie Whitetree, sat somberly around a long, rectangular table awaiting him.

"Forgive my tardiness," Sanooke began. "I was out of town when I received the call." Sanooke took his place at the head of the table next to Eddie. "We shall dispense with our normal meeting procedures—let's get right to this."

Attle Armstrong, one of the council elders and a representative of the deer clan, rose to speak. "Chief Sanooke, with the park being closed to the west of us and the Blue Ridge Parkway closed to our east, our little town will soon begin to feel the isolation very quickly. We all believed many tourists would be here this summer, and now it looks as if they won't be coming at all. Something must be done."

Another elder and a representative of the blue holly clan, the heavy-set and bull-nosed Watty Hartford, rose to join in before Sanooke could reply. "My brother-in-law and I placed most of our savings in our motel, Sanooke. We refurbished the entire place this past winter. New draperies. New carpet. And we have advertised so much this year. To be honest, I don't know if we will survive this."

Sanooke, himself a member of the wolf clan, rolled his eyes toward the fat man. "You will survive, Watty. As will we all. A tragedy has befallen our park neighbors and we shall help them weather this storm. It is true, we will see a significant drop in our tourist trade for a few weeks, but hopefully this will not last throughout our entire summer."

"And if it does?" Watty asked.

"Then we will cross that bridge when we get to it. None of you should be panicking at this point."

Eddie who was seated next to Sanooke simply turned in his seat to be heard. "Even a little hitch in the economy is going to prove problematic, Chief Sanooke. Perhaps we could ask for an extension through the Qualla Grant...."

Sanooke cut him off. "No, Eddie. That money is ear-marked for the housing project. Asking for an extension now may cause delays in its progress and that project is something our community desperately needs at this point. Besides, we will not start asking for more handouts from their government. It is not our way."

Sanooke looked up addressing them all now. "We must not react in haste or with indiscretion to this matter. We must remain strong for our neighbors as well as ourselves. Let our people look to you for guidance and stability. Weather this storm."

After the meeting had broken up, Sanooke and Eddie remained seated at the conference table. Eddie waited for all the council members to exit and then leaned over to Sanooke.

"You can put on a good show for them, Sanooke, but you can't fool me. Something about this is scaring the hell out of you, isn't it?" Eddie said with a raised eyebrow.

Sanooke remained stone-faced. "It is an unpleasant situation. The reservation will suffer financial difficulties. There is nothing more to it than that."

"C'mon, Edami, I wouldn't ask if I didn't know you so well."

Sanooke paused and took a long, hard look at Eddie. "You have heard details of this latest attack?"

Eddie furled his brow but nodded.

"Another man...ripped apart...by one of our bears perhaps?"

Eddie continued his simple nod.

"And no tracks were found, as none were found near the Oconaluftee?"

"Yes, that was what was told to me," Eddie confirmed.

Sanooke took a very long pause and then leaned toward Eddie to whisper. "And what do you know of yo-nv di-gi-ti-lv-s-di?"

Hearing the ancient words, Eddie sank back into his chair as if he had been suddenly shot right between the eyes. He stared off at the wall in front of him—his mind racing at the possibilities.

"I see you understand, Eddie," Sanooke said in his soft voice. "And then you must also understand that what I have said must never leave this room."

4:43 PM

The wind whistled threw the thick laurel brush and cooled its tempered skin. Judaculla sat back in the pit, exhausted—its work was nearly complete. In front of it was a mound of the black unearthed soil that it had achingly dug with its claws—caked over now with the rich sediment and its own drawn blood.

It stared in fascination at its work. The decomposing heads of those hikers he had encountered at Roaring Fork, the arm from the fat man fishing in its river, the remains of skin and organs taken from Graveyard Fields. They were all fitting tributes for the Judaculla, satiating its great hunger. It was getting more and more powerful. Soon the words of the ka-i-e-le u-de-li-da would be realized.

Soon no one would be able to stop it.

7:35 PM

Amanda walked up the steps of Cole's simple wooden, ranch-style cabin in the ranger complex located just a mile from the station. After leaving Gatlinburg, she had driven like a bat-out-of-hell back to the paper and fired off her story of the past two days. She took it straight to her editor's office and plopped it right on his desk. She didn't even wait for a response—she knew it was hot—perhaps the most tantalizing piece that the *Chronicle* had ever ran. She told his assistant that she'd call back before the paper was put to bed, but she still had other angles she needed to follow up. She then had gone home and showered and now looked quite relaxed in her jeans and her favorite white oxford shirt with its sleeves rolled up to mid-arm. She had her hair pulled back into her usual ponytail and she had applied a little makeup to hide the stressors of the past two days. She was herself again—confident, renewed, and ready to go wherever this story would take her.

As she knocked on his door, Amanda thought about the man inside. She wasn't sure yet of what to make of the relationship she was developing with Cole—friend...foe...confidant...something more? But she knew he had an ear to the heartbeat of the park and that was at least worth keeping in his good graces. She had called him from the paper to find out about this falling out with Sheriff Thurmond, but he had only invited her to dinner saying that he would explain things then.

She knocked several more times on Cole's door with her right hand—her left hung by her side gripping a bottle of red wine. She looked at her watch, shook her head, and then gave a good pounding with her fist. Finally, she heard Cole mumbling something and then the tumblers on the lock being turned.

Cole opened the door. He stood there shirtless—a bit bleary-eyed.

"Seven-thirty?" he asked

Amanda smiled. "Yeah, you sure you want to do this?"

Cole nodded and scratched his chest. "Sure, sure. Just give me a minute to get ready, will ya?"

He held the door open and Amanda walked inside. "I guess I overslept. Came back from setting bear traps this afternoon and just crashed."

"It's been a long couple of days," she agreed.

As she entered, Amanda's eyes swept the small living room. Its simple décor and untidiness spoke volumes to Amanda about Cole, but there was no real disappointment—it was, in fact, exactly what she would have expected from such a man.

The room was barely furnished with just an over-sized couch and mismatched La-Z-Boy recliner. A dusty black and white TV with tin-foiled rabbit ears sat unplugged on a bookshelf. A small fireplace fronted the room; its block wood mantle had several framed and unframed photos leaning against the stone facade.

Cole picked up some discarded laundry from the couch and headed toward the back of the cabin. "I'll just jump in the shower and be right out."

"No problem," she uttered. She held onto the wine with both hands now and moved to the center of the room.

"Just have a seat, or get yourself a drink, if you like. I don't have much, but I know there's some beer in the fridge," Cole called out as headed to the back of the cabin.

"I'll be alright," she answered.

Amanda could see the tiny kitchen from where she was standing. She felt a twinge of sadness as she could imagine Cole eating his TV dinners there alone at the small counter or maybe even standing over the sink. She knew from her own experiences that being lonely was all it was cracked up to be.

Amanda heard the water to the shower turn on in the back. She went to the couch, but it smelled a bit old and musty, so she thought better of it and just ambled around the room. She took note of the beautiful mallard which was mounted spread-wing on the wall above the couch as well as several large trout stuffed in various poses around it. The woodsman, the huntsman, the ranger—it all made sense for a man like Cole.

After poking around cabinets and peeking through drawers, the pictures on the mantle finally drew her in. She began to pick them up one by one. Most of the photos were of a Native American family—a young boy seemed to be a favorite of the camera's eye. There was one unframed photo of Cole with his arm around a Cherokee man who was dressed up in full Native American regalia. They both had huge grins and squinty eyes as if they had just shared a long night of laughing or drinking or perhaps both.

Two more photos on the end of the mantle struck Amanda as they were the only ones with any hint of age to them. The first was a black and white photo of an old woman fishing in a small creek. She had her hand on her hip and was leaning back as if she were straining to bring in her haul. Amanda guessed grandmother, but she couldn't be sure.

She then picked up the other photograph. It too was black and white and was weathered in its tiny glass frame. It was a family on a porch in front of their simple wooden home. A father, mother and two children, both boys. She focused on the boy sitting on the bottom wooden step. He had dark skin and dark hair. It kind of looked like Cole, but again she wasn't positive. The photograph looked about thirty years old so the age of the child would have been about right.

The photographer had framed the shot from the dirt road that ran in front of the house. There was an enormous oak tree to the left of the house and an identification post that was in the bottom right corner. The sign numbers were fronted by the image of a small, twisting mountain. Amanda could read the postal numbers 617, but she couldn't make out the name entirely. The first letter was definitely an M followed by the letter I and then what looked like a double LL. After that, the letters bled off the photograph. Her best guess was *Miller*. But if this was truly Cole, then that couldn't be right—not if this was his house.

She continued to analyze the child for several minutes—she could see Cole's high cheek bones in the boy's face and a possible widow's peak like Cole's despite the boy's close shaved crew cut. She became lost in the picture, drawing her fingernail around the smiling boy several times. And then it hit her. An image flashed in her mind. The small knife. C…T…*M*!

"You ready?"

Amanda jumped; startled by Cole's voice. "What? Yes, yes, of course…" She turned toward him and laid the picture back on the mantle in a nonchalant fashion. Cole had showered and dressed in no time. So used to seeing him in his uniform, Amanda was taken aback by his attire—dark jeans and a wine red button-down. His hair was still wet and was combed back to reveal his taut face. He seemed different. Less the authority-figure now. More approachable. One might be tempted to say handsome even.

"Are we going out? I thought you promised me a home-cooked meal?"

Cole smiled. "And you'll get one. Just not from *this* home."

Amanda returned his witticism with a genuine smile.

Within minutes, they were in Amanda's red Mustang pulling out of Cole's driveway. They had both offered to drive but then Amanda came up with a compromise—take her car with Cole behind the wheel. With the convertible's top reattached they were finally able to travel and talk peacefully without the whistling competition from the wind.

"Where are we going?" Amanda asked.

"Friends of mine. Live over in the Qualla Tract. I've been putting off an invite from them for several weekends now. You'll like 'em. Kina is a helluva cook."

Amanda just nodded to Cole's static answers. She was getting used to his punch and duck method of giving only the slightest information to her questions. Feeling gamey though, she decided to press him on another issue. "I thought maybe we were heading to see your buddy,

Sheriff Thurmond. Ya'll seemed to get along so well in the superintendent's office." She said it with a hint of a smile but then squinted her eyes as if bracing for his reaction.

Cole sighed but kept his eyes focused on the road. He then tilted his head in her direction and cast a relenting look her way. "No, I don't think I'll be sharing bread with him anytime soon."

Amanda kicked off her clogs and pulled her right leg up under her leaning towards him. "Why, Cole? What happened between you two?" Cole just shook his head. "C'mon. I really want to know," she insisted. "You promised you'd tell me."

"It's nothing really…" he started. But he looked back at Amanda with her cute quirky smile. She was really beginning to work on him, and he relented.

"Okay…okay…. It happened over ten years ago when I was first starting out here in the park. Thurmond was still a deputy sheriff with Swain County at the time. He was out doing traffic duty when he'd pulled over a logging truck from Brevard which he suspected was running moonshine to the Georgia hills. It was a common route, and Thurmond had gotten pretty good at sniffing out the runners."

The headlights of a passing car distracted him momentarily, but then he continued.

"Anyway as Thurmond was checking out the rig, the bootlegger got the goods on him and pulled a pistol out from under his seat. He forced Thurmond to surrender his weapon and then used the sheriff's own handcuffs to pin him to his patrol car. As you can imagine, this pissed Thurmond off to no end. The logging truck then made a u-turn and headed back this way up Highway 19. Thurmond eventually freed himself somehow and took off after him."

"How did you get involved?"

"Well, the logging truck tried to escape through the park which meant it became our jurisdiction—our problem. We got wind of what was happening and they sent me to intercept. I was instructed to cut off Thurmond's pursuit. Which *is* park policy by the way." Cole rapped the tip of his index finger on the steering wheel for emphasis. "And again this did not sit too well with the future honorable sheriff."

"I see…. And did they ever catch the guy? The runner, I mean."

A grin spread across Cole's face. "Yeah, after turning Thurmond and the rest of the sheriff's department around, I managed to locate the abandoned truck off a maintenance road near the Oconaluftee station. An hour later I tracked the guy down—found him hiding in a tree of all places."

"*You* made the arrest?"

Cole shook his head affirmatively and bit his lower lip. "Three days on the job and I was front page news. Got a couple of accommodations from the park service—and it just made ol' Thurmond madder than dirt."

"And you two have been bumping heads ever since?"

"About six years ago I ran into him at a Park Service sponsored dove shoot and tried to strike up a conversation, but given half a chance he'd as soon blown off *my* head as a dove's that day. And I still see him around Cherokee ever so often, but I think we've resigned ourselves to sticking to our own side of the street...as it were."

"And his plan to border the park is encroaching on your side of the street."

"Exactly. And he knows it too." Cole waited and then added, "The jack ass."

Amanda nodded her acceptance of the story. Her smile, however, evaporated as her thoughts turned to the more serious side of the dilemma. "This latest attack is going to cause problems though, isn't it? Thurmond's right about the people...the poachers, I mean. They'll be coming."

"I hope not, but it is possible."

"And Superintendent Lawton said in his office that a group from Wildlife Services may even get called in. You called them assassins. How do you plan on stopping all this?"

Cole gripped the wheel just a little bit tighter and stared at the road ahead. "Once the attacks stop, everything else will take care of itself."

Amanda gave a bit of a sarcastic laugh and looked out the passenger's side window. "Yeah, well, that *is* the problem then, isn't it?"

Cole didn't respond. He just kept his eyes on the road—his thoughts to himself.

More than you'll ever know.

8:25 PM

Cole pulled the Mustang quietly through Big Cove, one of the neighborhoods in the Qualla Tract. Amanda eyed the simple block houses and dilapidated trailers, but there was no empathy on her part—only acceptance. Her years of covering crime in D.C. had taught her that life was not always fair and she took societal partialities with a grain of salt.

Cole wheeled into the dirt driveway of Eddie's modest home. Firewood and a child's overturned tricycle were scattered about the front porch. Smoke billowed out of a brick chimney on the side of the house.

The screen door flew open and Eddie greeted Cole and Amanda before they even had a chance to reach the porch. "Hello there…. Come in, come in…" His deep voice was booming yet warmly receptive.

"Hello…" Amanda returned—her disarming smile in full glow. She instantly noted that the man standing before her was the same one she had seen in the picture with Cole.

As they walked into the house, Eddie whispered playfully into Cole's ear, "About damn time."

Cole smiled and half-whispered back, "Well, you know women—they're always late."

Amanda overheard and shot an incredulous look at Cole. "Excuse me?" she said jokingly.

Cole threw up his hands and cocked his head. "You're right. It was my fault. Just trying to pass the buck."

"As usual," Eddie added with a laugh. "He's always blaming someone else."

As they entered the front room, Kina came quickly out of the kitchen wiping her hands on a flowered apron. She pushed strands of her long black hair away from her round face and greeted everyone with her own warm smile. Eddie took her by her hand.

"Amanda, this is Eddie and Kina Whitetree, my friends," Cole offered. He then pointed to Amanda. "And this is Amanda Rivers."

"It's nice meeting you. I want to thank you for including me at your table tonight," Amanda said handing the bottle of wine over to Kina.

"It's our pleasure," Kina returned. "As a friend of this one, you'll always be welcome in our home."

"Yeah, were just glad the lone ranger here decided to bring someone with him tonight," Eddie joked. He then began to move forward and added, "C'mon on in here, Amanda, I'll introduce you to the rest of the Whitetree clan."

Eddie led them into a smaller sitting room where a warm glow radiated from the fireplace. Amanda noticed a young boy playing in the center of the room on a red and blue madras rug. And like she did with his father, she immediately made the connection to the photographs on Cole's mantle.

Well, at least those pictures make a little sense.

The boy ran from where he was playing and latched onto his mother's leg—his big, brown eyes staring up at Amanda.

"This little guy is Jonathon, our son," Eddie said.

Amanda bent down to say hello, but he just hid behind Kina's apron. They all laughed.

"Give him a few minutes and he'll warm up to ya," Eddie followed. He then pointed to the corner of the room. "And over there, smoking her pipe—*although she has been warned several times not to*—is my grandmother. Everyone calls her Unilisi."

Amanda stood and faced the corner of the room. She saw the frail old woman rocking in her chair—the wispy smoke curling out of the pipe. Unilisi turned slightly and glared at Amanda. Her face was leathery and veins bulged from her thin and spotted skin, but Amanda immediately blocked that all out locking in only on the woman's eyes. There was something different about this woman and Amanda picked right up on it. She had a kind of awareness to her as if she had the power to see right through people. It immediately got to Amanda and made her feel uncomfortable.

Amanda also sensed the old woman was constantly doing something with her right hand. Amanda forced herself to break eye contact to look down at the object. It appeared she was rubbing a small bear paw which hung from a silver necklace. She kept kneading at the paw with her thumb and forefinger.

Amanda finally turned back to Eddie and Kina and forced her smile to return. "Well, it's very nice meeting you all."

An awkward silence followed until Cole finally broke the tension, "So...let's eat."

After a filling meal of venison flank steaks, fried squash blossoms and bean bread, they all returned to the small side room and the slow dancing flames of the fire. Amanda's gift wine had passed quickly during the meal and now Eddie had brought out some of his scuppernong wine to keep the evening flowing.

"You make this yourself?" Amanda inquired to Eddie.

"Yeah, we've got several vines growing wild in the backyard." Eddie paused and then added, "Makes it convenient for an ol' bottler like myself."

Amanda smiled and took another sip. "Well, it's very good. Very sweet." She looked at Kina. "And that meal was excellent. I haven't had anything that good since I moved down here."

"I told ya she was a great cook," Cole quickly interceded.

Kina leaned forward on the couch. "I know you live in Asheville now, but where exactly were you before, Amanda?"

"D.C. I actually worked for the *Post* for five years—mostly covering the crime beat down town."

Eddie and Kina both reacted with impressed looks. "The nation's capital, huh? A far cry difference from our quiet little Smokies, I'll bet." Eddie said. "What with all the impeachment hearings and political fallout happening up there now with Tricky Dick and his crew."

Amanda agreed. "Yeah, you would think that's where a reporter would want to be—knee deep in all that. But to tell you the truth, I had had enough of life in that city, the D.C. life. While everyone else seemed glued to Pennsylvania Avenue, I was reporting on the rapes and beatings that were taking place in the projects just a few short blocks away. And really no one seemed to care too much about it—those people or those crimes. No matter how terrible the child murder or the gang rape, my stories never made to the front page. To be honest, it just got to be a little depressing." Amanda paused as she finished her wine. "I needed a break from it; and when Sam…Samuel Cox, the *Asheville Chronicle's* publisher and a former instructor of mine from college, called, I knew it was time to make the change. My colleagues warned me that I'd grow bored reporting on the weather and the openings of new resorts in the mountains. But it's been anything but boring lately, hasn't it?" She then added, "I guess it's impossible to totally get away from the negatives."

Eddie nodded. "We definitely have our share. Although I must confess, a crazed bear running through the park is something new even for us."

Cole shot Eddie a disappointed look.

Kina joined in. "To have two such attacks occur out here like that…it seems almost impossible."

118

"It's going to be tough on our people as well as the park. The town is already feeling the effects," Eddie offered. "I sure hope this is over with soon."

Everyone turned and looked to Cole as if he had all the answers. Cole sighed deeply as if he had explained it a million times already and placed his wine glass on the small coffee table in front of him.

"The thing is...black bears are so unpredictable. And now we're supposed to round them all up...." he started. "But Kina, you're right, you know it. Despite being wild animals, two attacks on humans in three days...it's just unheard of. I can't imagine it will happen again. I just can't imagine it."

Unilisi, who after dinner had returned to her rocker and was sitting quietly near the hearth, suddenly began blurting out in her native tongue. Eddie looked up sternly at his grandmother and told her to be quiet, but despite the warning, Unilisi kept rambling. She began to work herself up. Amanda couldn't understand a word, but she knew the old woman was furious about something. Kina finally got up from the couch and went over and calmly but firmly took Unilisi's hand and whispered into her ear. Like a disgruntled child, she jerked her hand away and turned back to the fire. She became quiet once again, yet the anger still smoldered in her face.

Cole leaned into Eddie tapped his knee and whispered, "Should we go?"

Eddie gave a quick shake of his head. "No, no...not at all. She just gets that way sometimes."

"What was it she was saying?" Amanda asked—a genuine mix of concern and curiosity.

Eddie waved a dismissive hand and smiled. "Oh, it's nothing really. It's just she and a circle of her friends don't believe the attacks were made by a bear at all...." He announced this with his voice trailing off—as if he regretted translating it in the first place.

Amanda had heard the rangers say the very same thing but this was different somehow. She could hear the hesitancy in Eddie's voice—furthering her curiosity. "What do you mean not a bear?"

Eddie sat up a little on the couch and cleared his throat. "Oh...a combination of legends and old people's vivid imaginations, I'm afraid," he began. "I know this will sound silly, Amanda, but many like my grandmother believe the attacks were the work of Tsul-kalu...what the white man called Judaculla."

"Judaculla?" Amanda repeated. She looked over at Cole. "The same one you were telling me about yesterday?"

Cole quickly nodded. "Yes. According to Cherokee legend, his dwelling is a cave on top of the Devil's Courthouse."

"Right…it's kind of like our version of the devil…" Eddie began but then decided to skip the biblical parallels. "The Judaculla was a slant-eyed giant of a monster, a seven-clawed goliath that allegedly lorded over these parts during the ancient times. It was a creature that became a source of trouble for my people—burning fields, destroying and devouring livestock…humans too…always causing pain and mischief. Many of our old stories dealt with those who had come in contact with this monster. His markings are supposedly found on several rocks throughout the Smokies."

"But your grandmother believes this monster actually has something to do with what's going on now?

"Yes, to many of our elderly and true believers, it is not so much legend as a part of nature. They believe it's intertwined—nature and these old stories. Some are fairly adamant about it."

Eddie smiled at the absurdity of the story, but Amanda continued to prod, "So why do they believe the Judaculla has killed these two men?"

"She said it kills others because of an ancient argument between the monster and our people. A struggle for power—if you will." He added with a shrug, "Typical old folk talk."

"What caused the argument?" Amanda asked in all seriousness—her throat growing drier with each inquiry.

Eddie laughed but seemed more annoyed than anything. "I don't know exactly…I think it was something over sacred hunting grounds. Certain parts of the Smokies were by all accounts given to us by the Great Spirit to hunt for food, but the Judaculla claimed the land belonged to it." He tossed in, "To this day, some of our hardcore believers won't even cross boundary lines into its supposed domain. They say there is a prophecy that foretells our destruction if we violate its territory."

Amanda caught a quick glimpse of Cole who was now staring blankly at Eddie.

"Please don't take her too seriously, Amanda," Eddie continued. "Anytime a tree falls across the road or a raccoon knocks over a trashcan many of the faithful blame it on the Judaculla's wrath. It's just their way of explaining things. That's all."

Kina returned and sat down cross-legged on the couch whispering, "Forgive us, Amanda. Unilisi is not herself tonight."

Amanda gave a slight smile and nodded as if accepting the explanation. But as the conversation that night turned to less intriguing subjects, she could not get the old woman out of her mind. She had sounded so convinced, so passionate in her speech. And as the evening grew, Amanda caught herself sneaking peeks in the corner at the slow moving rocking chair. And every time she looked, as if reading her mind, Unilisi turned slightly and flashed her powerful right eye in Amanda's direction.

11:20 PM

Cole pulled the Mustang to a stop in front of his house and cut the engine. He looked over at Amanda. "As promised, one home cooked meal and one quick tour of the reservation all in…" He looked at his watch. "…under four hours."

Amanda smiled, "It *was* nice. Thanks. I enjoyed meeting Eddie and Kina."

"Yeah, they're good people. They've been especially good to me over the years. That Unilsi is something though, isn't she?"

Amanda paused. "Cole, why did you invite me out tonight?" The question had been on the tip of her tongue the whole ride home. She finally felt brave enough.

Cole hesitated and then looked hard again into her eyes. "Well, I was feeling a little guilty. I mean, I wasn't exactly the most gracious host when Tully assigned me to you. Fact is—I could hardly stand you at first…."

They both laughed.

"Same here," Amanda replied.

"We got off on the wrong foot. I thought I should make it up to you in some way."

Amanda nodded.

"Anyway, I'm glad we did this tonight." He waited and then, "Maybe we can get together again sometime?"

Amanda didn't respond. She just looked at him—lost for the right thing to say.

"Well, anyway…goodnight," Cole said with finality.

Cole popped opened the door and climbed out. Amanda quickly followed out the passenger door.

"Cole, wait," Amanda called out. She went around the front of the car and stood with him face to face—the street light from above cast their long shadows against his cabin. "I wanted to apologize too. I know I was a bit pushy at first and I should have approached you differently." She paused. "It's just the way I am sometimes. My job leads the way in which I think."

Cole simply nodded having already accepted this. He reached out and stroked her arm. "You don't have to apologize. I understand completely."

Amanda sensed his touch and for some reason it just felt right to her. As if guided by her wishes, Cole grabbed her arm a little tighter. They both went silent as the connection intensified. Amanda looked deep into Cole's eyes. "Cole, I don't know if it's the wine or the…"

Cole didn't wait. He pulled her in and kissed her deeply. Amanda put up no resistance wrapping her arms around his neck. Cole felt the warmth of her chest against his. An electrical sensation fired throughout his entire body. At once he felt the weight of his ongoing pain vanish—his mind was finally at ease. He was able to focus only on the moment—only on Amanda. They broke from the kiss.

"Cole…"

Cole placed his finger against her lips. He picked Amanda up in his arms. She felt his strength and gave in to it. She wrapped her legs around him and buried her head into his shoulder. He carried her up the steps of his house and they disappeared inside.

May 23, 1974

6:51 AM

Amanda's arm slipped off the side of the bed jarring her awake. She held her position and her breath as she batted the sleepiness from her eyes. She looked down at the wooden floor of the tiny bedroom trying to get her bearings and saw her clothes intermixed with his. This drew a satisfied smile followed quickly by a concerned raised eyebrow. Having spent her young adult life in the uninhibited sixties, nothing sexually ever threw her anymore, but this was different somehow. It wasn't guilt or shame playing with her head. It probably wasn't even related to the actual *drop of a hat* moment they had shared last night. Perhaps it was just the revelation that she had awakened in the bed of a man whom she had nothing in common and vehemently detested only three days prior.

Where are you going with this one, Amanda?

She rolled over quietly to the center and took a look at Cole. He was sleeping on his stomach; his head was turned so that she could not see his face. The covers on his side of the bed had been tossed back around his ankles and her eyes lingered on his nude body. She reached her hand out and lightly ran her fingers down his strong back. She admired his lean, muscular tone and the exotic tint of his dark skin. She noted with concern several deep scars that crossed parts of his body; but otherwise, he seemed to be perfect physically.

But what of the man himself? What of those sudden changes in personality? The short, brusque answers to her relatively innocuous questions? Or those agonizing moments of dead end silence?

What is that darkness that holds you, Cole Whitman?

"Good morning…" Cole muttered as he awoke on cue and turned to face her.

"Good morning," she returned.

She moved over to kiss him. He held his arm out and she leaned back into his chest. They remained quiet for a while as he kissed along her neckline and ran his hand tenderly over the curves of her body.

"Cole..." she finally stated. "No secrets between us, okay?"

"I already told you...I'm not married," Cole said in jest.

Amanda laughed and then sat up. "No, you know what I mean. Let's keep this honest—you and me."

Cole smiled. It was the same old act. There was so much he wanted to tell her, but he held firm, keeping everything in check. "I'm a very simple man, Amanda. I am what you see. There are no secrets...I promise."

Amanda nodded but then added quickly, "Tell me about that scar."

Cole gave a puzzled look and then followed her eyes down as she indicated his hip.

"Oh...that. A climbing accident...several years ago. I was out practicing my repelling techniques when I fell about twenty feet down a rock face. Dangled upside down in mid-air for about three hours until I was rescued. They got me down, but I think I left half of my ass cheek up there on that rock."

Amanda grinned, satisfied, but then reached out and turned his right arm over. "And these?"

Cole paused. He looked at the faded white slashes on his arm and then back to her. "It was a helluva fall."

Amanda gave a slight nod. She so much wanted to believe him, but her instincts were screaming at her. Her whole life—trust was never her strong suit. They sat again in silence until the moments of doubt faded.

Cole finally stretched and got out of the bed. "You want some coffee? I think I have some in the kitchen?"

"No, I'll just wait 'til I get to work," Amanda said as she also slid out of the bed and began throwing on her clothes. "I'll probably be late as it is."

They finished dressing and Cole followed her out to the front door. Amanda opened the door but then turned back around.

"I know you've got a busy day, but call me if you find out anything new about the attack in Graveyard Fields, okay?"

Cole nodded. "Yeah, of course, no problem. I was gonna call you later anyway."

Amanda smiled. She cupped the back of his head with her hand and then leaned back and kissed him.

As they broke, Amanda took a quick look in the direction of the fireplace. Her eyes then zeroed back in on Cole.

"By the way, Cole, who is that boy sitting on the bottom step in that last picture on your mantle? The black and white photo on the end?"

Cole didn't bother to look; he just continued to stare at Amanda. He then forced a pretend smile that somewhat unnerved her.

"Just family."

9:47 AM

Tarvus Jackson, a fifty year old furniture salesman from Cherokee and an avid weekend sportsman, brought the scope on his Winchester 7 mm rifle up to eyelevel. The crosshairs peered through dark branches and heavy foliage and fell right into place between the base of the outstretched blackie's neck and right shoulder. The four hundred pound bear which had been marking its territory suddenly released its hold on the small conifer and came down on all fours. It yawned, twisted its head and then dug at some nearby grass stalks—blissfully unaware of its impending death.

Jackson maintained it all in his sights. Within seconds he regained the preferred shoulder-neck target. He then felt his right index finger go tight—the *squeeze* was about to happen…then the *pop*…then the *drop*. As he always did, Jackson saw it happening in his mind first. He held his breath…just a few seconds more….

A twice forced *cough* interrupted the moment's flow. It was made just a few yards to the right of where Jackson had set up for the kill. Jackson eased off the trigger and slowly turned his head in the direction of the startling noise. Leaning against a giant oak with an open twelve gauge shotgun in his hands was Cole. He smiled broadly at the stunned hunter.

"Now the way I see it, ya got two options…You can put that rifle down and come peacefully with me or…" He locked the barrel down on the shotgun. "…you go ahead and shoot that bear and end up with an ass full of buckshot."

Cole secured the weapon from Jackson and loaded it and its owner in the back of his jeep. He drove the jeep through a well-traveled ravine and then popped back out on the parkway heading east.

Within forty-five minutes he wheeled the jeep into the station at Oconaluftee. The lot was a steady mass of confusion at this point as tractor-trailer trucks were lined up with stacks of iron bear cages waiting to be unloaded. Several rangers were standing around talking and gesturing to the truck drivers. Three of the cages located in the bus parking zone were already tagged and had medium-sized bears crammed into them. The animals were rocking their cages wailing their pitiful cries to get out. Cole spied Horace and Nic in the middle of it all and pulled up right next to them.

"Got an extra cage for this one?" Cole asked jamming his thumb toward Jackson.

Horace looked at the guy and frowned. "No, but we can always squeeze him in with one of the blackies."

Nic joined in, "Another poacher? Goddamn, this is gettin' outta hand. Where did ya find him?"

"Rocky Spur. I caught fresh tire tracks as I was makin' my rounds this morning. We'll need to go back later and impound his truck."

Nic nodded and then got face to face with Jackson. "You were over at Manny's the other night, weren't ya?"

Jackson remained tight-lipped.

"Yeah, I remember you," Nic continued. "So, how much is a blackie goin' for these days anyway?"

Jackson turned his face away in defiance.

Nic leaned over the jeep and stuck out his jaw. He gave the man his best drill instructor voice. "I said *how much*, shit-for-brains!?"

"Five hundred with proof of kill," Jackson mumbled under his breath.

"Yeah? And who's puttin' up the ante, tough guy? Wouldn't be anybody *we'd* know, now would it? Somebody from town maybe?"

Jackson turned to Nic with rage in his eyes. "Fuck you!"

Nic leaned back, rolled his shoulders but kept his cool. He only gave the man a slight grin. "Well, I hope he paid you in advance cause that's how much it's gonna take to get your sorry ass outta jail."

Horace stepped in and prevented any further escalation. "Come on." He calmly grabbed Jackson out of the back of the jeep and led the dejected man inside the station.

Cole put a steady hand on Nic's shoulder to measure any further hostility in his partner. Nic bumped his hand away. "Oh, I'm alright.

That's just the second one I've had to deal with this morning. This whole thing is really starting to piss me off."

"Me too. But its priority one, you know?"

"Yeah, yeah, yeah...I know."

"By the way," Cole said. "You really got some idea who might be flipping the bill for this bear hunt?"

"Just a theory...but think of all those people who stand to lose from the park being shut down, Cole." Nic turned and looked directly at him. "Merchants...business men...The sooner the bears are out, the sooner the money goes back in their pockets. There were a lot of 'em there at Manny's the other night. And a lot were Cherokees."

Cole nodded but said nothing.

"Stands to reason there are quite a few of them who would want this situation resolved now. Somethin' to think about anyway." Nic shrugged and then began to stomp away.

Cole called after him. "Where ya headed?"

"Elkmont—promised Dale I'd help secure the Little River access road. I'll check-in around lunch. We can pick up the asshole's truck then."

With that, Nic climbed into a park maintenance truck and flew out of the lot. Cole turned back to the chaos behind him as he heard the *slam* of iron cages on the asphalt. He watched for a moment as the cages were being unloaded from the trucks and then reloaded on park flatbeds. He knew he was needed to help facilitate the dispersal but he lingered instead in front of the three captured bears. He bent down in front of one of the cages and looked at the miserable creature. The bear nudged its nose through the wire.

"I know just how you feel," he whispered.

10:10 AM

Amanda sat at her desk in the newsroom swiveling in her desk chair and staring at her IBM electric typewriter. She had taken a chance and stopped by her apartment to change and to freshen up after leaving Cole's house—hoping her publisher wouldn't notice her tardiness—but it was difficult trying to get anything past Samuel J. Cox. He had strolled by her desk purposely and tapped firmly on his watch; she had given him the quick nod in return. *Message received.*

Cox was a man of only fifty-seven years, but his slight build combined with a lifetime of chain smoking made him look eighty on his good days. Some of Amanda's fellow journalism majors at Virginia Tech had hated Professor Sam because of his penchant for perfection and expected work ethic from his students, but Amanda saw him differently. His need for excellence was right up her alley; and in that, he kind of reminded her of dear old dad anyway. They had hit it off as pupil and master go; and although he never said so, Amanda knew he was instrumental in her landing the *Post* job right out of college. And when that call came that fateful night, when Amanda was suffering the lowest of the lows, she knew it was in her best interest to drop everything and follow him to this new job in Asheville. And now together again, Amanda was already making good on her vow to help him turn the *Chronicle* around. The bear story had become the biggest seller in recent memory.

But now she was stuck. And she wasn't sure if it was story related, a lack of sleep, or maybe it was the fact that she couldn't stop thinking about…

"Cole Whitman."

Amanda looked up from her desk. Ted Anderson, the pudgy, assistant copy editor and would-be office lothario, stood smugly in front of her, a folder in his hand and his eyes squarely focused on her breasts.

"Sorry…?" Amanda mumbled.

Anderson frowned. "Whitman, Cole. The guy you asked me to check up on a couple of days ago."

Amanda gave a half smile. "Oh, yeah…of course. You've got something?"

"Well, a little bit. See for yourself."

He tossed the folder on her desk. Amanda didn't hesitate and opened it right away.

Ted leaned into her cubicle—his jiggly chin hanging over the side. "What's this guy to you anyway?" he asked as she fished through the papers.

"Just part of the story, Ted," Amanda lied. "Trying to be thorough."

"Okay, if ya say so. Holler if ya need somethin' else," he said as he began walking away.

Amanda kind of waved without looking up. "Yeah. And thanks, Ted."

"Anything for you, sweetheart."

Ted's parting words fell on deaf ears as Amanda had quickly become engrossed in Cole's file. She had forgotten she had ordered a write-up on him as well as some of the other principals involved, and now she rapidly flipped through the pages on Cole—her eyes narrowed in focus. Most were copies of business and governmental forms—old tax returns, loan applications, etc. There was little for her to sink her teeth into—they were about as useful to her as her one-sided conversations with the mysterious ranger had been.

She did find the newspaper write-up of Cole's arrest of the bootlegger from years ago and read through it twice. She was particularly amused at the *no comments* of the unidentified source from the Swain Sheriff's Department. Still, nothing new was forth coming and she began to question what it was she was after anyway.

And then…something resonated. She went back to the form copies at the front of the file. She found Cole's application he had submitted to the National Park Service twelve years ago. She traced her forefinger through several boxes of the faded document until she found what she was looking for. She looked up and leaned back in her chair.

"But that's not what you said…."

10:47 AM

A cool rain from the west blew quickly over the Appalachians and began to settle in the mountain chain's fertile basin. Grey clouds formed and hung like heavy spheres in the sky and the temperature made a steady plummet—destroying what had been a promising start to the crisp mountain morning.

Nic had just completed his security check at the Elkmont access road ahead of schedule and was thankful to be back in the maintenance truck despite its broken heater and busted radio. As he headed back to the station, he rubbed his hands and blew on his finger tips to keep warm. He managed to entertain himself by humming an old Hank Williams tune to the beat of the thread-bare window wipers as they scratched across the windshield. His walkie-talkie slid back and forth on the dashboard with every turn into the mountainous curves. He lunged for it as it suddenly rung out.

"Oconaluftee Two—this is Turner, go ahead."

"Nic, its Horace…What's your twenty?"

"I'm two miles due east of Little River—headin' back to the Bear Cave. What's up, Horace?"

"I hate to ask, but Cole said as long as you're working your way back here, would you mind checkin' them traps in the east end of Chimney Tops?"

"Now?" Nic made a sour face.

"Yeah, he said the ones at the creek entrance have those chain-snaps and he didn't know if they were set properly yesterday."

"But it's rainin' like a bitch out here, Horace. Can't they wait til later?"

"C'mon, it's only three. Right near the trail entrance."

"Only three? Then you come do it."

"Sorry, Nic. It ain't my request. Just lettin' ya know what the boss said..."

"Yeah, yeah, yeah…just give it to the new guy—he won't care if he gets wet," Nic said in his best sarcastic tone.

Horace laughed. *"You'll live. Besides, I'll fix ya a cup of my famous chicken soup when ya get back."*

Nic sighed. "Better be some damn good soup, Horace. Nic out."

Nic threw the walkie-talkie on the floorboard next to him. He leaned forward in his seat and looked up at the threatening sky. He blew out a dispirited breath and cursed Cole, Horace and the whole damn day.

Within thirty minutes, Nic had made the drive down a gravel road to the trail entrance of Chimney Tops. The shelter at Chimney's was a good two and a half mile hike from the point of entrance but thankfully the traps were hidden near a tributary of the Little Pigeon River which ran only a few hundred yards from where Nic had parked.

Nic begrudgingly threw on his poncho and slid out of the truck. He took no more than a couple of hurried steps when his left foot sank several inches into the loose mud that fronted the riverbank. He shook the mud from his boot and plodded carefully along the bank looking for a secure area to cross.

With the rain now in a relentless pour, Nic made it across and began his search for the traps. The traps themselves were of simple design—a long metal rod attached to a chain that when sprung clamped a rubber clip down on a bear's unwitting paw. The rangers had designed the traps years ago as a much more humane way of rounding up their persistent panhandlers.

Nic hadn't been the one to put out the traps, but he knew what to look for. Two of them he found rather easily as they were hidden near blackberry thicket bushes that ran alongside the stream. Nic knew black bears were notorious berry pickers so those trap placements made good sense. He checked their chains and made sure the springs were pulled taut—both had been set correctly.

The third trap was less obvious, but he stumbled upon its yellow marker as he moved upstream. It was backed against the trunk of a giant oak and had several green kudzu vines hiding the attached rod. This one was not set properly so Nic pulled the chain back into locking position and engaged the spring. He took a step back, wiped the rain from his face and took a final look at the trap. Satisfied, he began to turn away, but then something near the base of the oak caught his eye.

Nic again wiped his face as he knelt down to get a better look. It was a lump of some sort encased in mud, but it didn't look natural—like it didn't belong there. The rain was pounding him in all directions but his curiosity eventually won out. He crouched down on all fours and stuck his head over the front end of the trap. Careful not to set off the spring, Nic slowly reached over the back of the trap and grabbed the object. As he stood, he brought it closer to his face.

What's this...?

As the rain washed it clean, the horrifying nature of what he held in his hand became a reality. It was an eye—mutilated and void of its vitreous gel but undeniably an eye. *A goddamn human eye!*

Terrified, Nic dropped it on the ground—his excited breath escaping him. As he began to back away, he heard a *rushing* noise moving up behind him. Nic turned and then froze in shock—staring at the unholy hell before him.

It can't be.

What he saw was not possible. He couldn't force his mind to accept it—it wasn't real. Yet Nic's blood ran cold when it made a sudden motion toward him. And following a high pitched, *animalistic cry*...Nic's blood just ran.

1:32 PM

Amanda drove her Mustang into the empty parking lot at the Cherokee Museum of Natural History. She pulled the hood on her raincoat over her head, slipped out the car and side stepped several pooling puddles as she made her way to the front entrance. It was a Tuesday; but with the parkway shut down, she was not at all surprised to see the *closed sign* hanging on the front glass door. She knew, however, Eddie was somewhere inside—a quick call to Kina had confirmed that.

She rapped on the door until the old curator shuffled to the front pointing at the closed sign.

"I need to see Eddie Whitetree," she said through the glass. "I understand he's here."

Not fully comprehending, the old man unlocked the door and cracked it opened. Amanda stuck her head inside. "Eddie Whitetree?"

The old man nodded and then held the door for her pointing to the back.

Amanda cautiously moved through the darkened museum. Bathed in low light, the gallery took on an eerie presence giving Amanda a slightly ill-at-ease feeling. There were ghostly images of spears, tomahawks and other melee weapons floating from the ceiling, and the walls were covered with sharpened arrowheads and oddly formed stone tools, vases and pots. She continued through the atrium until she emerged into the main section of the museum. It was dark as well, but Amanda could still make out much of its design. There was a giant stone statue of the Cherokee leader Sequoia centering the room surrounded by individual dioramic scenes of Cherokee history.

She heard some make-shift noise and followed the sound around back. Eddie was there on a well-lit stage standing on a step ladder. He was adjusting the lapel on the long blue coat of a cavalry officer astride a replicated horse. The mannequin soldier bore a stern, insolent look and had his right arm stretched in front of him as he gestured to several sad Cherokee figures that followed. Amanda studied it briefly.

"The Trail of Tears....?" she finally asked.

Surprised by her voice, Eddie whipped his head in her direction. He then smiled and nodded as he looked back at the soldier. "Yeah, that's right. Over four thousand died on that forced march to Oklahoma in 1839." He began to climb down the ladder. "I think they should have stuck around with my ancestors and fought it out, don't you?"

"Circumstances compel us to err on the side of caution sometimes. I'm guessing they were thinking of the safety of everyone involved—their wives...children..."

Eddie nodded in agreement. "Yes. But sometimes the safe move is not always the right one."

Amanda smiled and moved closer to the scene. "I certainly hope the incidents of the past few days won't be as equally devastating."

Eddie jumped off the stage and got face to face with Amanda. "We're not packing it in just yet." Eddie looked at her for a moment. "Let me guess...you're concerned about the Cherokee's response now...a new story angle perhaps?"

Amanda grinned. "I am curious, Eddie. Now that I know you have a finger on the pulse of your people—it seemed logical to come to you."

Eddie wiped his brow with his shirt sleeve and reached for a drink from a Dixie cup. "Okay. So, shoot, what exactly do you wanna know?"

"How this situation will affect the reservation. You said at your house last night that the strain will be hard financially—tourism is going to take quite a hit—but how long *can* the Cherokees hold out?"

"That's the big question, isn't it? We hope long enough obviously. We took a hefty lost this past weekend during our Qualla Arts festival. This time of year is just so vital to us...the tourist season. In fact, this weekend we are supposed to start production of our historical play, 'Unto These Hills', one of our summer mainstays, but now...who knows."

Amanda began jotting his comments down on her pad. "And what about the reservation's state of mind in all this? What about their emotional ties?"

"Emotional ties? Emotional ties to what?"

"To your neighbors? More specifically to the park?

Eddie finished his drink and threw the paper cup at a nearby receptacle. "What are you driving at, Amanda?"

"Simply, do you trust the park to handle this situation to your liking?"

Eddie paused—the wheels turning. "Of course...but this isn't really about the park, is it? You really want to know if I trust *Cole* to handle the situation." He lowered his voice. "I know you two spent several days together. Did you find out something about him?"

Amanda gave a feigned quizzical look. "No, nothing, I was just..." She stopped and looked directly at Eddie. "Why? Is there something about him that I *should* know?"

Eddie shrugged. "No, of course not. I mean he's a great guy. My good friend. My o-gi-na-li. I just thought maybe somehow you had wandered inside that head of his and got lost as I have on many occasions."

Amanda gave a reluctant nod—puzzled at Eddie's words. "So you *do* trust him to solve this situation?"

Eddie gave a booming laugh. "Amanda, do you have any idea how much Cole Whitman has done for me and my family—not to mention how helpful he has been to the Boundary over the past several years? I have no doubt he and his fellow rangers are doing all they can do to solve this problem. I mean we're a team, the park and my people...a family."

Amanda bit the end of her pencil and smiled. "Family...I like that. It'll make a great headline for the story." She then raised a finger coyly; she was determined not to let this opportunity slip away. "By the way, Eddie...what do you know about *Cole's* family? He's so tight-lipped about his personal life sometimes. I could barely get him to tell me anything."

Eddie's eyes shot up to the ceiling as he considered the question. "Uh, not much. Like you say, he's not one to talk a lot about personal things."

"Do you know where he's from?"

"I assume from around here, but I really don't know."

"Does he ever talk about his life...his home, school, brothers, sisters, parents?"

"No, I can't say that he ever...."

"Did he ever mention any of their names? Did he ever say he was going to visit anyone?

Eddie shook his head 'no' to both questions.

"And how long have you known Cole?"

"Seven...eight years now."

Amanda gave Eddie a surprised look. Eddie returned her look with a half smile and a shrug of his shoulder. "Sorry, I guess those things just never came up."

When the interview wrapped up, Amanda paid Eddie her thanks and left. As she drove out of the lot, Eddie watched her through the front glass door. He had convinced himself that he had done the right thing. He truly believed that keeping Cole's secrets was in the best interest of their friendship.

In a few days, he would regret ever knowing him.

3:10 PM

Amanda swirled a spoon in her coffee cup as she sat in a booth at the Shoney's in Asheville off I-26. With the parkway closed she had to drive the long way around from Cherokee and she was feeling every mile of it. More importantly she was frustrated. Her concerns over Cole were getting in the way with the larger story, but she just couldn't let it go. Something was pin-pricking the back of her neck about him. Call it intuition or bad vibes, but she just couldn't leave it alone. It didn't help that she felt that Eddie was covering for him either. A guy just isn't friends with someone for eight years without knowing *some* details about his life. And then compound that with the fact that she really was starting to care for Cole, and Amanda began to feel a little confused. She needed to talk. She needed a friend.

Etta Darby walked through the door of the restaurant and Amanda waved her over to the booth. Etta was tall and thin with a long neck that helped to accentuate her height. She had a fair complexion for an African-American with slight European features on her slender, oval face. Amanda had only known Etta for a little while having answered her ad for a roommate after moving to Asheville. But they got along famously, both young, good-looking professionals working long hours, finding their niche in life. And Amanda was grateful to have someone like Etta to keep her balanced and to lend an ear every now and then. The fact that she worked in the coroner's office had been an unexpected bonus.

Etta threw her car keys on the table and slid in. "Nothing like eating lunch at three in the afternoon." She grabbed at her stomach. "No wonder my system is so screwed up."

"Sorry, but I was at a late interview; I got here as quickly as I could."

Etta smiled. "Oh, it's alright, Amanda. We were extremely busy at the hospital anyway."

Amanda leaned forward. "What's the word on the Graveyard Field's victim? Another bear attack, right?"

"No claw fragments like last time but, yeah, it's gotta be. You wouldn't believe the amount of damage done on that man. Maybe more than what was done to the first victim."

Amanda raised her eyebrows in disbelief.

"I'm serious. Not only was he splayed open from the chest down, but that animal ripped off the man's entire lower abdomen—genitals and everything."

"Jesus…"

"Yeah, it was bad. Melvin said he'd never seen anything like it. There was trauma done to every inch of his body."

Amanda took a sip of her coffee—more than a little unnerved by how close she may have been the one lying in Etta's morgue.

"How about the boys in the park?" Etta continued. "Any news?"

Amanda shook her head. "No, but they're convinced it couldn't be the same animal. Smokemont is too far away. Has to be just an extreme coincidence or something."

"Well, what about the missing hikers?"

"No word. Just another mystery right now."

Etta scrunched up her face. "Doesn't sound like they have a good grasp of what's going on in their own park. You might have been right pegging them as incompetents like you did in your first article."

Amanda squirmed in her seat at the assessment. "Having spent time with 'em now, I don't think that's true. In fact, they're probably as good a group of rangers as there are. The circumstances are just so damn strange in this case. I really don't think it's their fault."

"Uh-oh," Etta smiled.

"What?"

"I think time spent in the backwoods with Mr. Ranger has had an effect on my girl's perspective."

Amanda coyly smiled back. "No, Etta, it's not like that. But they have been a bit more compliant with information through all this…we've been working as a team lately."

Etta just continued to smile—content to let her roommate hang herself with her words.

"C'mon, you know what I mean."

"Are you sure? I know you were supposed to have dinner with that Whitman fellow last night. And don't think I didn't notice that you didn't make it back to our apartment either."

Amanda smiled again and reluctantly nodded. "You're right about that. Things have gotten a little complicated with him."

The Shoney's waitress interrupted and took their orders before Amanda could continue. Afterwards, as they lunched their way through their chicken salad, she got Etta up to speed on the bears, the time in the park and her relationship with Cole.

"Truth is, Etta, I don't know anything about him. He seems to keep everything so wrapped up inside."

"Sounds like a million other men."

"No, it's not that. It's like I told you—he will act one way and then be somebody totally different a second later. He even gets his own personal history screwed up. He says he went camping with his father when he was eleven, but the information I have on him clearly states his father passed away when he was eight. He said that he grew up not far from here, but again the paperwork shows he grew up in Mississippi—never lived in North Carolina until he started working at the park. He shows me a knife that he said was a family heirloom but the initials don't even match his last name. And then he is at a lost to explain it. He has these pictures...."

"Look," Etta interrupted. "All of that is kind of weird—I'll grant you that. But he wouldn't be the first man to tell a few white lies about his past, Amanda. I mean did you ever stop to think the guy was doing it to make an impression on you? Ya'll were camping out all alone in those beautiful mountains. Maybe the mood struck him. Maybe he was just trying to get inside your pants. It happens all the time."

Amanda shook her head. "No, I'm telling you—I know those lines— this wasn't anything like that."

Etta smirked and shook her head. "Amanda, Amanda, Amanda..." Several *beeps* then emanated from her purse drawing a puzzled look from her roommate.

"What's that?' Amanda inquired.

Etta pulled out a Motorola Page Boy. "It's my pager. When we are on call now, we have to carry them with us. The hospital won't let us go anywhere without them."

"Hmmm. That's convenient."

Etta shook her head. "Yeah, sometimes too damn convenient. Excuse me, I better call this in."

Etta hopped up from the booth and went to a pay phone outside the restaurant. Amanda sat there for a moment mulling it all over. *Is she right? Was Cole just giving me a line? Am I misreading this man again?*

Within thirty seconds, Etta came back inside and solemnly sat down. There was apprehension in her eyes, and Amanda picked right up on it.

"What is it, Etta? What's wrong?"

"It was our dispatcher at the hospital. She said there's another attack victim in the park."

Amanda's face went blank. "Oh, my God…"

Etta nodded and leaned over and grabbed her hand. "Amanda…the victim was a ranger."

9:22 PM

Cole stared at the fire as it popped and cracked before him. The screams echoing in his head had finally subsided. They existed now only as the squeaking of wood on flame. All was thankfully calm at the moment. His eyes drifted to his surroundings. He was home. Somehow he had made it there, but again he wasn't sure how. He must have started the fire in his fireplace, but he didn't even remember that. Apparently, he had been through another grueling session—another one of his living, breathing nightmares. This one had been severe—he had slipped into one of his unaccounted-for blackouts, what the doctor use to call a *phasing episode*. Nothing from the past several hours came to mind—nothing was clear. He noticed his clothes were soaking wet and his boots and hands were all muddy. And he felt exhausted—both physically and mentally.

Headlights flashed through a front window and he heard someone jump out of a car and head toward his house. There was a rapid-fire series of *knocks* on the front door, but Cole remained seated—afraid to answer it. He wasn't altogether sure if the sounds were real anyway. The door finally swung open and Tully Lawton rushed inside from the pouring rain. The storm followed him in.

"Where the hell were you, Cole?" Tully demanded. "Why didn't you answer your phone? Why didn't you check in, goddamnit?"

Cole stammered to answer, "My phone? I…I'm not…"

"Where have you been all afternoon? We've been trying to contact ya. We've had the whole goddamn park out looking for ya."

Things began to register and Cole stood up to face his boss. "I'm sorry, Tully, for cryin' out loud. I've been out checkin' traps—just doing my job. Why? What the hell is goin' on?"

Tully ran his meaty hand through his wet, silvery hair. "We tried to raise ya on your radio…we tried to contact ya." Tully pinched the bridge of his nose and began to pace in front of Cole's fireplace—the weight of the world now squarely on his shoulders.

Cole was back to full strength now and was anxiously processing it all. "For God's sake, Tully, what's happened? Why were you lookin' for me?"

Tully held out his hand palm up to Cole's face. "Cole…there ain't no easy way to tell ya…." His voice started to shake.

"What? Tell me what, Tully?"

Tully swallowed hard but said nothing. Cole suddenly became irritated and leaned into the old man. "Tell me goddamnit!"

"Cole…. It's Nic. He's dead."

Cole backed off quickly as if punched in the nose. The words hung ominously in the air. "What? What do you mean…? He's dead?"

"Just like the others…. Just like 'em."

"Like the others…?"

Tully nodded and resumed his pacing. "They found him near Chimney Tops. Went out there to check traps apparently. He had been attacked…there was blood everywhere." He paused and drew in a pained breath. "He failed to report in this afternoon so Horace sent Buck out to check on him, but by the time he got there…Nic was already dead."

Neither spoke. Cole's mind was racing, spinning out of control. He slowly managed to find his way back into his chair. Tully held onto the mantle of Cole's fireplace. But after a few moments, he finally turned and faced Cole.

"There's something else, Cole. Something worse…"

Cole looked up from his chair—apprehensive, afraid.

"They found something next to Nic's body. It's hideous. Beyond belief."

"What?"

Tully paused, biting down on his lip. He then measured his words carefully. "They found a bear paw with razor sharp claws…drenched in Nic's blood. It had been gutted."

"Gutted? What do you mean?"

Tully held out his hand again. "The inside of it gutted—dug out. Like it had been fitted for a human hand—like a glove."

Cole's face twisted in anguish. "Fitted for a *human* hand?

"Yes, a *human* hand, Cole."

Cole's voice lowered to a whisper, "But it's an animal…an isolated bear attack…."

Tully nodded. "Oh, it's an animal alright, but not like what we were thinking. We were so sure it was one of our blackies. Had to be one of our blackies they said. Now to find out it's just some…*sick…deranged…fuck.*" Tully spit out the words in disgust and then walked back toward the fireplace patting himself down for a cigar. He chomped down on the unlit Smokin' Joe's and stared at the fire with a sullen, out-of-it look.

They became silent again—the seconds between them passing like hours. Tully finally slammed his hand against the mantle. "We've got to do something, Cole. We can't let this happen. We gotta find this son of a bitch. That's all there is to it." Tully looked up from the fire and back at Cole. "You've gotta help me, Cole. Help me bring an end to this. Promise me. Promise me, Cole."

Cole had never heard his boss plead in such a despondent way. In fact, he had never heard angst of any kind in Tully Lawton's voice until now. It seemed the old man was on the verge of tears. Cole looked Tully straight in the eye and gave him an assured nod of the head. Of course he would help. Of course he would do whatever it takes to rid the park of this madman. Cole would find him and stop him.

But who's gonna stop me?

11:47 PM

The ceiling fan in Eddie's bedroom swished and hummed in monotonous fashion. With Kina curled up on her side of the bed asleep, Eddie laid on top of the covers wide awake staring at the fan's rhythmic spindles. Unlike the constant fan, his thoughts were all over the place. If the reports he had heard were right, then all hell was about to break loose.

Yo-nv di-gi-ti-lv-s-di. Yo-nv di-gi-ti-lv-s-di. He repeated the words over and over. Ghost-bear. The words Chief Sanooke had whispered to him at the Qualla Center had come squarely back to haunt him. The old folks may have been right about one thing—there was more to this than some wild animal. And if this was indeed a man, then the authorities would no doubt discover what ghost-bear was, and the finger of blame would most assuredly be pointed at his people.

He remembered the first time hearing ghost-bear while out tracking in the forest with his father. He had told Eddie of the ancient Cherokee fighting tactic in which select warriors would use the dismembered paws of bears to covertly attack and kill members of warring tribes. These silent assassinations were done as individual attacks so as not to precipitate a full scale battle, but they were effective means of reprisal nonetheless. They often made these *hits* near water and rock as to negate the attacker's footprints and leave the impression of a singular animal attack. Both the attack at Smokemont and the one in Graveyard Fields had this distinction and now the young ranger's murder could be grouped with them as well.

Murder. The word played like fire in Eddie's head.

He finally shot up out of bed and headed into the kitchen. He poured himself a jelly glass jar full of his scuppernong wine and sat at the kitchen table. Large sips of the wine soon loosened his apprehension but served only to entice his curiosity.

Someone with a possible knowledge of ghost-bear...warrior fighting...

Eddie drummed his fingers along the kitchen table top.

Has the ability to move in and out of those areas undetected...

Eddie got up from the table and looked out at the starry night sky through a small window over the sink.

Is physically strong enough to overpower someone...no, more than that, has animal, brute strength...

He moved to the kitchen counter and picked a mountain apple out of a basket of fruit. He rolled the apple back and forth on the counter.

Would be able to have his victims under surveillance...know where they were going...

Eddie took a slice out of the apple with a large kitchen knife. He then dunked the cut of apple into the scuppernong wine until it dulled with pinkness. He flipped the cut into his mouth.

Is obviously unstable enough to murder someone...

Eddie drained the remainder of the wine and tossed the rest of the apple in the trash under the sink. He washed the knife and carefully replaced it in its cutlery block. He moved to the kitchen door and flipped off the light. He paused for a moment in the darkness.

Don't even think that way. Get that out of your head.

Eddie returned to his warm bed. He lay on top of the covers as he always did. He stared up at the ceiling watching the spindles of the ceiling fan as they swished and hummed. It was going to be a long night.

May 26, 1974

11:45 AM

Three days had passed since Nic was found dead and what Eddie had prophesized that night in his home had come true—all hell had indeed broken loose. The Great Smoky Mountain National Park and its surrounding little mountain towns had gone into immediate lockdown and became the focus of one of the most sensationalized crime scenes in recent memory. The reservation itself became immobilized with fear and suspicion—very few ventured outdoors—blame and mistrust were rampant.

The local Cherokees, under Sanooke's orders, refused to give interviews to the press and were uncooperative with law enforcement. The Tribal Council had agreed that the less said in the open forum the better for their people. But their silence was interpreted by many to be an admission of guilt. Speculation of their involvement ran high in the white community. The good-will that had existed between the Cherokees and the mountain folk began to seriously erode. The incidents at Pine Ridge and Wounded Knee had nothing on the powder-keg building in the Smoky Mountains.

The case itself had been handed over to the FBI, and Cole and the rest of the park division along with all local authorities had been reassigned as a special task force to assist as needed. The FBI was convinced that Nic's murderer was still around hiding out in the park, and they were now in the process of organizing a massive search for the killer.

Meanwhile, the story of Nic's murder had garnered national attention. The nature of the killings and the exotic locale added flavor to a story in which its interest had temporarily surpassed even the impeachment process in DC. Reporters from all over the country were sent to cover the story and they could be found lurking around all of western North Carolina. Save one notable exception.

Upon the news of Nic's death, Amanda, like the area she covered, went into a self-imposed seclusion. She found it impossible to continue to write about the story, and other reporters at the *Chronicle* had taken up the lead for her. She was of course upset over Nic, but she was equally upset over her relationship with Cole. She still cared for him, despite his lack of total honesty with her. And even though she had placed several calls to him over the past three days, he had refused to answer her. She knew he was hurting and realized he needed time, so she backed off. In reality, they both needed the time to process it. It just didn't make it any easier on her.

"You got too close, that's all," Sam Cox said to her as they drove down the highway. He was leaning away from her in the passenger seat blowing cigarette smoke through a cracked window. "Happens to all reporters. Few days…and you'll be fine as wine."

Amanda dressed in a black dress could only nod. Even Sam's calming tone wasn't enough to steady her. She thought about all the violent cases she had covered in DC, but nothing came close to this one—nothing she covered ever felt so personal.

As for Cox, he had agreed to ride with Amanda to the small town of Cedar Falls, North Carolina for Nic's funeral—partly for support but also to get his lead reporter back in the game.

"You have a unique perspective on this story, Amanda. I don't feel comfortable with anyone but you handling it," Sam said.

"I've given it some thought," Amanda lied. "Maybe I can find my angle up here at the funeral."

Sam flicked his ashes. "It's a good place to start. Just don't let the leads you've built up the last few days go cold." He then turned and looked at her. His eyes narrowed. "I don't mean to be presumptuous, Amanda. But whatever *feelings* you may have developed in all this need to be put aside. See it through to the end, okay?"

Amanda again nodded. She even managed a half smile at her boss. She knew he was right.

It's just going to be hard as hell.

2:00 PM

The Holy Trinity Baptist Church of Cedar Falls sat high on a hill overlooking a frontage road which ran adjacent to the Wicker-Lovell main thoroughfare. The parking lot and attached cemetery of the tiny church were packed with quiet mourners who had come to pay their final respects. Rain had eased into the grey afternoon and a variety of colorful umbrellas were now sported throughout the otherwise gloomy crowd. Amanda stood with Sam at the back of the crowd under a single umbrella waiting—watching everything. Amanda found herself shivering not knowing if it was from the cool, damp air or something much deeper.

Two black limos and a hearse finally pulled up in front of the church. Nic's parents, his older sister, Dottie, and her husband emerged from the first car while Cole, Horace, Tully and several of the other rangers serving as pallbearers came out of the second. The family was met by the white-haired funeral director who comforted them in hushed tones. The rangers then solemnly moved as a singular unit to the back of the hearse. They removed Nic's casket and followed the precession into the tiny graveyard. Amanda focused in on Cole who kept his head down throughout—seemingly oblivious to all around him.

Nic's other relatives and several former friends, some in military dress, emerged from the church and joined his family under a tarp for the graveside burial. The preacher, a tall, angular man named John Gervais, walked calmly through the cold rain and stood just inside the covering next to the casket.

With only the sound of the raindrops on the canvas tarp, Reverend Gervais addressed the parishioners, "Friends, let me open this sad occasion with the comfort of the good word." He opened up his Bible and read with deliberation the marked passage, "Fear not, for I have redeemed you; I have called you by your name; you are mine. When you pass through the waters, I will be with you; and through the rivers, they shall not overflow you. When you walk through the fire, you shall not be burned, nor shall the flame scorch you. For I am the Lord your God, the Holy One of Israel, your Savior…"

In their meeting place in the forest, several of the older Cherokees had returned for their own ceremony—clandestine as it was. They believed their worst fears had been confirmed—all signs indicated that the legendary Judaculla had returned. There was no question in their minds now. They figured all along it couldn't have been an animal, and, despite the mounting evidence, they rejected the possibility that it could be a man—let alone one of their own people—utilizing the ghost-bear tactic. Only a monster of such ferocity could have committed so much harm and destruction. Only the Judaculla. And they knew the authorities would not be able to take care of it, so they had taken matters into their own hands.

Unilisi, her face covered with the white stripes of the ancient ones, emerged from the forest and broke into the circle around the fire. Stoical in face and manner, she took her role as shaman in the proceedings very seriously. She was followed by Luga, another elder, who was stripped to the waist and made rhythmical timing beats of the procession on a small ancient drum.

The circle grew tighter around the fire as Unilisi began making the secret chants and throwing the sacred powder into the flames before her. Luga lead the others in a repeating chant in support of Unilisi.

"And I know that *you* are troubled today, but let me assure you that Nicholas Ryan Turner is troubled no more," the reverend continued. "Because of these events, our world may seem a worse place, but you must know that he is in a far better place—a place that knows no murder, no hatred, no death."

The elders followed Unilisi's lead and went down to their knees. She called out in her native language to the sky invoking the ancient Cherokee prayer of death. "Tsul-kalu. Your spittle I have put at rest under the earth. Your soul I have put at rest under the earth. I have come to cover you over with the black rock. I have come to cover you over with the black cloth. When the darkness of the storm comes, your spirit shall grow less and dwindle away—your brother shall come and take you away—you shall never reappear."

"And it is in His name that we shall endure. Amen," Gervais concluded. He nodded at the rangers who then stood and walked in a single file in front of the burial platform. Each removed the carnation from the lapel of their uniform and deposited it on the head of the casket. Cole was the last in line. He rubbed the flower between his thumb and forefinger and then placed it gently next to the others.

Unilisi held a mixture of geranium root, grape leaf and deer blood in a clay bowl with both hands. She raised it high above her head. She called to the deer's spirit to give them strength against the monster. "A-da-ne-di u-du-gi-gv-di…a-da-ne-di u-du-gi-gv-di. Di-ga-ti-le-gi Tsul-kalu." She then dipped her hand in the mixture and wiped it across her forehead. She passed it to the others who proceeded to wet their faces in the thick concoction and metaphorically in the animal's spirit.

With the rain in a heavier pour, the crowd had gathered as close as possible to the tarp for the concluding hymn. "When we've been here ten thousand years, bright shining as the sun, we've no less days to sing God's praise then when we've first begun. Amazing Grace, how sweet the sound…." The words echoed through the tiny churchyard. Amanda continued to glance over at Cole. She noticed he wasn't singing—he didn't seem to be involved at all—he was just staring off into the distance.

Energized, the Cherokee elders now stood and were calling the monster in unison. They called it to the fire—to its grave—and away from their world.
"Tsul-kalu! Tsul-kalu! Tsul-kalu!"
Unilisi walked away from the others and stood at the edge of the forest. She had done all she could do, but it would not be enough. There was only one thing that could stop it now.

4:11 PM
Doctor Hatcher sat alone at his desk reading *The Asheville Chronicle*—within his reach three jigs of Jack Daniels swirled in his cracked coffee mug. He ran his fingers through his thinning hair and then dragged them down to his temples. The *crackle* of burning wood in his buck stove was the room's only discernable noise.
Hatcher suddenly got a pained look on his face. He took up the mug and drained it clean. He then stood up at his desk and walked over to the metal filing cabinet. He fished a small key out of his front trousers' pocket and dropped to a squat position and manipulated the lock on the bottom drawer.

With a great straining effort, Hatcher reached to the far back of the drawer. He pulled out several yellowing manila file folders. He thumbed through a couple and stuffed them back in the drawer. He then pulled out one and held it up to the faint light of the room's overhead bulb.

The folder was a half inch thick and the inscription on the front where it said Patient's Name had been blacked out.

Hatcher returned to his desk and opened up the file. A medical chart and a few prescription copies were stapled in the front. He ignored this and dug deeper into the file. Finding what he was looking for, he pulled out several old copies of newspaper. The newspapers were yellow and brittle and he handled them with great care.

He spread the newspapers out on his desk and ran his finger along the heavy print headline of the first one:

LOCAL FARMER PUZZLED OVER SLAYING OF HORSES

Hatcher leaned back in his office chair until it *squeaked*. "Omophagia," he whispered to himself.

6:35 PM

Cole sat at his desk filling out forms in robotic fashion. Despite the park being closed, there were still the day to day operations to be performed and he had fallen way behind schedule.

He still had on his dress uniform although by this point he had loosened his tight-fitting tie. His desk was a royal mess with a crumpled Hardee's fry bag and a discarded Big Twin container sitting on top of stacks of files and time sheets.

Amanda walked through his office door unannounced still wearing the black dress from the funeral. Cole looked up; and for a moment, they just stared at one another. No words were needed. Despite all that had happened between them over the past few days, there still was an immediate connection.

Cole finally got up and walked around to face her. "You alright?" It wasn't much, but it was the best he could come up with. *Typical Cole.*

Amanda's eyes were wet and she had trouble getting the words out. "Why didn't you answer my calls? I've been a wreck for these past three days."

Cole grabbed her arms. "I know. Me too. I just couldn't face you…or anyone for that matter. I'm sorry, Amanda." He reached down and grabbed at her right hand. He slid his fingers in next to hers. Again they went silent.

Amanda put her free hand on his chest. "Cole, its time for you to talk straight with me. I want to be able to understand you. To trust you. But right now I feel like you're holding back. And I can't help you unless I trust you. Unless you trust me."

Cole nodded as if he understood but he remained silent.

"Can you be honest with me, Cole? You promised earlier you always would."

"Soon, Amanda…soon you'll know everything. Just give me a little more time, okay?"

Amanda squinted in confusion. She leaned over and pushed strands of his black hair from in front of his eyes. "What happened to you, Cole? It was something terrible, wasn't it?"

Cole's eyes locked with hers—*so much to tell her*—but he then broke away. "There's no time for this now, Amanda. It's gone—it's…dead. My past is not the issue—it's unimportant. I've got to help end this thing. I've got to help 'em stop whoever did this to Nic." He paused. "This isn't about me."

Cole moved back to the desk and started fishing aimlessly through his papers.

Amanda decided to drop it—she would have to be satisfied for the moment that they were at least talking. "Cole, he was out there with us, near us—wasn't he? That same monster that did this to Nic." She suddenly sounded much clearer, more focused. "That may have even been him that walked past me in the fog that morning not a bear."

Cole agreed. "Yes…"

"It's just so damn surreal. To think we could have been right there with him."

Cole only nodded continuing to look through his papers. Amanda grabbed at his arm and forced him to look directly at her. "Do you have any idea who could do such a thing?"

"Some maniac, obviously. A psycho. Somebody that needs to be put away…and soon."

"Of course, that's true. But how?"

Cole smirked. "Unfortunately, the FBI has control over the case now. They're certain that the guy is still somewhere in the park—planning on launching a massive search starting tomorrow."

"What do *you* think?

"Who knows at this point? Anything is possible I guess."

Amanda briefly closed her eyes and shook her head. "Unbelievable. I don't mind telling you this thing scares the hell out of me. It's like a nightmare come to life. And I know it's strange, but I just can't help but feel that it's not over. The worse is yet to come."

Cole put the paper down and stood in front of her. He wrapped his long arms around her and drew her in close. He wanted to tell her that everything would be alright—that he would protect her from whatever was out there. But he didn't. He couldn't. He just held her and comforted her knowing that she was probably right.

The worse is yet to come.

8:47 PM

Eddie ran down the stone slab steps on the back of his house with garbage bags slung in both hands. The weather was clear, and the starry night had brought with it much cooler temperatures. Barefooted and shirtless, he hustled across the thick-leaf grass of his backyard, past the muscadine vines and over to a small shed. He quickly deposited the trash into a waiting can behind the shed and started to head back to the house.

But he stopped in his tracks as he heard something *moving around* in the woods behind him.

"Hello?" he called out. "Anybody there?" He slowed for a moment peering through the darkness hopping from one foot to the other in order to keep warm. Seeing nothing, he quickly shrugged it off as some animal running around in the woods and headed back to his house.

But the noise came again—louder...closer...and this time, Eddie came to a complete stop. Eyeing a shovel that was leaning against his shed, he picked it up and braved his way through the vines. At the edge of the tree line he stopped and repeated sternly, "Who's there?" Again there was no response.

He increased his awareness and kept his ears tuned to the sounds around him. There were slow, heavy-paced footsteps coming up behind him. *Someone* or *something* was approaching. Eddie heard the slight breaking of the twigs under foot and sensed the pall of a cast shadow. His body stiffened as he clutched down on the handle of the shovel. Now feeling it to be within striking distance, Eddie wheeled around with the shovel raised high above his head. He yelled out, "Eiyahhhhhhh!"

"Whoa, whoa, hold on, Eddie! It's just me."

Eddie froze. And then with the realization, Eddie's wide-eyes narrowed and he brought the shovel down to the ground with relief. "Cole, for God's sake, you scared the living shit out of me."

Cole stepped out from the shadows into the light of the back porch. "Sorry, Eddie. I didn't mean to."

"Yeah, well, don't worry…. I'll just send you the cleaning bill later," Eddie said with a nervous laugh. He then pitched his brow. "What the hell are you doing sneaking around back here anyway?

"I needed to see you. I wanted to talk…but just you and me. I had to be sure."

Eddie nodded. "Of course—next time how about a little warning though, okay?"

The two old friends exchanged uneasy smiles in the faint yellow light.

"Hey, listen," Eddie continued. "I'm sorry I didn't make it to Nic's funeral today. We thought it best if our presence wasn't felt, you know, during the actual service."

"I know, it's okay," Cole agreed.

"Things are getting kind of heavy in the community now. You can almost cut the tension it's so thick."

"No one is calling for a lynching just yet, Eddie."

"Try telling that to my people. Anytime we venture outside the Boundary we've been getting some nasty eat-shit looks from the whites. Most of my people are just gonna stay home until this thing blows over."

Cole paused; he knew it was pointless to argue about it—paranoia seemed a racial polarity mainstay these days. "Eddie, they found a gutted bear paw next to Nic. And I've been around these parts long enough to know the significance…"

"Everybody knows the significance," Eddie said flatly.

"No, not everybody. It's not exactly the most commonly known aspect of Cherokee history."

"But thanks to the press, it soon will be. I can just see the editorials now—*the ghost-bear murders* they'll start calling it. Believe me, Cole; once the people hear about it, and understand it, they'll see plenty of those bloody bear claws in ol' Injun' Joe's wigwam if they want to."

"But you've got to admit ghost-bear comes directly from the whispers of the ancient community. It must be on the lips of every...?"

"No, it's not," Eddie said.

"But surely there's been talk...?"

"No...."

"C'mon, Eddie, you know what I'm asking. What have you've heard from the inner circle? The elders, the council, someone has to know something...."

"There's nothing. Absolutely nothing," Eddie said—his voice rising in pissed off fashion. "We are as surprised by this as anybody. You're in law enforcement, for crying out loud. I would hardly call this damning evidence against my people, would you? I mean, any sick-o could have committed those crimes. In fact, if I were leading the investigation that's where I would start...with the psychopaths—maybe *anybody* who's got a screw loose, right?"

Cole paused at the not so subtle hint. He jammed his hands into his coat pockets and turned slightly away in anger—he couldn't believe Eddie would go that far, but on the other hand...*point well-taken.*

"I didn't mean it like *that,*" Eddie followed. "It's just...don't let 'em railroad us on this one, Cole. You know perfectly well how easily this could blow up on the Cherokees." He reached out and grabbed Cole's shoulder. "We're counting on you, partner." He paused and forced Cole into his stare. "We've been friends a long time—a lot of water under the bridge as they say. We've done so much for each other."

There were layers to everything that Eddie had said, and Cole knew eventually he was going to need his old friend on his side. He finally grinned. "Look...I know you're freezing your ass off, so I'll let you get back inside. Just give me a heads up if you *do* hear anything, okay?"

"Of course...and you do the same."

Cole nodded and turned to go but then spun back around. "By the way, Amanda didn't happen to come by to see you, did she?"

"Yeah, she stopped by the museum the day Nic was killed. Why?"

Cole bit his lower lip. "She ask about me?"

"A little," Eddie said. He then added softly, "Don't worry, Cole. I didn't tell her anything."

Cole thought about it for a moment and finally held up his hand to Eddie as a gesture of thanks. He then slipped away, disappearing into the darkness of the night.

9:26 PM

Amanda arrived at her loft in downtown Asheville. It was a two bedroom high-rise that she shared with Etta on the east end of the River Art District. It wasn't that big, but it was secure and functional and for now it served her purposes well.

She kicked off her high heels at the door, flipped on the light and meandered down to the bathroom at the end of the hallway. She let her black dress slide off her shoulders and gather around her feet. She decided to skip the shower and just wrapped herself up in her oversized Virginia Tech sweatshirt—a favorite leftover from her college days.

She moved to the small kitchen, grabbed a Budweiser from the fridge and plopped down in front of the television in the adjacent living room. She was beat—tired as hell.

Hearing the commotion, Etta emerged from her bedroom in her fuzzy pink bathrobe and joined Amanda on the couch. "How'd it go?" Etta asked softly.

Amanda closed her eyes for a moment. "Okay, I guess." She sighed. "God, but I hate funerals."

Etta nodded. "Did you see Cole?"

"I saw him—went to the station after the funeral. We talked, but I don't know if anything was really said, if you know what I mean."

Again Etta nodded. "Did you ask him directly about the inconsistencies?"

"He said he'd tell me everything later—said he was too wrapped up in the case right now," She took a sip of the beer. "I don't know if I should believe him or not."

Etta opened her mouth to respond but caught herself. She got up, went to a bookcase near the couch and poured herself a glass of port from a decanter that sat on the end of the primary shelf. "I left you a copy of my notes from the Turner autopsy on the kitchen table. I don't know if you'll find anything useful...it *ain't* pretty that's for sure."

"Thanks," Amanda said without much enthusiasm—the emotional day had taken its toll. The thought of going over the nauseating details of Nic's autopsy made her head spin.

The wine suddenly loosening her resolve, Etta sat back down and looked at Amanda pensively. "Amanda, have you considered...." She stopped. "No, never mind."

"What? Considered what?"

"No, it's not my place really."

"C'mon, what is it, Etta? It's not like *you* to hold anything back."

"Well...have you considered the potential role that this guy Cole may have played in all this?"

"Role? What do you mean?"

"You know...the possibility that maybe Cole might have had something to do with these...murders."

"What!?" Amanda asked with half-laugh.

"No really...think about it. You've gone on and on about this guy's strange behaviors—his night and day personality—his dangerous mood swings. Plus—we know he knows the park, the forests, the rivers...he's a ranger after all. He could have moved in and out undetected while all this was going on."

Amanda put her beer on the coffee table. "No, Etta, this is ridiculous."

"Is it? He's also had opportunity, right? I mean, he was right there when that guy in Graveyard Fields was killed."

"No, he was camping five miles away. He was with me."

"All night? Are you sure?"

Amanda tried to dismiss the idea with a shake of her head.

"Think about it, Amanda. What do you really know about this guy?"

"I know he wouldn't *kill* someone," she said defiantly. "Look, he acts strange sometimes...he's a hothead definitely...but he's not some homicidal maniac."

"Why? Because you slept with him?"

"Jesus, Etta, that has nothing to do with it. All those little weird things I was freaking out about him just days ago you dismissed as nothing. Now you want to accuse him of killing three people based on that same shit?"

Etta paused for a second. "*Somebody* has been killing these people."

Amanda looked at her hard. "Yeah, but it's not *Cole*. Nic was his friend. They were partners for God's sake. He couldn't possibly do something so abhorrent." She paused—a faraway look in her eyes as she digested Etta's accusations. She finally looked back with conviction. "It's *not* him."

Etta gave up with a relenting smile. "I hope you're right." She laughed and then softened her tone. "I just don't want anything to happen to my roomie, that's all." She reached over and patted Amanda on the knee.

Amanda grabbed her beer and took a big gulp. "Oh, don't worry about me. I'm a big girl. I can take care of myself."

Etta smiled, got up again and headed to the kitchen. She would not speak another word about it, but the damage was already done. As the TV continued to flash a wave of forgettable images and sounds, Amanda sat there curled up on the couch—an overwhelming sense of dread crawling up her spine.

11:35 PM

Judaculla stood atop the pinnacle of the Devil's Courthouse—the steady wind cooling its skin. It closed its eyes and took in the medicine of the night feeling the wind's rush and the droplets of moisture in the heavy air. It needed this; it needed solace—for it had finally returned home to heal.

The last human had fought hard against Judaculla and had inflicted much pain upon it. He had even dared to lock arms with the monster and test its great strength, but to no avail. Judaculla had ultimately taken the life blood from the arrogant man. It had slit the man's throat and ripped him from the inside out.

It had momentarily infuriated the creature to have lost its claws in the struggle, but it knew they could be replaced. It would make new ones. Better ones. Sharper ones.

As it stood there, it meditated on its next move. Others would be coming now. They would be searching for it. And it knew what it had to do. It would have to go into hiding. It would blend in until the time was right—until it could strike again.

But not now, not tonight. Tonight it would put its pain in the past. The hurt would be buried deeper and deeper. Finally, it had time to rejuvenate.

The monster leaned over and grabbed the congealed mass of human remains at its feet and brought it up to its face. It was the only remaining tribute from its latest victim, but it would have to do. It bit down into the dirt-covered mass and tasted the flesh. The dried blood possessed a rank smell of strong iron, but it devoured the meat anyway—right down to the tough cartilage.

It felt the surge of power throughout its giant body. It was becoming strong again. It was becoming complete, whole—and soon no one would be able to stop it. It would make them pay for trying to take its world. It would make them pay.

11:57 PM

Amanda rolled over and looked at the clock. *Shit... almost midnight.* She turned back over on her side and again Etta's words turned over with her. What she said may have been out of good intentions, but just the thought of Cole being behind the murders was now burning right through Amanda's soul. It almost seemed cruel that her roommate would say such things, but Amanda knew that Etta was a logical, dispassionate person. Perhaps she saw things as they really were. Perhaps she saw Cole as *he* really was.

Is there really a killer behind those eyes of his? Is he really capable of such madness?

Maybe the truth was she wasn't upset that Etta had made the accusations, maybe she was just worried that she had tapped into a dark fear that Amanda had been forming all along. Maybe it took her roommate to help her see what she was really feeling for some time now. The pictures, the knife, the scars, the family history, the bursts of anger, maybe it did add up.

Amanda sat up in bed and turned on the light at her bedside table. She heard the voice of Sam Cox coming through loud and clear now, or was it that of her father's? *Follow through. Eliminate prejudice. Get to the truth.* She grabbed a pad and pencil. She started making a list of Cole's actions since she met him beginning with their heated exchange at the

156

visitors' center. She was going to create a profile and hoped to find the real Cole Whitman in the process. This wasn't a story angle anymore; it wasn't about selling papers or pleasing her boss. It was about finding the truth. And no matter how frightening or upsetting the truth actually was Amanda was now bound and determined to uncover it.

May 27, 1974

6:24 AM

A heavy fog blanketed the entire Smoky basin but did little to slow the inordinate amount of traffic heading through New Found Gap Road, the park's central thoroughfare. Fifteen hundred National Guard Units, the largest call-up in North Carolina history, combined with over three hundred park personnel, local law enforcement, US Marshals, ATF Agents, and an assorted array of police and professional investigators descended on the halfway point of New Found Gap at the Rockefeller Memorial. Militarized vehicles and trucks of all kinds were lined up on the shoulder of the road for two miles deep in both directions.

Cole and the rest of the park personnel had been assigned to assist with the traffic and were catching hell in trying to coordinate the gathering for this massive manhunt. They had been in position since five a.m. and the surge of people had been steady ever since.

As Cole waved in trucks and gave instructions to the gathered men, he found he was simply going through the motions and that his true thoughts centered only on Nic. He kept expecting to see his face every time a ranger or guardsman walked passed him. And his absence was beginning to work on him. It was more than sadness he was feeling now, more than guilt—it was like a burning sickness—as if someone had gotten a hold of *him* and ripped out *his* insides.

At the back of the parking lot rose a gray stone observation platform like the turret from some medieval castle. It was here at the same storied locale that FDR had made the dedication to the park years ago. Now it had been transformed into the command center for the manhunt complete with tables, maps, heavy lights, generators, radio equipment and a wide, army-green tarp that covered the entire platform.

Paul Meyers, the FBI veteran who had been assigned the lead in the case, was busy in the center coordinating information. Standing out in his

158

blue blazer and tie, Meyers looked the quintessential federal agent. At fifty-five years of age, he still possessed a wiry yet athletic frame to go along with his head full of salt and pepper hair. And his thin, oblong face was saddled with a crooked nose—the result of having been broken in the line of duty three times. He was a confident and intelligent investigator, at times a hard-ass and generally unrelenting in his views. He played the part of the man-in-charge well, and Meyers came to the Smokies with a clear objective and years of experience in getting his man. But nothing in his unblemished career could have prepared him for the magnitude of what awaited in this case.

Three other agents came down from Washington with him that comprised the rest of the FBI team. Jones, Krazenski, and Dole were all three good men. Solid, professional detectives, who by this time in the investigation, had left the running of the operation to Meyers and were already out into the field with their assignments conducting interviews and prepping certain spots for the search.

Meyers was joined in the command center by Colonel George Pertand of the North Carolina National Guard. The balding, paunchy former police chief of the town of Marlboro, Pertand had an amiable spirit and an even-tempered sense of command. He never took himself too seriously, which made him a good counter to the overtly dour Meyers, but he was all business when it came down to crunch time, and he was very protective whenever he had to implement his men. He knew the difficulties involved in searching for what amounted to the proverbial needle in a haystack, but years of living and working in these mountains gave him good credentials as the leader of the foot soldiers.

Sheriff Thurmond and Superintendent Lawton were also there representing the local authority. Thurmond had been assigned to work with the police volunteer units, help coordinate their movements and to be the local liaison for Governor Bob Scott's office. He was feeling important and acting all gung-ho, relishing the opportunity to work with the law enforcement heavy-weights. And it gave him just the greatest of pleasures to be high upon that platform watching Cole directing traffic directly beneath him.

As for Tully, he sat in a folding chair near the edge of the tarp—his ample gut lapping over his belt and his cigar twisting away in his mouth. He watched the proceedings with a skeptical eye. With his influence in his own park now diminished, his contempt for the manhunt was thinly veiled and he didn't care who knew it. "Excuse me there, Agent Meyers," Tully began slowly.

Meyers turned from studying a map to squint in the superintendent's direction. "Yes, Mr. Lawton?"

"Well, I don't mean to sound so negative before you and your posse here even begin, but where do ya'll figure to start this little expedition? I mean, after all, it's been three days now since the last attack."

Without looking back, Meyers thumped the map in the area of a meticulously drawn circle. "As I indicated in my correspondence to you earlier, the initial plan is to work the site of the last known incident here at Chimney Tops. Given the time and terrain, we have determined it best to form a perimeter of twenty miles around that site and work our way toward the center."

"Twenty miles? But what if he's already outside that perimeter? Do you have any idea how big this park is? We have over eight hundred square miles of mountains and forests. He could be hidin' anywhere. Or he coulda made it to one of the local towns by now and hopped a train clean outta here."

Meyers lifted his chin and gave a weak smile. "I suppose that's possible, but given the nature of the attacks, there's a good chance he's still hiding somewhere in the vicinity."

"*My* men," Tully asserted with a bit of rising temperament, "along with Anson's deputies, have searched that area high and low already and couldn't find a damn trace. What makes you think this will be any different?"

Meyers turned his back to Tully and looked at the map again. "Perhaps, Mr. Lawton, *your* men missed something."

Tully just shook his head and spat cigar remnants at the ground.

Meyers continued as he studied the map. "In most of the cases we've handled like this, the suspect will generally stay close to the area where he's been active—either to see the reaction to his attack or perhaps to plan his next strike. He also no doubt feels safe in this environment—a way for him to blend in if necessary. We saw a similar incident with the murder of several young girls in the Northwest this past year. We used to call it backyard homicides—one of our fellow agents, Bob Ressler, has started using the term serial killing."

Tully withheld his comment—grinding hard on the cigar.

Colonel Pertand, also studying the map, picked up on the conversation, "And Superintendent, your men covered all these tributaries shooting off of the Little Pigeon River, yes?"

Tully nodded. "Yeah...well, at least as deep as they could go."

"That's gotta be his key. He uses the streams and rivers. Wades in, attacks, and then disappears without leaving any tracks or prints. Probably hanging out in a cavern or cave near one of the river sources," Pertand stated.

"Agreed," Meyers said. "And that's where I want your units to concentrate as we tighten the circle." He turned back to Tully. "Within our specified radius, Superintendent, are there any caverns or caves in that direct area?"

Tully laughed. "Are you kiddin'? Tons of 'em. And thick forest too. If a man is hiding out there...well, you'd have better luck pulling gold outta yer ass."

Everyone but Meyers laughed.

"Don't worry about our search specifics, Superintendent. With the right concentration of manpower..."

Tully stood up and sucked his teeth. "It won't matter, Agent Meyers. Your just gonna be stirrin' up dust, that's all." He paused for a moment and looked out at the parking lot. "Besides, from the looks of some of these jokers ya got running around up here, they could walk right past that lunatic and never even notice him."

"My men are highly qualified and these search experts have been approved," Pertand interjected.

Tully moved face to face with Pertand. "Approved? Approved, my ass, Colonel. I didn't approve anybody. Now if you wanna load up a bunch of good ol' boys with guns and bullets and send 'em out into the chunk on some kinda wild goose chase, that's your business, sir. But it sure as hell sounds like a recipe for disaster to me. Somebody's gonna get hurt out there." Tully pulled back and gathered in everyone in the command center. "And make no mistake, gentlemen, I don't want any more tragedies in *my* park!"

Thurmond reached over and grabbed Tully by the arm pulling him aside. "Listen, Tully. We've got to do this, and you know it." His grasp tightened forcing Tully's attention. "Look at it this way: either we go along with this manhunt—find this son of a bitch—or we lose the park altogether."

"Lose the park?" Tully pulled away from Thurmond's grip. "It's already lost, Sheriff." He walked behind the command center and looked wistfully out onto the smoky blue horizon. "I shoulda known from the start…only *man* coulda fucked things up this bad."

9:34 AM

Drew Hopkins, the Chief Supervisor for the Asheville Post Office was leaning back in his chair admiring the pretty woman sitting across from him. He wasn't really listening to her; he was just nodding his head in pretension smitten by her blue eyes, her auburn hair and her tight blouse. But as she continued to explain her predicament he realized he had to get his focus out of her shirt and back to the matter at hand.

"So, what you're saying Miss Rivers is that you only have a partial known address and you were wondering if we could help you ascertain the rest of the *where to's* and *what for's* and so forth?"

Amanda gave a slight grin. "Yes, Mr. Hopkins, as I said, it's not even an address really. It's just the house number, but the route sign had a drawing of a mountain in front of it. It was in the corner of an old photograph, and I could just make it out."

"Do you have the photo?"

"No, but I've drawn the emblem here." Amanda pulled out the paper from her purse and spread it out on his desk. "As best I could anyway…"

Hopkins studied it briefly. "Is it at least a North Carolina address?

Amanda stared blankly—thinking back on her conversations with Cole. "I think so. I don't know for certain. The photograph was old— maybe thirty years or so."

Hopkins frowned and drew in a deep breath. "Well…it ain't much to go on, now is it? Certain communities sometimes have these emblems on their postal markings. I remember old beach towns on the Outer Banks use to have a seagull fronting the route numbers, college towns often use their team logos…but a squiggly mountain like this could be just about anywhere in the western zone. Although, I know positively it ain't Asheville or anywhere in Buncombe County."

Amanda leaned back in her chair biting her lower lip. She began feeling a bit desperate and more than a little foolish.

Hopkins read her disappointment. "Still…" Hopkins stood and leaned toward the open door of his office. "Al? Al, could ya come in here for a sec?"

A tall, grey-bearded man soon appeared in the doorway. "Ya call me, Chief?"

"Yeah, Al. Uh, Miss Rivers, this is Al Dixon, one of our veteran couriers, been here since the dark ages—served all over the Tarheel state. Ain't that right, Al?" Al just smiled and nodded and then amiably came up to the desk. "Anyway, Al, Miss Rivers here is trying to locate an address. How about take a look at this drawing, will ya? Do ya recognize that emblem there? She believes it to be part of an old N—C postal number sign."

The old courier adjusted his glasses and took a brief glance. "Yep, could be...I think I done seen it before—up north, I believe. You might wanna try th' twenty-eight seven-oh-fivers along th' Tennessee line. Bakersville...Roan Mountain...."

"Are ya sure?" Hopkins asked first although Amanda was about to.

"Yeah, I'm pretty sure it's un ol' design they use t' use up in them hills. Bakersville...a lot of their rural routes up there use to have that un. Especially the ones off 'un th' Roan Mountain Road—near the border."

"Bakersville?" Amanda asked for confirmation.

Hopkins nodded. "Yeah, well, it's a possibility. Bakersville is the base for most of the mountain routes on the Carolina side of Roan. It'll be a good starting place for ya anyway."

Hopkins went to a heavy-bound file notebook with all types of names and numbers in it. "Let's see...Ben Calhoun is the post master up there—met him once—good guy. He might can help with ya next step. At least, anymore than what we can do for ya at this point."

Amanda quickly thanked the gentlemen and made her exit. Within minutes she was back in her Mustang tearing up I-40 towards Bakersville. With all that was going on in the park, she felt uneasy devoting this much time to what amounted to an improbable thread of the story. However, none of the official information on Cole had checked out. There was no Cole Whitman from Mississippi—in fact, there wasn't a Cole Whitman from any of the addresses he had reported on file. He had lied about his past and she wanted to know why. Perhaps it could be explained away, perhaps there *was* a logical reason. And if there was, she knew then that she could put her mind to ease about Cole. She could then finally concentrate on the case and help locate the *real killer*. But suspicion is its on master, and Amanda knew she couldn't stop now even if she wanted to.

10:17 AM

A squadron of Bell 209 Huey Cobras from the Guard base in Asheville screamed over the tips of the southern Smokies heading west toward Chimney Tops and the Little Pigeon River. Once used as small troop transporters in Vietnam, the refit birds were now an instrumental part in Meyers' plan to search for the elusive killer. The *thumping* of their blades caught everyone's attention on the ground and would become a daily reminder of what was happening in the park. Most of the searchers saw the helicopters as a welcome element to the hunt, but some, especially the rangers, saw it as affirmation that the park was no longer under their control. They saw them like they saw the FBI, the guardsmen, and all the others—as an unwanted and unwarranted invasion.

Cole sat wearily in his jeep at the Oconaluftee entrance to the park as the choppers flew overhead. The noise from their search drew pain to his already aching head. It seemed an unfit punishment that he and the other rangers had been given the odious task of guarding the gates while the real search went on without them. And it left Cole feeling shell-shocked, tired and just plain pissed off.

A group of the local Cherokees he now eyed hiking up Highway 441 wasn't going to help matters either. They were walking quickly and seemed intent on heading in his direction. He noticed some of them were carrying heavy tribal walking sticks while others had hunting rifles slung over their shoulders. Neither was a particularly good sign. *Soldiers off to war*.

Cole then centered his focus on the leader of the group. And once recognized he could only laugh to himself. *Unbelievable*.

He hopped out of his jeep and made his way toward them. Eddie greeted him with a solemn face and a low tone of voice. "Cole...."

Cole looked the group over. "Out for a little stroll, gentlemen?"

"Just doing our part. Keeping an eye out like the sheriff requested."

Cole nodded but then leaned in to whisper. "Take these people home, Eddie. It's not a good idea."

"Look, Cole, I know you aren't exactly thrilled about all this, and I'm not too sure if I'm altogether happy about it myself, but this manhunt may be our best chance to prove our innocence. If we can only catch this guy..."

"The last thing we need is more civilians walking around with firearms. It's already a goddamn zoo up there, believe me. If you really want to help, then *take* these men home."

"Cole, we had a meeting this morning. My people know where this investigation is headed. Left up to the FBI, it won't stop in the woods. There are agents already snooping around our town, staking out our businesses and our homes, wire-tapping our phones...."

"Just sit tight. They'll go away."

"You're only kidding yourself, partner. They ain't leaving till they get one of *us* hanging from a totem pole. It's their way." Eddie emphasized his frustration by slapping the butt of his rifle with his hand.

"Damnit, Eddie. Take these people outta here. You of all people should know better. Don't give them cause."

"Don't give *them* cause? And who gave 'em cause to harass my people, Cole? Who gave cause for a bunch redneck punks to write obscenities on the doors and windows of our store fronts and sign posts? We haven't done a goddamn thing. Since we talked about it last night, I've gotten twenty calls from my neighbors worried sick how all this is gonna play out."

"Last night, we talked about trust, Eddie—you and I."

"*Trust*." Eddie repeated with emphasis—he then hesitated. "That's right. U-du-gi-gv-di. And when it does go down, Cole, when they start locking us up and throwing away the key, where will *you* be standing? That's what they want to know." He then lowered his voice, "And that's what I gotta know."

Cole looked at the men surrounding him and then back at Eddie. "I'll be standing where I always stand, Eddie...and you're a sorry son of a bitch to have to ask."

For a moment they only stared at one another. The fragile truce that existed between them had been torn up, rewritten, torn up and rewritten again over the past several days. Its status was again uncertain—but Cole had left the next move up to his friend.

Finally, Eddie gave a simple nod of his head and a hard-pressed grin and Cole followed with his own. Eddie then turned, and with his arms wide he began to usher the rest of the Cherokees back down the road.

A few yards away, he turned back and took a final glance at Cole. His o-gi-na-li looked haggard, worn-out. Eddie wanted so much to believe him, and he had given him the benefit of the doubt one more time. But despite Cole's words, he still couldn't tell what was truly going on in that head of his. Amanda may have been on to something. In all these years of friendship, he still didn't know who Cole Whitman truly was.

As for Cole, he just stood there; his hands in his pockets, watching them walk away. Events were spinning out of control, worlds were colliding and at this point he knew he was helpless to prevent any of it from happening.

3:47 PM

Amanda pulled the collar of her overcoat tight around her neck as she stood at a payphone outside the Creekside Restaurant near Bakersville. A misty rain had begun and the temperature of the little mountain town felt much colder than its posted fifty degrees. Amanda had found little success at the town's post office. They were able to confirm the route design on the house marker was used for the Roan area, but any further inquiry generated little more than confused looks and whole-sale indifference. And her brief visit to the Bakersville City Hall also proved fruitless as their record keeping was limited to land transactions and taxes paid for the past five years. She found the name *Miller* three times in the local taxpayers' registry, two Milner's and a Milly, but she was able to rule them all out with a quick glance into their family lines. There seemed to be no connection to that picture on Cole's mantle and anyone living in the area.

On the verge of giving up, Amanda had decided to pull over and put in a call to the office. Perhaps talking to someone at the paper would make her feel less guilty about taking on this wild goose chase. "Yeah, Ted, it's me, Amanda. What's the word from the park?"

"Nothing, so far. We've got our people in Cherokee and Sugarland, but they're not letting us anywhere near the search—they got rangers at all the entry points and they're not talking. Sam said he's been gettin' the run-around from Lawton's office as well as the Sheriff's. Typical press block, I guess." He paused. *"How goes it on your end?"*

"Bleak," Amanda replied. "I think I might be headed for a dead end here too."

"What was so terribly interestin' up there anyway?"

166

"Thought I might've been on to something, but now…." Amanda gave up on the thought—not wanting to get into it with Ted.

"Well, Viv and Larry got the go-ahead to do pieces on the victim's families. You know, give the people a face to go along with the dynamics of the story. Larry is already making his way up to see the Jacob man's sister in Nashville, the one who was killed out in Graveyard Fields…"

As Ted continued to prattle on and on, Amanda found herself tuning him out. Her focus soon drifted across the sleepy Bakersville street and centered on a small sign that was angled in her direction. The odd-shaped sign was painted grey with a singular white cross in its center and an arrow pointing toward an adjacent street. She had to squint, but she could also just make out the words on the bottom: *Penland Cemetery*. As she studied the sign, she suddenly heard Cole's voice echoing in the back of her mind: *There's no time for this now, Amanda. It's gone—it's…dead.*

And suddenly for Amanda something clicked.

"Ted…" she interrupted. "…how long do we keep obit write-ups on file at the *Chronicle*?"

Ted stammered for a moment, a bit put off for having his thoughts disrupted. *"Well, we don't necessarily keep separate files, but we do have copies of all of our old papers on microfiche since day one, including the obituaries. Why? Do you want me to look someone up?"*

"No," she said quickly. Amanda then looked to the front of the restaurant and smiled. "Ted, I gotta go. I'm going to hang out up here for awhile. I may not be back in today, okay? Tell Sam for me, will you?"

"Uh, sure, sweetheart. Whatever you say. And you just watch those slick mountain roads."

The line went silent. Amanda hung on to the receiver for just a second—mulling it all over.

It's gone—it's…dead.

She then moved out in front of the plate glass window of the restaurant and pulled a copy of the *Mitchell County Weekly* from an orange coin rack. It was the local newspaper that covered Bakersville and much of the mountainous area. She ran her finger under the nameplate at the top of the paper: *Since 1942.*

Amanda pulled strands of her windblown hair from in front of her face and looked back at the Penland Cemetery sign across the street. She'd been checking property tax receipts, voters' registration records, mailing addresses looking for a connection to Cole Whitman among the living. But what if his link to this area no longer existed? What if it had been wiped out entirely—if his past was truly dead?

Maybe it's time to start looking among the buried.

4:16 PM

In the woods on the outskirts of Cherokee, Zeb Tucker sat on the gate of his pickup truck with a rifle sprawled across his lap. He was surrounded by an anxious group of his fellow mountaineers. Each one was loaded up with backpacks, weapons and enough heavy ammunition to start a small scale war.

Zeb cleared his throat and then looked up to address those gathered. "Cole and the rest of 'em don't want us out here that's fer sure, but I reckon we're here anyway. Ain't no better trackers and hunters than what we got right here amongst us. Nobody knows this land like we do." Everyone nodded their approval. "Fact is, they's concentratin' all their searchin' in the same spot and this madman could be anywheres in our park. So whether they like it or not, we're here and we gonna find this sumbitch fer 'em." Again the rest of the hunters enthusiastically agreed.

Zeb slid off the back of the truck and slung his rifle over his shoulder. "Fan out. Keep a tight eye. Look to your hiders, fox burrows, bear slogs, anything that six feet will fit intah. And if you do see 'im...put a damn hole in his head."

4:39 PM

As the cold rain precipitously changed to sleet and back over to rain again, Amanda rode the brakes back down the mountain curves to Spruce Pine, a neighboring town of Bakersville. She was now resolved to find the publishing office for the *Mitchell County Weekly*. She figured that in covering this area for the last forty years, they would have the best insight into the people of the vicinity—both living and deceased.

Located on the main street next to the North Toe River, the paper was housed in an old, red brick building under the banner of Appalachia Printing. The building itself had at one time been the front offices for a mining company long since defunct, and the *Weekly* only used the first floor for its publishing needs—the rest of the enormous building had simply been abandoned.

Amanda walked through the front door shaking the rain from about her. She immediately caught the distinct smell of fresh print—reminding her of her days working the school paper at Virginia Tech. Two women, Barbara and Corkie, both well into their sixties were busy typing at their respective desks. Corkie, stationed to the right, looked up at Amanda as she continued to type.

"Good afternoon, Ma'am. May we help you?" she asked in a distinctively squeaky voice.

Amanda placed her umbrella next to the door and walked over to her desk. "I certainly hope so. My name is Amanda Rivers. I'm a reporter from Asheville."

Both women stopped typing having instantly recognized her name.

"From *The Chronicle*? The one who is writing about the attacks in the park?" Corkie asked.

"Yes," Amanda said tentatively having not as yet gotten used to her sudden fame. "I know this may sound like a strange request, but I was wondering if you could help me locate someone from this area. If you're not too busy…"

Barbara got up, a bit intrigued, and moved behind Corkie's desk. "Is this related to what's happening down there in the park now?"

Amanda hesitated and then nodded. "Possibly."

"Well, we will do what we can. We've both been in Spruce Pine all our lives. Corkie here, her family owns this company. Her son is now publisher of the *Weekly*."

Amanda smiled in the old woman's direction.

"You might have better luck looking up records at the town hall though. Spruce has grown so much over the years; I doubt we know everyone," Corkie added.

"No, I'm not looking for someone living here now. The family use to live near Bakersville, in fact—maybe on the Roan Mountain Road. I have reason to believe they aren't there anymore. Either deceased or perhaps moved away."

"I see. Well, we do cover Roan with our paper, but if it's been awhile…" Barbara said.

"Yes, and our articles covered general type of things; we weren't people specific, if you know what I mean." Corkie added.

"There may have been a tragedy associated with this family…. Again, I'm just not too sure," Amanda said with her voice trailing off.

Barbara frowned. "How about the name then? We could start there."

"Miller…" Amanda blurted out. She then paused and added, "Milner maybe. Mill something or other."

Corkie swiveled around in her seat to give Barbara a long, knowing look. She then turned back to Amanda. "Millwood?"

Amanda squinted at the possibility. "It might have been. Millwood did you say?"

Corkie gave a weak smile. "You're definitely not from around here, are you, dear?"

"No," she answered quickly. "Tell me about the Millwood's."

Barbara measured her next words carefully. "Have you ever heard of the story of the Roan Mountain…butcher?"

Amanda felt her stomach go tight—a sudden buzz in her ears. She felt like she was very close now. She shook her head 'no' as she leaned over and braced her hands on Corkie's desk.

"It's a long story. Very tragic. But it may indeed be what you're looking for," Barbara continued.

"Oh, and I do remember it as if it were yesterday," Corkie said lowly. "What that monster did to those people. Especially the Millwood's. I'll never forget what happened to them…all murdered…except for the little one, Cole."

Amanda gasped. Despite her best efforts to restrain herself, an avalanche of emotions began to pour over her. "Cole?" she managed to repeat.

"Yes," the old woman announced flatly. "Cole Millwood."

5:47 PM

Amanda was now seated in Corkie's chair with the two women pulled up on either side of her in folding chairs. Fetched from the press's vault, several old but pristine copies of the *Weekly* were now stacked neatly on the desk. And Amanda gave each one her rapt attention as she read through the articles one after the other.

170

Amanda blew out a breath and leaned back in the chair as she finished reading the last one. "God...."

"That's how most people felt about it," Barbara concurred.

"According to their neighbors, they were thought of very highly. It's upsetting to think something like that could happen around up here. We're just simple mountain folk really," Corkie added.

"You have no idea what that madman did to this area, Miss Rivers. For those several horrifying weeks, time stood still. It's something Corkie and I will take to the grave."

Amanda turned towards Corkie. "You wrote these articles, didn't you?"

"Yes. We were the only press for this area for years. As a weekly we generally wrote about upcoming festivals, business openings—you know, small town stuff. This though...this was different. It was...difficult."

Amanda gave the old woman a look that someone of only shared experiences could give. She then looked back at the last article refocusing her purpose. "You wrote here that after the Millwood's were killed, the sheriff took the young boy into his own custody. What happened to him after that?"

"Taken by family...a foster home...nobody knows for sure...except Red...Sheriff McClane, that is," Corkie answered.

Amanda sat up in the chair to ask them both. "The sheriff. He's not still alive, is he?"

"Red? Shoot yeah. He and his wife Alma got a place not too far from here. Getting old, but still got their wits," Barbara offered.

Corkie held up her hand. "But I should warn you though—if you plan on going out to see him, you should know he never liked talking about this with anyone. It was the roughest time in his life, and I know he would just as soon forget it."

Amanda nodded that she understood. "I know that feeling. But this is vital—I have to speak to him."

5:55 PM

At the Qualla Civic Center, Sanooke sat at his desk in his small office. He was sitting uncomfortably upright in his chair—an imposing look on

171

his face. Special Agent Krazenski of the FBI sat directly across from the chief—a pad and pen in his hands. If Meyers was the brains of the FBI unit, then Ed Krazenski was definitely the muscle. The former marine was two hundred and twenty pounds of bad attitude with an equally daunting scowl to go along with his crew-style haircut and his stuffed, brutish body.

Both men had already sized each other up and the intimidation game had begun in earnest.

"Thanks again, Chief Sanooke for *finally* agreeing to see me," he said in a sarcastic tone. "If I didn't know any better, I'd say you people weren't too interested in helping us find this guy running around in your park."

Sanooke said nothing continuing his blank stare at the FBI man.

"Of course, I know that not to be true. I mean, why wouldn't you want this crazy-ass killer stopped? Am I right?" Krazenski said not really expecting a response.

He got none.

Krazenski shifted in his chair. He tried another approach. "So tell me…how did you lose that arm, Chief?" He waited again through the prickly silence and then added, "I guess it must have fallen off by itself then, huh?"

Sanooke raised his chin. He had had enough. "What do you want?"

"What do *I* want?" Krazenski repeated. "I want to find the man responsible for these murders. I want to put an end to all this. What do you think I want?"

"What do you want from *me*?" Sanooke clarified.

"Okay, Chief, let me lay it out on the table for you. We got a guy out in these woods killing people with bear claws. Ripping 'em to pieces real good, right? A real psycho. Well, what I want to know from you is who do you think could possibly be behind it? I want to know who *you* think it is. It's that simple really."

"I have no idea."

Krazenski laughed. "Oh yeah? Well tell me this then, Chief. What do you know about…uh…?" He glanced down at his pad. "…ghost-bear?"

Sanooke breathed deeply but remained a closed book to the FBI man.

"You have heard of it, right?" Krazenski paused again—waiting. "Alright, let me tell *you* about it then. Ghost-bear is an ancient Cherokee fighting tactic. Your ancestors use to use it to do away with neighboring tribes. They'd dismember the paws of a bear, sharpen the claws, and then use them to gouge the enemy. Messy but effective. I imagine it's kind of like what we got going on in the park right now, don't you think?"

"That was long ago—in ancient times."

Krazenski peered back at his notes. "Yeah, but it also says here that a similar tactic was used as recently as 1939. A Mister Dan *Bighawk* Taylor, member of the wolf clan, used a single bear claw to nick the carotid artery of one James Hapner Jones, a member of the...what's this say? The *potato clan*? In what was described as a struggle for land ownership during one of the tribal council meetings." He looked up from the notepad. "I guess some things just never change, huh, Chief?"

"Killing one's enemy is not inherent just to my people. Besides, anyone could perform the ghost-bear ritual."

"Yeah, but your people know all about it."

"Apparently, so do you," Sanooke said matter-of-factly.

Krazenski grinned. Realizing what he was up against, he leaned forward. "Well, let me put it to you another way then, *Chief*." He said *Chief* distastefully. "We ain't gonna be pussy-footing around on this one. If we find out that you or the council or anyone else in this shit-bag town has any knowledge of who the perpetrator is and is just sitting back covering for him, then we're gonna come down hard on you and your entire reservation. And you ain't got enough fire water, snake oil and tomahawks to do anything about it. Got it, *Chief*?"

Sanooke let the agent's moment pass and then he too leaned forward—his eyes smoldering. "And let me tell you something—if you think you can come here and threaten me or my people with baseless accusations and innuendo then you're sadly mistaken. I know your laws as equal to any one of you assholes stumbling around in our mountains. And make no mistake...if you do try to come down hard on us, *you're* the one who's gonna need the snake oil...to loosen that tomahawk you're gonna find stuck up your ass."

"Is that a threat?" Krazenski stood and the kicked the chair back as he asked.

"No more than your threat, policeman." Sanooke waited and then added, "This interview is over. Now, get the hell outta here."

Krazenski flipped his pad closed and kind of shook it in Sanooke's direction. "Sure thing, Sanooke. But don't worry, we'll be in touch." The FBI man then stormed out the room slamming the door behind him.

Sanooke held at his desk for just a moment contemplating. He rubbed the back of his neck. He thought about the murders...the effect it was having on him and his people....

He then stood at his desk and turned to the wall behind him removing a picture of the Cherokee seal that hung next to the framed document of the US government's guarantee of Cherokee autonomy. He placed the frame on his desk and removed a thin skeleton key that was taped to the back of the picture. He held the key up to the light and momentarily closed his eyes. Sanooke then opened his eyes with sudden conviction. "No, old man, don't be a fool," he whispered to himself.

7:20 PM

Having backtracked up Highway 261, Amanda found Red McClane's home on a country road halfway between Spruce Pine and Bakersville. The two women at the *Weekly* had given her precise directions to the retired sheriff's house, and she now wheeled into his muddy driveway.

Amanda was quick out of her car and made her way to the covered front porch on the small wooden framed house. She wiped the cold rain from her face and knocked on the door.

A grey haired woman with bad posture appeared behind the screen of the main door. She scrunched up her face as she tried to discern who could possibly be standing on her porch so late in the day. "Yes?" she finally said.

Amanda inched forward. "Mrs. McClane?"

"As I live and breathe, honey."

"Mrs. McClane, my name is Amanda Rivers. I'm a reporter with the *Chronicle* in Asheville. I'd like to ask Sheriff McClane some questions please—only take a sec."

The woman looked behind her and then turned back to Amanda. "Watchya want to talk to Red for? He ain't sheriff now. He's retired. Besides, he don't hear too good no more." Her thin voice dipped and cracked behind the screen door.

"That's okay. I'd just like to talk to him about an old case of his—some things only he would know about. I promise not to take up much of his time."

The old woman hesitated and then disappeared—closing the door behind her. Amanda waited patiently taking brief glances at the chipped paint splotches on the siding of the house. It momentarily dawned on her how closely it resembled the house in the picture on Cole's mantle.

The door suddenly reopened and Red McClane in a robe and dirty t-shirt shuffled out front. The man who had once gained his namesake from a stout thick head of red hair had now only a thin, silver patch along the ear line. The rest of his head was covered with wrinkles and unsightly liver spots. He also had a three-day stubble of grey beard—further evidence of a man quietly slipping into decay.

He squinted at Amanda. She imagined, like most lawmen she had known, he was used to judging a person quickly with his tell-all eyes. She hastily tried to give off her most pleasant vibe.

"Alma tells me you're a reporter," he said abruptly.

"Yes, sir."

"Ain't never cared for reporters too much."

Amanda cleared her throat. "Sir, I'd just..."

"Aaaah," he interrupted. "C'mon, let's get this over with."

Instead of inviting her into the warm house, Red opened the screen door and moved on outside. He led Amanda to a wooden bench at the end of the porch. He sat there cross-legged, his bony knees jutting out from under the tattered robe. Amanda sat down beside him and leaned forward so he could hear.

"Mr. McClane..." she started out in a loud tone.

He waved her off. "You don't have to yell. I just pretend I don't hear so good so I don't have to listen to Alma yappin' all the time."

Amanda smiled and began again, "Mr. McClane...Sheriff, I'd like to ask you some questions about a case you worked back in fifty-three—the Roan Butcher incident."

Red furled his brow and sucked his teeth. "Aw, shit. I shoulda known it be sumptin' like that. Why the hell you wanta go diggin' up them old ghosts fer? Nobody round here wants to go through that pain again. Makes my belly tighten to the core just thinkin' 'bout it."

Amanda bit her bottom lip. "Sir, I know this isn't easy, but I have reason to believe that that case may have bearing on another case now. But I also need to be sure. It could directly affect the lives of others, Sheriff." Amanda paused and used her own eyes to plead her case. "Please, sir…tell me what you know."

The old man crossed his arms and bounced his leg a few times as he thought about it. Finally, he turned to Amanda. "Okay. Seeing hows it might be important, I'll tell ya what I know—least what I can remembers anyway."

Amanda thanked him with a half-grin and took out her pen and pad from her coat pocket.

"It was late summer in fifty-three when we got a call from Art Stone— one of our local bean and cabbage farmers who lived this side of Roan— off'n the mountain road up there. He asked us to come out to his farm and take a look at what had happened up to his barn. Buddy Wilkes…Deputy Buddy Wilkes…was the first to respond. After his initial investigation, he immediately called me and told me I *had* to come out and take a look for myself. Said I wouldn't believe it. So, I finished up what I was doing and made the hour drive out there." He paused for a moment as the dreadful memory swelled in his head. "It was the goddamnedest thing I ever done seen. All of Art's horses—must have been five or six beautiful quarter horses he had—all of 'em had been hacked to pieces somehow. Jesus, God, there was a bunch of blood everywhere. The smell was awful. Damn near made me puke just to step foot in there."

"Could you tell at that point how the animals were attacked?"

Red shifted his eyes quickly to the reporter. "Well, no. Ziggy…uh…Mike Zeigler, another deputy of mine at the time, thought he used a hatchet or an axe—some kind of sharp knife maybe." He drew his right hand in a cutting fashion over his left palm.

"And was it? The reports I read didn't mention the instrument of death."

Red paused looking hard at Amanda. "We weren't too sure…I'm still not convinced…." His voice trailed off as if he were still trying to come to grips with what happened. Amanda decided to move on.

"And then there was another attack a few days later?"

Red nodded. "Yeah…and then another and then another. The good people of Roan were losing animals one right after the other. Big animals. Expensive livestock. All in the same manner. And there wasn't a damn thing I could do about it."

Visibly upset, the sheriff paused again and rubbed his hands on his robe as if blood stains were still there. He then looked up at Amanda. "A lot of these animals had parts of 'em missing too. Legs, ears, eyes, organs, chunks of body meat.... Some thought it was a cult, you know, devil worshipers or some shit living up in the hills using the parts in rituals. It scared everyone half to death."

"And then people began to disappear," Amanda stated.

"We had two missing person cases over the next two weeks. We had no idea they might be related…we still don't—never found the bodies, but most people were convinced they fell victim to the butcher." Red grunted *butcher* as if he had sworn never to mention the word again.

"Tell me about the Platt girl. She managed to escape him right?"

"That's right. He kidnapped her from her home—held her for two days. He tortured that poor child…beat her…did terrible things to her…" Red stopped. He was having a difficult time trying to get it out.

Amanda waited. The sheriff looked so frail at the moment—so vulnerable. She hated making him go through this, but his memories were everything now.

"But before he could finish her off," he continued, "she managed to escape somehow. They found her in the woods—naked—bleeding.…Thing was she was so messed up she couldn't help us at all. She was in what they called a *cat-a-tonic* state. So, we continued the search."

Amanda bit the end of her pen. "And not long after that he went after the Millwood's."

"That's right. It was a Saturday night. From the evidence at the crime scene, they must have all started out sittin' 'round the kitchen table. Maybe they had just finished eatin'—I don't remember exactly. Anyway, he busted out their back door and came stormin' in. From there it's purely guess work as to how it all went down. But I imagine it was like a scene from your worst nightmare. There was an obvious struggle—but that son of a bitch was just too strong for 'em. We found the bodies of Mrs. Millwood and the eldest boy in the kitchen. Both had their bellies ripped open and their throats slashed. Half the boy's face was actually torn from its skull…*goddamn* it was awful." Red's voice began to shake.

"What about the father? Mr. Millwood?"

"He was found in the boys' bedroom—face down in his own blood. His head was angled toward one of the beds." Red breathed deeply. "And when we arrived at the scene, that's where we found the little boy—under that bed. He must've hidden there when the bastard came tearin' through the house. I'm pretty sure he watched from under there while his father was killed."

Amanda suddenly pictured Cole as a young boy—the one from the picture—going through that horror—alone.

And then she remembered what he said: *All good fathers are in a way, don't you think? Proud of their sons? No matter...what we've done...or didn't do.*

"He blames himself," Amanda whispered.

"What's that?" Red said looking up.

"Nothing. It just all seems so horrible."

"It was. In my fifty years of law enforcement nothing this bad ever took place—before *or* since. I never knew a more evil man than John Early...that was the man's name, the butcher."

"How'd you catch him, Sheriff?"

Red rubbed his hands vigorously to keep warm. "We had our eye on him for some time. We had begun to profile all those living in the area, and he just kinda fit. He lived alone off the Roan Mountain Road. Small time farmer. Dirt poor. Crazy as hell."

"You couldn't have stopped him any earlier?" She didn't mean the question to come off sounding as if she were criticizing and thankfully Red didn't seem to take it that way.

"Not enough evidence. But after the Millwood killings, I got a warrant to go out and search his place. While we were snoopin' around inside the house, he ran out back to his barn and hung himself. He had 'parently been plannin' his suicide for awhile. It was...a strange crime scene. We found bits and pieces of the animals everywhere."

Amanda paused and then forced the sheriff to look at her. She felt this was the moment—the time for affirmation. "Did you find anything else in that barn, sheriff?"

Red hesitated—stunned by her question. "What do you mean?"

"The instruments of death. Did you find bear claws in there, Sheriff?"

Red dropped his eyes to the porch and nodded that he understood. "I'm an old man, Miss. I don't watch the TV or keep up too much with what's happenin' in the world, but I know where you're a-goin' with this. The murders in the park—down there near Cherokee. That's what this is all about, ain't it? You think it's connected somehow."

Amanda leaned forward—resolved. "Did you find bear claws?"

Red shook his head slowly. "No. We didn't find claws. But there was something else…"

A thousand possibilities swirled in Amanda's head. She gripped down onto the edge of the bench.

Red coughed into his fist. "In the barn, where he hung himself. On either side of the barn walls…painted in blood…a message…for us…for everyone."

"What did it say?"

Red looked hard at the reporter and then said the words as if they were emblazoned in his memory forever: "Only the butcher…only the eater of flesh…shall escape his death…only the butcher shall return…"

May 28, 1974

6:02 AM

The low murmurs of people talking and the banging of pots and pans over a breakfast fire awoke Tully from his deep sleep. He was a bit disoriented by the morning camp sounds, but he soon put it together. He had pledged to remain at the FBI's command center until the manhunt was completely finished, and he decided it was best to camp out along with Pertand's crew at Newfound Gap. As long as *they* were there in his park, he wasn't going anywhere. He wanted to make sure that every tree, plant and rock was back to its rightful place after all this nonsense was over.

He climbed out of his cramped two-man tent, stretched his achy bones and threw a Smokin' Joe's into the corner of his mouth. All around him hundreds of other tents were springing to life with weary guardsmen climbing out for their first taste of the morning, mountain air. Tully gathered from talking to the men throughout the night that they were mostly satisfied in helping with the manhunt in his Smokies. It gave them a chance to enact their skills and ultimately validate their time spent in the guard. And like most of the park's visitors, they enjoyed being out here in a relatively safe natural setting. It sure as hell beat waking up in the rice fields of Cambodia or Vietnam as some had recently done.

The Superintendent looked across the lot and saw that the overnight crew was still maintained under the canopy of the command center. He hitched his suspenders onto his shoulders and waddled over to see what they were up to.

Meyers was sitting in a director's style chair at the command table—already with his sunglasses on. He was eating a biscuit and talking to whom Tully assumed was another FBI agent. *Just what the world needs*, he thought.

Thurmond had also returned to the center and he greeted Tully with a Styrofoam cup of black coffee and a solemn face. "Morning, Tully."

Tully took the offering. "Morning, Anson. And thanks." He sipped lightly at the strong brew. "Anything yet?"

"Nope, not a thing. Every sector checks out clean so far. Meyers is talking about broadening the perimeter today. Maybe use some more guard units."

Tully nodded but also smirked in an I-told-you-so fashion. He then paused and took a playful up and down look at Thurmond and his disheveled appearance. "You look rough. Did you sleep in your patrol car all night?"

Thurmond smiled. "As a matter of fact, I did. And you're one to talk. You're looking pretty rough yourself, Superintendent. I believe I'd rather wake up next to *my wife* than have to look at your ol' ugly mug in the morning."

Tully chuckled. "Is that a fact? Well, I believe I'd rather hump one of my blind hogs than have to wake up next to *your wife*, Sheriff."

They both laughed—effectively burying whatever tension had seeped into their friendship over the search specifics the day before.

The smile on Tully's face vanished however as Meyers approached him. It would take more than a few off-color jokes to establish goodwill between these two.

"Good morning, Superintendent," the agent said wiping the biscuit crumbs from his angular chin.

"You ready to call this damn thing off, Agent Meyers? I hear you haven't had much luck yet."

Before Meyers could respond a team of Huey copters exploded into view overhead heading back toward the west. Meyers looked up at them and then back at Tully.

"We're just warming up, Superintendent. We're gonna catch *your killer*. And soon."

Tully gave a half-hearted smile to this and then looked up at the helicopters as they banked against the rising sun. He scratched at the silver hair on his head.

Not damn soon enough, he thought.

9:33 AM

Macon Eldridge made his way through the thick, wet weeds in a darkly wooded patch that ran parallel to the Oconaluftee River. A local farmer and hunting enthusiast, Macon was one of the volunteers from Zeb Tucker's *illegal search* groups.

Although he was born and raised in the outskirts of Bryson City no more than ten miles from the park, he was not familiar with the area he was presently in. He knew, nevertheless, that if he stayed close to the riverbank he could eventually find his way out. And now after being on the hunt all night without food or sleep and without finding any signs of anyone, let alone the elusive killer, Macon wanted exactly that—a way out.

His progress of getting back to the outside world, however, was slow as his clothes were heavy with rain and sweat and he had developed painful blisters on both feet. He also kept straining his neck to look for breaks in the tree line—looking for an open passage to a trailhead, power line or road—but none were forthcoming. And now he had become quite frustrated.

Macon took a breather on a multi-leveled stone slab near the river. He removed his bill cap and wiped the sweat ring from across his brow. This wasn't how he envisioned the search going at all. He figured by now he would have tracked the bastard down and put him in the dirt with a blast from his granddaddy's deer rifle. It all had sounded so good and glorious when the men were talking it up just the day before. He laid the old Browning across his lap and watched as sweat droplets slid down his nose and leaped onto the gun's wooden stock.

A *moving noise* in the woods behind him suddenly grabbed at his attention. It sounded as if something heavy was breaking through the forest. Macon slid off the slab and raised his rifle in the apparent direction. He put the butt against his shoulder and leveled the sights to the breaking bushes behind him. Bear, deer or man-killer—whatever was coming through the brush was going to feel the heat of his barrel in just a matter of seconds.

As the person emerged into view, Macon lowered his rifle with an honest-to-goodness laugh of relief. "*Ho-ly cow*. I almost blasted yer head off," he said.

The individual continued to approach him in a non-threatening manner.

"I've been out here all night by myself. I sure didn't expect t' see anyone out here now—least a' all you," Macon added.

They came face to face.

"That sure was close." He paused and then followed, "What the hell is ya doin' way out here anyways?"

Bewilderment grew on Macon's face. He looked down in time to see the double serrated edged hunting knife being thrust into his stomach.

He opened his mouth to beg for his life but only the milky pour of fresh red blood emerged. Macon's eyes blinked several times before they found the back of his eyelids. Within seconds the thrill-seeking hunter crumpled to the ground.

He gasped one last breath and then he was gone.

12:14 PM

At 120 feet, Mingo Falls was one of the tallest waterfalls in the southern Appalachians and with the diminutive Unilisi standing just a few yards from its casting spray, it looked all the more immense. Across the fallen waters at the head of the Pigeon Creek trail, stood Sanooke having just made the short hike from Big Cove Road. He moved closer to the bank so that she could hear him over the din of the falls.

"I know what you want. I know why you have asked me here," Sanooke said.

Unilisi remained quiet, but she straightened her back and lifted her chin to form a demanding pose. She hoped it would be enough.

Sanooke shook his head. "No...we have come too far to fall back on the old ways, Unilisi. What you ask for is not a simple matter. There's more to it than just giving you the ka-i-e-le u-de-li-da. Besides, there has been no indication that the prophecy is coming true."

Again Unilisi does not respond but lets her disappointed look say it all.

"Yes, perhaps there is someone using ghost-bear. I don't deny that," Sanooke followed. "Yes, it may even be one of our people...and certainly our town has been hurt by all this. But that doesn't mean we are at war with the ancient enemy." Sanooke paused but then became more assertive in his voice. "I can't just give in to this anytime one of the elders has a vision or a premonition about these kinds of things." Sanooke rubbed the bridge of his nose. "I will become a laughing stock…*we* will become a laughing stock if I allow our people to believe what you say. The old ways are finished, Unilisi. After some time, you will see that I'm right."

Unilisi held for a moment and then mumbled a parting shot in her native tongue before she disappeared into the woods behind her. Sanooke breathed in a heavy sigh and went down to one knee. He picked up a smooth stone and skipped it across the river. He weighed it all very carefully and tried to reassure himself in his thinking, but her brief words were now dancing circles in his head.

It may already be too late.

2:37 PM

Ranger Buck Matthews pulled his park truck down an access road behind the trail loops at Mingus Creek. He had seen whiffs of black smoke filtering across the forest from a mile away, and he decided to venture in to investigate. He knew the manhunt was happening thirty miles from there; and with the park sealed off, there should have been no one remotely near this area.

Buck loaded his rifle, slung his pack around his shoulders and made the trek through the lush woods. Within ten minutes, the power of the Oconaluftee could be heard pushing through the trees before him. He then broke into the clearing. Buck followed a thin deer path through the clearing until he reached the river. And there on the opposite side of the Luftee was the small unattended fire.

Buck found a shallow pass and began to cross the river when he realized that he had not called in his position to the ranger station. He had gotten so caught up by his own curiosity that he had forgotten all about proper procedure. *That'll be your ass*, Buck figured. *If something happens, Cole'll never let me hear the end of it.* It had been Cole's idea to use those rangers not patrolling the border to keep an eye on the rest of the park—just in case—but he had strictly admonished them on the safety factors.

Once on the other side, Buck shook the river's icy water from about him as he slowly approached the smoke-producing fire. He held his hand out to the now nearly invisible flames and allowed the fire's limited warmth to seek out his damp legs. He noticed that the fire was comprised mostly of broken twigs, moss and pine cones. It was being used as an obvious signal—*but by whom?* Buck twisted his head up and down the river bank and along the forest in both directions. He let his pack drop to the ground and he grabbed hold of his rifle with both hands.

"Hello?!" he finally called out. "Anybody hear me?"

His calls were met with the rushing sound of the river only. Buck figured a multi-slab rock a few yards away would provide a good stand to do a visual search so he sauntered over. As he raised his right leg to climb up, he noticed something etched into the base of the rock. It was crudely carved but Buck could just make out the letters:

CNCSKF

What's this? Initials? Hunter markings? He said the letters out loud, "C-N-C-S-K-F."

It had been an unfortunate sign of the times that many of the recent visitors to the Smokies had developed the bad habit of carving their name or initials into the wood railings at observation points throughout the park. Usually they professed their love for someone encased in a sloppily drawn valentine shaped heart. Or they followed their name with the obligatory *was here*—as if it were the only way they could possibly be remembered in life. But this didn't strike Buck as the case. For one, the area was too remote. Very few came back here. And secondly, the way the letters were carved into the rock one would have to be right up on it just to be able to see it—not the *modis operandi* of the normal attention-seekers.

He scratched his head.

And then something else caught his eye. On the left side of the rock a dark pooling substance. Buck went perfectly still. Now the ante had been raised.

A bunch.

Buck didn't need a medical analysis to tell him the substance was blood. He drew the chamber back on the rifle and cautiously put his foot against the base of the rock. He hesitated—imagining what could possibly be bleeding so much on the other side of that rock. His breathing was heavy but he quickly got it under control as he summoned up the courage. He decided he would make his move fast. No thinking. He would swing his whole body around with his finger on the trigger—ready to blast away if necessary.

He then pushed off the bottom of the rock with his foot and leapt to other side. He had his rifle dead-aimed at the source of the blood.

"Coooh Laud A'mighty!!" he shouted as he took in the cold dead eyes of the crumpled, lifeless Macon Eldridge.

4:18 PM

A guardsman stationed at the top of the riverbank led Cole down the same path Buck had used to cross the river before, but now the scene had taken on an entirely different look. Two of the National Guard's helicopters sat powered-down in the clearing on the far bank of the river and several men with high-powered weapons were now standing around the slab rock where Macon's body was discovered. The natural setting of before was all but eradicated. It was a crime scene now and everything was different. The small signal fire which had drawn the initial curiosity had finally died out and was nothing more than a charred spot amongst the rocks.

Cole saw that the entire command team including Thurmond and Tully had been brought in to investigate. Everyone though seemed to just be standing around—waiting. Special Agent Meyers was kneeling in front of the body—his eyes searching. Cole waded across the river and made his way over.

"Hold your positions, gentlemen. No one else is to get within ten meters of the victim yet," Meyers announced. He pulled a tape measure from inside his coat pocket and began to measure various angles in proximity to the body.

Cole quietly made his way toward where Thurmond and Tully were standing. He ignored the sheriff, brushing past him, and he sauntered up next to Tully. He went to a whisper. "Who'd they find?"

"Macon Eldridge. One of our locals," Tully answered in a dispirited tone. "Do you know him?"

Cole nodded. "Macon? Yeah, I've known him for some time. He goes into Manny's a lot—he's a regular down there. What was he doing out here?"

Tully didn't answer. He just shook his head, seething. "I told these bastards...I told 'em somethin' bad like this was gonna happen."

Meyers finished writing down numbers in his note pad and walked over. He put his hands on his hips and looked up to address everyone.

186

"Well, it appears to be just a straight simple cut. A knife. None of the thrashing mania like before. No bear claws."

"Maybe he knows we are on to him, and he's just trying to get it over with quicker," Thurmond said trying to get his two cents in.

"Maybe," Meyers said with doubt. "The angle of the cut, the fact that he didn't put up a fight—all of it seems to suggest he knew his attacker. We'll know more once my forensic team gets in here."

Tully stepped forward. "But we do know that another man has been killed, Agent Meyers. And all outside your *vaunted* perimeter. What do you have to say to that?"

"He wasn't one of *ours'*, Superintendent. And if *your men* had been doing their jobs patrolling the border as they should, then this man may not be lying here dead."

Tully gave an incredulous laugh and looked at Cole. "Can you believe this? Next thing you know, he'll be blaming *us* for the Kennedy assassinations."

Cole ignored his boss's comment and looked directly at the FBI man. "What about tracks? Do we have prints of any kind?"

Meyers shook his head 'no'. "We've checked several yards in all possible directions—nothing discernable. But it looks like he may have left us a message this time." Meyers pointed to the carved letters in the base of the rock.

Cole walked a bit closer and went to a squat position squinting at the writing.

"It doesn't appear to be a real word per say," Meyers continued. "It could be a code...maybe an acronym of some kind. I believe they were written with the tip of the same blade used to..."

"It's Cherokee," Cole said bluntly. "Da-na-da-s-ka-gi."

The gathered men went silent at Cole's understanding. It was a moment of clarity and perhaps the biggest break in the case yet. Meyers knelt next to Cole and looked at him waiting for the translation. Cole turned to him.

"Enemy."

6:55 PM

"I still say we should drag the reservation now. With all the manpower we got, we could spearhead through the upper district in Big Cove and pull the net all the way through to Bryson City. We steam-roll the reservation so fast, they won't even know what hit 'em," Thurmond barked to the others as he paced back and forth with a map of the Qualla Boundary rolled up in his right hand.

Most of the gathered contingents had agreed to return to the station at Oconaluftee after Meyers forensic team had ordered them out of the woodland crime scene. Cole had offered his office as a regrouping point and everyone except the FBI made the brief jaunt over. They were now sprawled out in the cramped office listening to the sheriff's rant.

"And if they ain't hidin' out in the reservation—one of 'em—somebody somewhere—will spill the beans as to where they're at."

Pertand crossed his arms, "What makes you think they'll squeal on one of their own, Sheriff? They seem a tight-lipped group. It just don't seem likely."

Thurmond flashed a dirty smile. "Just watch after we kick in a few of their doors...they'll come around—they'll cooperate."

Cole jumped from a seated position on his desk. "Oh, for crying out loud, Thurmond. You're so full of it sometimes." He stopped and looked at all the others. "Are we seriously going to listen to this?" He turned back to the sheriff and got in his face. "I mean let's just forget about the law and how illegal that kind of search would be for a minute—do you honestly think that a Cherokee would actually take a blade to someone and then conveniently leave his autograph for everyone to see?"

Thurmond's eyes narrowed. "Are you trying to tell me that this ain't the work of one of our Cherokees, Ranger Whitman? For God's sake, man, what else do you need to know? Bear-ghost tactics...silent executions...even the word—enemy...it don't take a genius..."

"You have absolutely *nothing* provable based on any of that. There are no hard facts in this case. None. Everything you mentioned is pure speculation and bullshit. But you're right about that one thing, Thurmond...your theory *sure don't take a genius.*"

Thurmond pushed Cole back as he thrust his hands into his shoulders. "I've been Sheriff of Swain County for ten years now, goddamnit! I know more about criminal behavior and the law than you'll ever know."

Veins popped in Cole's neck as he got chest to chest with the sheriff. "You don't know anything, Thurmond. You're just a bag of shit with a badge—that's all. You think if you huff and puff enough you'll scare the Cherokees into a confession, and it ain't gonna happen."

The rest of the gathered lawmen shook their heads and some shifted in their seats trying to hide behind nervous smiles. Tully's eyes went back and forth between the combatants.

Thurmond sneered down at Cole who was giving up three inches in height. "It ain't, huh? Well, what the hell have you got hot shot? You're always so goddamn sure of yourself...why don't you give us your list of suspects? C'mon, tell us who the great Ranger Whitman thinks it is."

Tully stood up. "Gentlemen...."

"Oh, that's right—*you don't know*," Thurmond continued. "Fact is, this whole case has been in your hands since the beginning and you haven't come up with a damn thing, have ya? You've just been pulling the park, my county and everybody else right down the shitter with ya."

"Shut your fat mouth, Thurmond. Shut it now, before I do it for you."

Thurmond showed his grey teeth. "You're welcome to try..." He leaned into Cole's chest and again pushed him back.

Cole felt the muscles in his body go tight. His breathing went hard like that of a mad bull.

Tully moved in between them and held out his hands traffic cop style. "That's enough! We don't need this...." He moved in closer to Cole. "Sit down...now!" he ordered. "This is the last goddamn thing we need." Both men held for a moment and then receded like weary prize fighters. Cole reluctantly plopped down again on the edge of his desk.

Colonel Pertand, who had been standing by the door, walked to the center of the room. "To be honest, I don't know what to do next, but if this little quarrel is any indication somebody better do something quick or we could find ourselves with an even bigger problem."

7:01 PM

The civic center in Cherokee was overflowing with its own concerned citizens. An impromptu town meeting had formed within the reception area of the center. Chief Sanooke and many of the tribal council were there but the majority of the crowd was those who had heard the rumors of the murder in the park and just wanted the latest gossip.

Sanooke climbed up on top of the reception desk and held up his hand to quiet the inquisitive crowd. "People…people, please settle down. I ask that you quiet down and listen to me now."

"What's going on out there, Chief Sanooke?" a voice abruptly shouted out. "Is it true that one of our people killed a white man? Are we to be blamed for what's going on in the park?"

Sanooke only managed to shake his head before the voices of the crowd intensified once again. "People…please…I know you have questions…as do I." The voices went quiet again as Sanooke continued. "We are getting very little information from the FBI. All we were told is that another murder has taken place within the park. That is *all* we know." Sanooke caught the blank stare of Eddie Whitetree who was standing three deep within the crowd. "I ask that you show patience and restraint…"

"Patience? We have been patient with their investigation. We have shown restraint, but they do not show respect to our people," said council elder Watty Hartford. The fat man ambled to the front of the desk. "And now they say we have been behind the killings all along. The time for talk is over. We must protect ourselves, Chief." He turned to the crowd. "They will come for us. We must act now!" The gathered Cherokees responded with wails and cheers.

With his control now seemingly lost, Sanooke gave up and climbed down from the desk. He saddled in next to Eddie who whispered in the old man's ear. "He's right, you know. It is what we feared the most. The FBI will come for us. It's Wounded Knee all over again."

Sanooke did not answer; he only surveyed the agitated people around him—conflicted by what he wanted to do and what he might be forced to do.

Parked just on the outskirts of the town of Cherokee, two trucks ominously waited on the shoulder of the road. In the lead truck, Zeb Tucker leaned over the passenger side front seat to address two men in the back. "You boys know what to do?" They both nodded eagerly as one held up a brown bottle—an oily cloth attached to the top.

7:34 PM

Cole stared at the floor of his office. His head hurt again and he was massaging his temples. Pertand had assumed the role of lead authority and was discussing their lack of tracking success with Tully and Thurmond. No one truly knew what to do but sit and wait. It was the FBI's game now and the feeling of defeat and helplessness permeated the room.

Horace gave a quick rap on the office door jamb and leaned in, "Cole…"

Cole looked up with bleary eyes

"It's Chief Sanooke on the phone. Says you better get to Cherokee fast. It looks like some kinda riot might be breaking out."

Cole straightened up and immediately shot his eyes over at Tully who returned the urgent look.

8:05 PM

Cole flew the jeep down onto the smoke-filled main street of Cherokee. Tully held fast in the passenger's seat as Pertand steadied himself with the roll bar in the back. They passed several raging fires painting the skyline a hellish orange. One had engulfed the roof of a motel and another was clawing away at the side of Mr. Penny's Cherokee Café. The reservation's fire department was there doing the best they could, but clearly they were outmanned and not prepared to handle such an overwhelming emergency.

The Cherokees themselves were running back and forth across the street trying to protect themselves and their businesses. In their arms they carried what they could salvage—small children clung to their sides. It instantly reminded Tully of those sad images on the nightly news of Cambodian refugees running from the vindictive Khmer Rouge.

As the jeep closed on the center, Cole noticed a large, angry crowd had formed out front. Cherokee men, women and even some children were yelling and jumping up and down—most held makeshift weapons of rocks or sticks.

The jeep came to a slamming halt and all three sprinted over. The entire front plate glass window of the center had been shattered and two of the Cherokee women sat on the ground nursing cut wounds. Pertand immediately stopped to administer first aid to these women, but Tully and Cole pushed further into the crowd searching for Sanooke.

"Do you see this!? Do you…?" Cole was greeted by the angry shouts as he pushed his way in. He wanted somehow to appease them but was overwhelmed by their sheer numbers.

He finally spotted Eddie, and he pulled him aside. "What happened? Who did this?"

"Who the hell do you think?" Eddie yelled as he pointed at the empty street behind him. "I told you this would happen. They blame us. And now we have to fight!"

Cole shook his head. "No…" he barely uttered.

"I must return home. I must protect my family."

"Eddie…!" Cole yelled after him. But it was too late. Eddie disappeared from Cole's sight and more angry faces and accusatory fingers emerged in front of him.

A sudden rifle shot *rang out* and everyone fell to the ground screaming. Cole immediately went into defense mode drawing his weapon and sprawling his body over as many of the trembling citizens as he could. He looked to the street and then the roof tops but he saw no movement. Cole hopped to his feet.

"Inside! Everybody move! Now!"

Cole held his .38 cocked behind his ear and waved the crowd of people into the center. Pertand had also drawn his side arm and he too helped to usher the citizens.

"Go! Get inside! Take cover!"

There was no argument from the Cherokees and they hastily dispersed into the various meeting rooms. They haphazardly huddled together; and then after few barked orders from some of the older men, they became completely quiet. Soon only the whimpers of a few crying children could be heard coming from the back of the center's conference room.

Back outside, Cole and Pertand surveyed all angles of the street in front of them—their chests heaving with excited breath and their eyes darting all about.

Several more shots *blasted* through the night and Cole immediately took off in the rounds' direction. "Stay here!" he yelled at Pertand.

He turned the corner behind the center and ran down the grass inlay between the center and the museum. He was running full out but then slowed as he approached the back of the museum. His run went to a jog and then to a complete stop. He grabbed at his aching head.

"Oh, no…"

His adrenaline had triggered his sickness, and he felt the first wave of psychosis creeping into his mind.

"No…no…not now…."

The images of death and rage flashed quickly. He heard the old screams. Cole bent over at the waist he pinched the bridge of his nose forcing himself to block the pain. "Stop it. Not now. I beg you." He was losing himself yet again….

Sirens blared. Lights were flashing. Shots were fired. Mayhem. Pandemonium. From his position of safety, Judaculla watched the carnage unfold in the streets of the Cherokee village. It knew that it was responsible for all of this. It delighted the monster that it could cause so much pain and suffering to those who had tried to destroy it—who tried to take his world. The prophecy was being fulfilled. The ancient words were becoming a reality.

Run, little Indians, run. Burn, little Indians, burn.

Cole stood up sucking in air and shaking his body as if he had just emerged from the depths of a frozen lake. The screams in his head were dissipating quickly.

It was much darker now. Time had passed but he wasn't sure if it had been five minutes or five hours. He finally steadied himself and gathered in his surroundings. *Cherokee…The riot…* He then ambled out to the adjacent street.

By the glow of a street light he saw a body lying in a near fetal position in the middle of the road. Cole walked over to it and then dropped to his knees. It was a young Cherokee boy. No more than fourteen or fifteen. Blood poured from an open wound on his chest. Cole grabbed his wrist and methodically checked his pulse, but he knew it already. He was dead.

It was too much. He had not the strength to deal with it anymore. Cole closed his eyes and leaned over the boy. He then collapsed on top of the dead child continuing to squeeze his hand. Wave after wave of the same sickening emotions continued to roll over him. Bitterness. Anger. Regret.

In a short time, Cole felt the presence of someone standing near him. He looked up. Sheriff Anson Thurmond decked out in full riot gear stood over him—a shotgun cradled in both hands.

"Great job of protecting the citizens, Whitman. Forgive the young man if he don't get up and thank ya."

May 29, 1974

7:03 AM

Cherokee was a veritable ghost town. All traffic in and out of the town had been stopped save the occasional rumbling of a National Guard truck bringing in more soldiers to keep a grip on her borders. The roads themselves were wet from an early morning rain, and they were filled with shards of glass and debris from the previous night's madness. The Smokies had also thrown down a cool mist from her peaks and the settled fog mixed with the still smoldering fires gave the mountain town an eerie, other-worldly presence.

The night had been a long and difficult one. The Cherokees had fought valiantly to defend their homes, their businesses and their lives against those who had sought to destroy them. But the face of the enemy kept changing throughout the late hours making their stance all the more challenging. It became unclear who was the aggressor and who was the protector—and so they ended up fighting against them all: the scum who brought the fight, the green sleeved militia, rangers, sheriff deputies, FBI—everyone. Cherokee strongholds in certain pockets of the town had been reported as putting up heavy resistance throughout the night but began to dwindle in the early morning hours. By sunrise martial law had been declared by the governor's office and all of Cherokee was officially roped in.

In the trashed Civic Center, however, a single dim light was on in a room near Sanooke's office. The room was small and plain with stacked boxes and file cabinets as its only holdings. It had been used primarily as storage for the reservation's forgotten business transactions. But for years, and without anyone's knowledge but the old chief himself, the tiny storage room also had held the Cherokee's greatest secret.

Sanooke knelt on the floor in the center of the room pushing the sealed boxes around like a madman—frantic in his search. Finally he cleared enough of the area to expose a small rectangular seam in the tile floor. Sanooke produced a hunting blade from his back pocket and carefully dug around the seam with its point until the piece of tile came lose. He removed the section and several pieces of block wood which was covering immediately underneath. He then reached under the floor with great difficulty and struggled to pull out a metal box. He dug down his shirt pocket and produced the skeleton key he had taken from behind the picture in his office. He used it on the lock and gently pulled out the contents—an aged, leather-bound tome. He took it to a small table near the room's only window and with his one hand proceeded to untie the cords which had kept the sacred book secure for decades.

He sifted through the old, brittle parchments carefully handling each section with a delicate touch. He found the one he was searching for and quickly became engrossed in reading the ancient words. So lost in reading the words that he did not realize someone else had come into the room and was now standing directly behind him.

"Whatcha say there, Chief?"

Sanooke whirled around and came face to face with Krazenski. The FBI man was smacking hard on a piece of gum and flashing a wise-ass grin.

"What are you doing here?" asked Sanooke.

Krazenski looked about the room and then back to Sanooke. "What? The town wasn't messy enough for ya? Ya had to come in here and wreck this place too?"

"You are not welcome here. Get out."

"Can't do that, Chief," Krazinski said enjoying every minute of it. "See, you gotta come down to the Sheriff's office with me *right now*. Alotta folks down there wanta talk with ya 'bout last night. Get your side of the story so to speak. We actually looked for ya last night; but strange enough, we couldn't find ya anywhere. You weren't hiding out from us, now was ya, Chief Sanooke?"

Sanooke turned back to the writings on the table. "I don't have time for your government's games. I must…"

"Oh, you'll find the time, Chief, or I'll help ya find it," Krazenski said as he whipped out a pair of handcuffs from his belt.

Undaunted, Sanooke turned and poked Krazenski in the chest with his finger. "I said I don't have time for you, now get out!"

Krazenski lunged at Sanooke. He overpowered the older man throwing him against the table. Sanooke grabbed at the ancient writings but his arm was whipped behind his back and the papers were sent scattered to the floor.

"You don't understand...." Sanooke yelled. "You must let me go..."

Surprised by the old man's strength, Krazenski had to exert an inordinate amount of pressure just to get the one handcuff on the chief's wrist. He then locked him in and began dragging Sanooke toward the door.

"Get the hell off of me! You don't know what you're doing! I must stop it! I must stop it!!"

Krazenski now had Sanooke's arm handcuffed to his own. He also had a sizable chunk of the chief's hair in his other hand as he pushed him out the Civic Center. A deputy and another FBI man were waiting outside and helped to usher the chief into the back of the deputy's squad car.

Back in the record's room the yellow bulb shown its light directly on the parchment that Sanooke had been reading. It was hand-written with great care taken in the calligraphy of the Cherokee language. There was also a hand drawn picture that stood out under the wording. It was an unmistakable likeness of the devil itself—a drawing of the claw-fingered, slant-eyed giant, Judaculla.

8:17 AM

Cole sat at his desk at the ranger station in Oconaluftee. It had been a long night and he had not the chance to return to his cabin. He ran his fingers through his black hair and rubbed his face as he tried to stay awake. The police deemed it imperative that he quickly finish his report and get to them his version of the *incident*.

As a fellow lawman he felt obliged to do so; but as he typed, he became less and less concerned about their wishes. He finally stopped in the middle of a sentence and gazed down at his chest and lap. For the first time he noticed there were blood stains all over his rumpled uniform. He looked like he had been through hell. And this time looks weren't deceiving.

The phone on his desk began to ring, but he just stared at it. He was almost afraid to answer. More bad news. It had to be. He heard Horace answer in the other room and then looked up at the door waiting for his appearance. Within a few seconds his friend appeared in the doorway. "Cole, phone for ya. It's Doc Hatcher."

Cole nodded and then waited for Horace to leave. He picked up the receiver and punched the line. "Yeah, Doc..." he said with the low voice of a defeated man.

There was a long moment of silence before Hatcher spoke. *"Cole, I know. I know...everything."*

Cole did not to reply. He hung up the phone and continued to stare at it. He then reached into the top drawer of his desk and pulled out a hand box of brass tipped .38 caliber bullets. He drew his weapon from his side holster and filled the six slots of the chamber before wrist-snapping it shut.

Cole stood and surveyed the room as if he were looking at it for the last time. He then slipped out of his office and the station without saying another word.

9:14 AM

Eddie had made the hour drive to Fletcher, North Carolina and was now waiting inside the Asheville Airport. He watched as Amanda's plane, an Eastern flight from Albany, New York, circled the tarmac and made its approach to the gate. It had been delayed coming in to Fletcher by an approaching weather system; but only for fifteen minutes, and Eddie was thankful he didn't have to wait much longer.

He had made his decision during the long night and after a few phone calls to the paper and then to her roommate, and after making arrangements for his family's safety, he had left Cherokee and tracked her to here. He had no idea why she had gone to New York, but it was irrelevant at this point. He just knew it was time for full disclosure. His decision to protect Cole until this moment had been one out of loyalty to a friend. But now...with all that had happened, Eddie wanted to set the record straight. And the sooner the better.

He decided he would tell her all he knew about Cole—all the unsettling details. He still couldn't bring himself to think Cole was capable of performing such detestable horrors like those that had been committed in the park. But if Cole did have something to do with the murders, and Eddie had kept those secrets to himself, he would never be able to live with it. Eddie decided Amanda would be the best judge of the information. She was close to Cole as well as the story. It would be her call.

Within minutes of coming to a stop, Amanda exited the plane and walked down the stairs toward the terminal. She was followed closely by a thin, sandy-blond headed man in his mid-forties wearing a charcoal grey suit and carrying a briefcase. Eddie surmised from the way that they were talking that there was more to it than just casual passenger to passenger conversation.

As they entered the tunnel connector, Eddie thought about the last time he had found Cole during one of his *seizures*. He had gone to his cabin to return a tackle box he had borrowed for a father-son fishing trip. When he got there he had knocked on the door but Cole didn't answer. It was raining so he went to the back of the cabin to leave the tackle under the covered back stoop. As he turned to leave, he heard bumping noises and Cole screaming like a madman inside the house. "No!! Stop! I'll kill you!!"

Eddie quickly kicked in the back door and ran to Cole's room. He found him lying in his bed with the sheets and pillows torn to shreds—bloody as hell. Cole was alone—still writhing on the bed—screaming and jabbing a hunting knife deep into his thigh. "I'll kill you! I'll kill you!! I'll kill you!!" Eddie jumped on the bed and wrestled the knife away from him. He pinned Cole down until he broke from his mania.

Eddie had found him several times before in varying states of confusion, but never with this much self-inflicted violence. Cole had made his friend swear to never tell anyone about his problem. He insisted to Eddie that he could control it. But because he never shared with Eddie the true cause behind his behavior, there was always an uneasy strain running through their relationship. And now it was going to be all out in the open. Several people were dead, the reservation was in shambles and paranoia ran rampant through the hills. It was the time for truth.

Friendships be damned.

11:22 AM

Sanooke sat crossed legged on a folding chair in the holding pen at the Swain County Courthouse. He leaned forward in the chair until it squeaked and stared out past the iron bars and into the busy detention area. He saw many of his people milling about—being questioned, being harassed. They ran the gamut of negative emotions: scared and confused; angry and resentful. He noticed they were in equal number to the number of law enforcement, and part of him wanted to scream out to them. He wanted to urge them to take up arms and to fight, but age and wisdom prevented it. He knew it was fruitless. Eddie spoke the truth when he said this was the same as Wounded Knee. The outcome would be no different. The American Indians were a dying breed socially, culturally, politically. And now they were about to lose their remaining fight— the one that meant the most.

I am such a fool, Sanooke thought. *I should have listened.*

It had indeed been very wise to strike now. Tsul-Kalu knew the Ani-yun-wiya were in a weak position. Its audacious plan to destroy the keepers was brilliant. And with the Cherokees now out of the way, it would inherit the Boundary and then do what the demon had always wanted to do—cause complete chaos. It would reign supreme. The blue-smoke mountains would belong once again to Tsul-Kalu—the devil—the Judaculla. The unholy prophecy would be fulfilled. The Cherokee were losing their sacred lands even now as Sanooke sat there in his cell.

Sanooke wished he could have done more to stop it. But now it was too late. Maybe if he hadn't doubted the signs and had given his full support to Unilisi and the elders in the beginning. If he had just given her what she and the elders had asked for. But it was not to be. He had told Unilisi earlier—believing in the old ways was over. It was a world that would only accept empirical evidence now. It would believe only what it could see. The police would blame the Cherokees; the Cherokees would blame the whites, and the whites would destroy everything including themselves to prove otherwise. And that was the beauty in Judaculla's plan. They would destroy one another and the blue mountains would be left for the taking.

Sanooke stood up and walked to the front of the cage when he saw Eddie enter the room. He was walking in a very hurried fashion with two white people—a reddish-brown headed woman whom he thought he had seen in town once before and a man in a grey suit whom he did not recognize at all. He surmised that it must have started raining outside as the three shook the dampness from all about them. They by-passed the Cherokees and several inquisitive deputies and headed into adjoining room where all of the major players had now gathered.

"I'm sorry. This is a closed meeting," Thurmond said as he looked up from his position at the head of the table. Meyers, Krazenski, Pertand, Tully and several others also turned in their seats as they took notice of the trio entering the room.

Tully rose from his seat. "Miss Rivers...?"

Amanda held her position—momentarily catching her breath. "Superintendent...Sheriff Thurmond...sorry to interrupt, but I have some urgent information. It's about a missing piece of the puzzle, sir—I believe we've found it."

11:29 AM

Doc Hatcher sat at his desk stroking his finger around the rim of his mug. The old medical file with the chart and newspaper clippings laid out flat in front of him. He checked his watch. He was still waiting on Cole—trying to run it all through his mind one more time.

This sure ain't gonna be easy.

A far-off *rumble of thunder* caused Doc to stir. He rose from his chair and checked the small window behind him. Pellets of rain streaked down the glass and he saw the tops of the mulberry bushes behind his office sway in the wind. He had always been fascinated by storms since he was a kid. But for some inexplicable reason, this morning storm seemed different. This one seemed to unnerve him a little.

Doc heard the front door to his office open. "Finally..." he mumbled. He then called out, "Back here, Cole!"

He waited a moment for Cole to answer or to at least hear him coming down the hallway. But he heard nothing. Doc moved toward the office door. "Cole...? Come on back here...I'm in the office."

Hatcher made it only one more step when he saw the barrel of the .38 appear in front of him. He heard the *click* followed quickly by the *explosion*. The bullet smacked him in the forehead sending a chunk of his brain to the wall behind him and his body slumping to the floor.

11:40 AM

"Now let me get this straight…you think Cole Whitman, the ranger, the guy from the park, might have had something to do with all this mess?" Thurmond asked with just a hint of hopefulness.

"We're not accusing anyone, Sheriff, but there may be a premise for that belief," Amanda answered.

Tully pushed away from the table—his face burnt red. "This is fucking ridiculous! What the hell do you mean Cole might have something to do with this? Are you suggesting my top ranger—*and good friend*—is the one behind these murders? Is that what you're seriously suggesting? Jesus H. Christ, this whole world has gone off the fucking deep end."

Amanda leaned forward. "Mr. Lawton, sir, I know how you feel. I felt the same way…"

The man in the charcoal suit interrupted, "As Ms. Rivers stated; we are not accusing anyone—only that Mr. Whitman's mental capacity may have given just cause in this case."

"Given just cause?" Tully snapped back. He then looked the man up and down. "And just who the hell are *you* anyway?"

The man took a pleading glance at Amanda. "This is Dr. Jack Snyder chief psychiatrist and head administrator at the Willard Psychiatric Center in Romulus, New York," she began. "He has Cole's record and much more information that may prove helpful."

"His record from what?" Tully asked.

"From the five years Cole spent there as a patient."

The room went dead silent. The news pricked Meyers' ears and made him sit up in his chair. Thurmond's face also lit up at the possibilities.

Tully relented and slowly sank back into his chair. "Okay, Miss Rivers, okay. I guess you'd better fill us in." He paused and then added, "I just hope *all* of what you got to say is worth listenin' to."

Amanda gave a deep breath and blew strands of her wet hair from her face. "Are any of you familiar with the Roan Butcher Massacre that took place not far from here in fifty-three?"

Meyers and Krazenski locked eyes and gave a mutual nod. Pertand raised his hand a little. "Yeah, the guy with the axe…killed a bunch of animals and some people too if I remember correctly. Most everybody from North Carolina remembers that. They use to tell stories about him around the campfires like he was the boogeyman."

Thurmond also nodded. "Yeah, we all know the case. And this ties into Whitman? How?"

"The butcher killed Cole's family when Cole was twelve years old. Killed them all right in front of him apparently," Amanda said—a sudden nervous lilt in her voice.

Meyers swung his head around and half-whispered to Tully, "Were you aware of this?" The superintendent still numbed by the accusations denied the query with a simple shake of his head.

"It obviously had a great affect on Cole's mental state," Amanda continued. "I know for a fact that the man who investigated the crime took Cole into his own home. He tried to help him overcome it all, but Cole became…violently unstable in the days after. So that's when they sent him to New York."

Everyone took a brief glance at Snyder.

Amanda led on. "For five years the staff at the Willard Psychiatric Center did their best to bring him back to some form of normalcy."

"Five years? I don't understand. I'm sure that had to be a helluva thing witnessing your family killed by a monster like that, but why did it take so long?" Tully asked.

Snyder went to his briefcase and opened it up. "The file will tell you." He began passing out copies of the medical breakdown. "Cole suffered from his trauma in an intense and unusual way to say the least. It was categorized at the time as an undetermined psychosis."

"Undetermined?" Meyers asked.

"Yes, no one at Willard had seen anything like it. They wrote that he acted with combined values of post-traumatic stress and various symptoms of schizophrenia: hallucinations, delusions, catatonic states and also these highly…*combustible* reactions. He often went for long periods of time without incident. And then he'd fall into these recessive emotional periods marked by deep, somber retractionary behavior. From that he'd suddenly lash out in fits of rage at anyone or anything nearby. His attacks were indiscriminate and often very brutal. They were summarily described as animal-like."

Eddie who had backed up against the door bit his lower lip at Snyder's use of the term *animal-like*.

"And nothing was done for him?" Tully again asked.

"Cole was turned over to the center's top psychiatrist, Dr. Paul Whitman—a specialist in the field of post-traumatic stress. He tried various therapeutic techniques to erase the tragedy from Cole's mind but was never fully successful."

"*Whitman*? That was the doctor's name too?" Tully followed.

Amanda jumped back in. "No, just the doctor's. Cole's actual last name is Millwood. He apparently began using the doctor's name after he left the center."

"Millwood?" Tully questioned again. He raised his eyebrows and clicked his tongue on the roof of his mouth—not sure of what to make of all this. "This is all just so insane…"

"Where is Dr. Whitman now?" Meyers asked.

"He died, unfortunately, of heart failure back in fifty-seven," Snyder responded. "According to our records Cole had grown very close to him. They said that after Dr. Whitman's death Cole had some of his most intense reactions—even wounding an orderly and a nurse with shards of glass from a broken hand mirror."

Pertand gave a matter-of-fact look. "Didn't they try medications? Shock therapy?"

"Yes, as I said, all of that and much more. But again with little lasting results."

The group went momentarily silent as they tried to digest it all.

Krazenski then leaned forward in his chair. "Well, what I don't get is how a guy that *buggsy* got out of your hospital to begin with—much less came to work as a park ranger down here."

"Amen to that," Thurmond concurred.

Snyder scratched the back of his neck. "Good question and one I don't have a good answer for. He was a minor and at the time of his disappearance from the hospital, there was a turn-over in administration. New doctors—staff." Snyder shrugged. "He must have fallen through the cracks somehow."

"Beautiful," Krazenski added. "Makes you wonder how many more crazies are out there running around who have fallen through the cracks."

"He had to go through fingerprints, background checks, the whole nine yards to come to work for us. And he has a *gun permit* for Chrissakes. This had to have shown up somewhere," Tully said.

Snyder indicated his shared puzzlement with a shrug.

"So, when was the last official data on this Cole person taken?" Meyers asked.

"Nineteen Fifty-Eight. Cole would have been seventeen. There is no record after that. No discharge. No follow-ups."

"And I've tried to check on his more recent records," Amanda stated. "It's a cold trail leading up to his time working here in the park. His home address, family records, everything was forged." She took another deep breath. "And you should also know his behavior has been suspect in the years since he arrived as well. Strange actions and reactions—even a suicide attempt. There are witnesses to corroborate all of this." She glanced over at Eddie.

Meyers rubbed his chin. "Well, it's a fascinating story, but it's hardly conclusive evidence. This man clearly sounds unstable enough to have reacted in some way, but what about the use of the bear claws…and the markings?"

Eddie stepped forward and faced Meyers. He felt like such a betrayer. It truly turned his stomach to do this to Cole. "He is well-versed in my people's lore and language. It would not be hard for him to use the ways of the Cherokee."

"Right. Remember, he's the one that knew the markings on the rock meant *enemy*," Thurmond eagerly added.

Meyers pointed to the handout. "But according to the medical records he is only reacting to his trauma." He looked over at Snyder. "You said he lashed out at people randomly. He's not conscious enough about what he's doing to plot or to frame anyone else…is he?"

"It's quite possible that when he goes through his episodes now he's acting under another persona. It certainly would make sense that he developed some kind of dual-personality through all this as a method of defense—a Jekyll and Hyde, if you will," Snyder confirmed. "Perhaps, when in the depths of his psychosis, his other persona is Cherokee derived. And perhaps when in this state he reacts to his surroundings with more cognitive ability—constantly developing, becoming more intricate in the planning of his actions. We simply don't know for sure. But it certainly wouldn't be beyond the scope of this patient to use stories he knew as a child to act out his aggressions under this split personality. And from what Ms. Rivers and now Mr. Whitetree have indicated, he knew much about the Cherokee culture at an early age."

"This is all horse shit," Tully commanded. "When I told Cole about Nic, he was visibly upset. There's no way he would have done those things to a fellow ranger—*especially not to Nic.*"

"He may not have even realized it. If he is indeed suffering from a true split-personality disorder," Amanda said.

"That's right," Snyder agreed. "He may have had an episode, emerged as this other person, committed the crime, phased out and woke up later with no memory of the murder at all." Snyder looked at the FBI lead. "That's why it's urgent he be evaluated as soon as possible."

Amanda weighed back in, "And if opportunity is a necessity, well, then, he's had that too. His whereabouts cannot be determined during any of the attacks." She paused before adding, "Not even out in Graveyard Fields."

Thurmond nodded eagerly. "I should have known. I mean, I knew the guy was crazy, but…"

Tully slammed his hands on the table rocking everyone's attention. "Wait a second here! Wait just a damn second! Ten minutes ago you assholes wanted to destroy my park and then the reservation looking for this madman. And now you sit here and listen to all of this psycho-gobbledygook and you want to start pointing the finger at Cole? You really want to throw all of this on one man? Based on *this shit*? I just can't…I just can't believe this…" Tully got up and started walking out the room. He stopped, threw a Smokin' Joe's in his mouth, lit it, and turned back for one final shot, "I don't want any more of this. I don't want any part of it. Ya'll can *all* go to hell."

Meyers waited as the door slammed behind Tully. He then took a hard look at Amanda and then at Krazenski. "Okay. Let's pick this guy up and bring him in. Certainly won't harm anything to question him."

Thurmond stood. "I'll do it. I'll go pick him up. I know the rocks he likes to hide under."

Meyers stood as well. "And I'll go with you." He looked over to his subordinate. "Ed, you stay here and finish up interviewing the locals—get whatever you can out of them."

Krazenski nodded.

"I'll also remain here—so I can set up and help evaluate him when you bring him back in," Snyder said. He then shot a look at Amanda. "And if I may…you might want to take Ms. Rivers there with you. She has made a connection with Mr. Whitman recently. He may not react as violently to the situation if she is with you."

Meyers began to nod his okay but then glanced over at the sheriff. "What do you think?"

"Fine by me. But don't you worry about Cole's reaction. I won't be taking any chances," Thurmond said patting his side arm as he made his way out the door.

11:55 AM

Eddie remained in the conference room after everyone else had gone. He was now seated in the chair that the bald-headed, National Guard commander had previously occupied. He felt drained—lifeless. He flipped through a series of papers which had been abandoned on the tabletop, perusing the aged handwritten copies, noting the terms *violent* and *dangerous* throughout the entire discourse on Cole. It was still so hard to believe.

He closed the file and thought of his good friend. Disconnected images of Cole mutilating his body, screaming like a madman, and then begging Eddie for absolution mixed in Eddie's mind with happier memories of the numerous times they hunted the Pisgah forest together, the infamous fishing trip to Abrams Creek, and those many times of drinking and laughing through the night. Eddie realized he would not find peace with his relationship to Cole this soon—it would take a lot of time. Besides, there were other issues now at hand.

Amanda's timely work on the case had certainly helped connect all the dots, but solving the murders was only the beginning. The madness which had inflicted the Smokies also had to come to an end. But at what cost? Eddie tried to calculate the devastation to the park and the reservation. He thought of the shops, the restaurants, and hotels. He wondered how long it would take for life to return to normal—if at all.

Frustrated by his thoughts, Eddie finally got up and wandered back into the detention area. He wanted to see if there was anything he could do to help expedite the proceedings now that none of the Cherokees could be held accountable for what had happened. The psychiatrist from New York was already out there helping. He was actively engaged in a conversation with an elderly Cherokee couple who had lost their business to a fire during last night's fracas. It was good to see that they were getting that kind of attention. Many of the other Cherokees remained at the deputies' desks giving depositions as to what they had witnessed the previous night. Eddie noted their sorrow too. *Not enough psychiatrists to go around.*

And then as he moved from desk to desk thinking how things couldn't get much worse, he peered toward the back of room. There he saw Sanooke, Chief of the Eastern Band of the Cherokees, head of the tribal council, the moral and spiritual leader of the Tsalagi, and his good friend, locked behind bars like a common thief.

Eddie rushed over to him. "Edami...?"

Sanooke waved him off. "It is okay, Eddie. I am unharmed."

"How long have you been here? They're not charging you with anything, are they?"

"No...not yet. This is *their way* of bringing me in to talk..."

Eddie grabbed at the bars. "To talk? Edami...let me get you a lawyer; I'll call the civil liberties office...AIM...somebody...there's no need for you to have to be here anymore. Maybe I could get them to contact Sheriff Thurmond..."

Again the old chief waved him off. "No. There is no time for that. Perhaps it is best that I am in here. Especially now that you have come."

Eddie scrunched his face—confused, pained by his inability to help. "But this is crazy. There must be something I can do?"

Sanooke held for a moment and then he looked long and hard at Eddie. He moved in close and went to a whisper, "There is. You must go to the civic center for me."

Eddie furled his brow at the old man. "The center? Why?"

"Next to my office is a small storage room."

"I don't understand..."

"The storage room, do you know it?" Sanooke asked firmly.

Eddie nodded. "Yes, of course, but..."

"On the table and now perhaps spread out on the floor are parchments of old writings. You must go and collect them all and take them to Unilisi," Sanooke commanded.

"Unilisi? *My* Unilisi?"

Sanooke gave a quiet nod. "She must have them now. She will know what to do."

"Why? What are they?"

Sanooke's eyes drifted past Eddie as he debated in his mind what to tell his young friend. He finally looked back at him with purpose. "They are the words of the ka-i-e-le u-de-li-da."

"Words of the *ancient secrets*? What is that? I never heard of it."

"They were written down by Sequoyah himself—mandated by our early nation leaders long ago."

"But his most important writings are in the museum. Are you saying there were others?"

Sanooke gave another slow nod of his head "Yes. They explain sacred Cherokee knowledge—beyond shaman, beyond the sacred rites. Passed down from the ancient times."

"Sacred knowledge of what? What the hell are you talking about, Edami?"

"What was once kept as whispers by a chosen few was given form on these papers. They have been in our trust from the beginning—passed from the chief of one generation to the next. They have been in my safe-keeping since the day I was chosen as chief."

"Why are they so important? And why on earth does *Unilisi* need to have them?" Eddie asked—his frustration rising. But then it came rushing to him like a wayward arrow and he momentarily closed his eyes to the realization. "This doesn't have anything to do with Tsul-kalu, does it?"

Sanooke did not answer, but he didn't have to. Eddie knew the old man's thoughts now and his disappointed look showed it. "Jesus, Edami, not you too. I thought you of all people knew we were living in the twentieth century now."

Sanooke's eyes narrowed at the insult. "There are things you are not aware of, Eddie. There are things that are at play here that cannot be seen. Don't be so quick to dismiss…"

"What? A giant, mythological monster? A horrid beast of seven claws and slanted eyes?" Eddie asked unable to hide his sarcasm. "You were the one who told us all that was all bullshit, remember? You said that was the kind of crap that kept our people from getting a hold in this world. That they would never accept us as long as we continued to dance around the fire and howl at the moon. Respect the past but live in the present. Those were your words, Edami." He paused and then blew out a sigh. "It's not Tsul-kalu. Nor is it someone using ghost-bear from the old clan rivals. It's not even one of our people. It's just a sick, sick man. And the police are on to him now. In fact, they just left to go pick him up." He waited and then added in a heavy tone, "It's going to be over with very soon."

Sanooke remained quiet. Eddie felt great shame for disagreeing so harshly with his chief and mentor, but he had had to live with those kind of old folk ramblings all of his life, and he never expected that kind of talk from someone as level-headed as Sanooke. Eddie held up his hand and was turning to leave. "I'll see what I can do about getting you released."

"No," Sanooke said with conviction. It was the chief's time to be direct. "You will do as I say, Eddie. You will go to the center and then take the papers to Unilisi. And you will do it *now*."

"But…"

"Eddie…if you value any part of our heritage *and* our friendship, you will do as I ask."

Eddie placed his hands on his hips and blew out another deep breath. He weighed it all very carefully.

Sanooke also mellowed in tone. "Years ago, when I ran for tribal chief, you said you trusted my judgment. You believed in me."

"Yes, of course I did."

"And now I ask you to trust me again."

Eddie nodded. "I do."

"Then go…and hurry."

Resolved, Eddie turned from the cell without another word and headed out across the room. Sanooke grabbed hold of the metal bars and squeezed them tight. He gazed up to the ceiling as if he could see past the courthouse's fluorescent lights and out into the sky above—daring to hope.

2:46 PM

The western flow continued to bring heavy black clouds to the eastern escarpment of the Blue Ridge with passing sheets of cold rain and the occasional disruptive clap of thunder. Thurmond shot an eye at the angry skies as he wheeled his cruiser into back lot of the Oconaluftee station. The weather was intense even for the Smokies, but at this point nothing was going to stop him from being the first to slap the cuffs on that murderous son of a bitch.

Thurmond and Meyers jumped out of the cruiser first followed closely by Amanda. All three made a mad dash through the rain and quickly ducked into the station. Thurmond then led them in a silent procession down the back hallway unsnapping his holster along the way. They bypassed Cole's dark office and made their way into the visitor's center.

Horace was alone in the building sweeping the floors when they seemed to magically appear before him. Just the sight of the three of them together sent up an immediate red flag. "Oh…hi…uh, is something wrong?"

"Whitman. Is he here?" Thurmond barked.

"No," Horace replied. "He left outta here several hours ago."

"Do you know where?" Meyers followed.

Horace tapped the broom on the wooden floors as he thought about it. "Not really. He got a phone call from Doc Hatcher this morning. Haven't seen him since."

The two lawmen caught each other's eye. "Come on, let's go," Thurmond said.

And all three turned to leave.

"Wait a minute," Horace called out. "Have you tried his place? I could try and contact him for ya."

"We checked. He's not there and he's not answering his phone or radio," Meyers said bluntly.

"Thanks anyway," Amanda added as they disappeared back into the darkened hallway.

Horace gave a brief nod of his head and with a shrug went back to sweeping the floor.

3:02 PM
Eddie returned to Big Cove and stepped inside his home. He fumbled with the switches by the front door as he stood there dripping rain all over Kina's good rug. The lights refused to come on, and he figured that his house as well as the rest of the neighborhood had fallen victim to the fierce storm.

He knew not to call out to Kina or Jonathon as they still would be at her mother's house in Maggie Valley. After the riot had broken out in town, he insisted they go there along with some of her friends from down the street until things cooled down. Kina protested, but eventually deferred out of concern for their son.

Unilisi, on the other hand, was a different matter. She had demonstrated her mule-headed stubbornness and refused to go anywhere. Eddie eventually relented but insisted that she stay in her room until he got back. And he prayed now that for once she had listened to him.

He went to her room and knocked on the door. "Unilisi…are you there?" He waited as he heard no response. "O-si-yo, Unilisi…ni-hi ha-hna?" He asked again knowing that sometimes she preferred the old language. She again did not respond, but as he pressed against the door, it opened wide into her room. It was dark, darker than the rest of the house, but Eddie immediately recognized the mild, vanilla aroma of her pipe's tobacco that always followed her. As he stepped in further, he could make out his grandmother sitting in a chair near the room's window. "Unilisi…?" Eddie asked as he moved closer to her.

Lightning abruptly flashed close enough to the window that it illuminated the room—coloring it a soft blue. It was not much, but it was enough for Eddie to see. He could tell now that Unilisi was not herself. At least not as he had ever seen her. She had streaked her face with lines of ceremonial paint and she sat there with her hands folded as if in a Christian prayer—fingertips rattling against each other and whispering a low moaning chant. Her pipe was recently doused, leaning sideways in an ashtray on the windowsill. As Eddie knelt in front of her, he could see that her eyes were closed. She seemed oblivious to everything around her.

"Unilisi…" he whispered into her ear. The old woman's body jerked and her eyes batted open. She turned to look into the face of her grandson. She seemed surprised but at the same time also relieved that it was him. "Unilisi," Eddie began again. "I have something for you." He opened his poncho and pulled out the leather bound book from a satchel he had tied around his waist. "It's from Chief Sanooke. He insisted that I give it to you. He said you'd know what to do with it." Unilisi took the book of parchments and laid it in her lap. She ran her weathered fingers down the entire casing of the book as if admiring a great work of art or a cherished family heirloom. "I don't know why or what good it will do…" Eddie started.

Unilisi suddenly rose and walked out of her room and toward the front of the house with surprising speed. Eddie hopped up and followed her out. "Unilisi? Unilisi, where are you going?"

The old woman stopped in the den and turned around laying her frail hand on her grandson's chest. She patted him several times, but said nothing.

"Unilisi…?"

Again the old woman did not respond. Eddie then watched in amazement as she nonchalantly walked out of the front door—the book protected by a fold of her Mother Hubbard wrap.

Eddie followed her out to the front porch and watched as she descended the steps. No words, no protection from the rain. She simply was walking away.

He was at a lost about her actions, but at this point it was just as hard for him to accept his *own*. He knew it was foolish. He knew there was no Tsul-Kalu. No Judaculla. No devil. And he knew it would have no bearing on what was happening with Cole or the murders. Yet as he watched her disappear into the wind and rain of the late afternoon storm, Eddie felt a pang of his ancestral blood pumping through his heart and all of this *craziness* suddenly seemed right.

3:33 PM

Doc Hatcher's '71 Ford F-100 pickup was parked on the corner of his office building like it always was—facing the road—ready to get away at a moment's notice. Thurmond pulled in and crept up the gravel driveway until he came headlight to headlight with Hatcher's truck.

"No sign of Cole's jeep. He may not be here," Amanda said as they emerged from the patrol car.

Thurmond gave a disappointed nod but then just as quickly turned and kept her at bay with a forceful hand warning. He had noticed almost immediately that the door to the building had been left partially open— never a good sign to a suspicious lawman. He and Meyers drew their handguns at the same time and made a guarded approach. They both took a quick glance back in the reporter's direction. Amanda didn't understand their sudden need for caution, but she understood fully they wanted her to stay put. She pulled the hood on her raincoat tight around her head and waited patiently in the downpour.

Thurmond pushed the door in all the way and leaned in his head. "Doc...? Doc Hatcher, you there?"

Hearing nothing but the rain on the roof, he gave a head tilt to Meyers and they both slowly entered. They bypassed the darkened front reception room and little by little began sliding down opposite hallway walls towards the back office. Meyers halted their progress for a moment while he peered into a tiny examination room. Seeing nothing of interest, they continued their way to the back.

As they neared his private office, Thurmond noticed Doc's windbreaker was hanging on a hallway rack and there was a slight scent of smoke in the air. A sudden chill sought out his spine.

"Doc...?" he called out. No response.

Thurmond eyed Meyers who silently gave him the go ahead. In one swift move Thurmond threw his body into the office while simultaneously going to one knee. He had his pistol cupped in both hands and leveled toward Hatcher's desk. Meyers swung in as well but remained standing tall aiming his weapon toward the front of the room.

"No, no...goddamnit, no!" Thurmond yelled as he rose from his position. Meyers looked to the desk and saw it as well. A large blood splatter like the web of a giant spider was imprinted on the back wall and window. From behind the desk, the doctor's feet protruded out in a twisted, unnatural fashion.

Thurmond holstered his weapon and moved to take a glance at the dead body. Doc's face had frozen at bullet's impact—his eyes were squinted shut and his mouth was gaped open.

There was no lament in Thurmond's immediate reaction—just rage—and it was rapidly boiling over. "That son of a bitch! That...bastard!" Thurmond leaned on the desk and pounded it with both fists. He snapped around at the FBI agent. "Is this enough goddamn proof for you?!" He rolled back around and pounded the desk once more. "If it's the last thing I do, I'm gonna nail that cocksucker!"

"Sheriff..." Meyers called out calmly. "Perhaps it would be best to back away from where you are—so as not to disturb any possible evidence."

Thurmond turned and held for a moment wiping the pain and anger from about his face. He recognized his misstep and gave a simple nod. "Yeah...yeah, sure," Thurmond stated in a now much calmer tone. "I'll go to the car and call the station—have our guys put the collar on Whitman."

"Good idea. Contact Pertand at his motel too. Tell him we might be able to use his men to help set up roadblocks."

Thurmond turned to leave but then hesitated as he saw Amanda standing in the doorway—her hand covering her mouth. Her need to know had drawn her inside the building and she flew down to the office after hearing the sheriff cry out. A line of anger still flashed in Thurmond's eyes and he really wanted to lay it on her hard. *What do you think of your ranger friend now?* But he suppressed the impulse to say anything. He figured she knew what everybody else was soon going to know—that the great ranger Whitman was nothing more than a cold-blooded psycho killer—and that thought in itself was enough for him. Thurmond continued on out the door simply turning his shoulders to slide past the shocked reporter.

Meyers pulled rubber gloves out of his coat pocket and slipped them on as he approached the body. He knelt down next to Doc and carefully extracted the bloody hair from around the bullet wound in his forehead. He then traced his line of vision back to the doorway and visualized the assailant's attack position—approximately where the reporter was now standing.

"Something's burning," Amanda said—surprising herself with her own voice.

Meyers turned in the indicated direction. He looked behind the desk and saw the source—an iron-cast wood stove. He tiptoed around the desk and knelt down next to the antiquated heater. Carefully he unhinged the latch and opened the small door. Whatever was inside had only been partially incinerated. He reached in and pulled out a wad of smoldering papers dropping them to the office floor. He put out the remaining burning edges by lightly tapping them down with the sole of his shoe. Then using the pen from his coat pocket, he began gradually to pick through them—charred and fused as they were.

Curiosity continued to get the best of Amanda and she too moved in to take a closer look. They appeared to be part of a medical file like the ones on Cole from the psych center as she noted the stock charts and health diagrams. But then something else caught her eye. "What's that on the bottom? Those yellow pieces there…"

Meyers lifted up the remaining pieces of the white forms and revealed several old newspapers encrusted on the bottom. As they fell apart and scattered to the floor, Amanda focused in on the closest one—its headline screamed out to her:

ROAN BUTCHER STRIKES AGAIN; THREE FOUND SLAIN.

Amanda backed up on her heels. It was the ultimate confirmation—the journey's end. *It had to be him now.* What started out as improbable suspicion and insinuation had finally evolved into this. For the first time since her roommate suggested it, Amanda now felt positive that Cole Whitman was indeed the murderer. Hatcher had known or figured it out. He was going to tell, and Cole came here to stop him. It was the only possible answer.

Amanda all of a sudden felt nauseated—a hard blow to the gut. Her knees became weak and she turned her head. It was too much—she became overcome by an onslaught of emotions.

"What's this?" Meyers asked.

Amanda turned back towards Meyers wiping a tear from her cheek. She was at least thankful that he had not noticed her reaction. "What's what?" she managed in response.

"This…over here…all over the floor," he said pointing to an area near the stove. "It appears to be some kind of grainy, chalky mud or…" Meyers leaned over and wiped the floor with his glove and then held his hand up for Amanda to see. "…white clay."

3:47 PM

Cole cut the jeep's engine on the fly and kept it in neutral so that it would roll silently the final twenty yards down the drive. He hopped out on the run and hurdled a small wooden fence that fronted the farmhouse. He drew his .38 as he leaped up the stone slab steps.

216

Raising his foot, he extended it toward the door, and with his gained momentum, made square contact with the wooden frame. The rusty iron hinges and bolt lock gave way and the door came crashing open into the house.

Ralph Chides had been resting in his favorite lounge chair, a newspaper covering his lap, when Cole attacked. He was so shocked that he barely had time to react only managing to work his way to the end of the chair before Cole was all over him. Cole stuck the cold barrel of the gun in Ralph's neck and grabbed him up by his shirt collar.

"What th' hell...?" Ralph cried out.

Cole pulled Ralph out of the chair and then slammed the surprised man against the wall rattling the house and sending a family portrait crashing to the floor. Ralph grabbed at Cole's arm, but he was way too strong. "What is ya doin', Cole?" Ralph managed.

"Did you think I wouldn't find out?!" Cole screamed. "Did you think no one would know?!"

"Know what, Cole? What the hell is ya....?"

"Doc! Goddamnit! You killed Doc Hatcher! You went to his office this morning and you put a goddamn bullet through his head." His grip went tighter around the man's throat.

"What? No...No, I swear it Cole..."

"You're the only one who farms in that white clay out there and you left tracks of that shit throughout his entire office," Cole said his eyes still ablaze.

The farmer continued to shake his head. "No, no...I swear it, Cole. I been out t' my fields 'til this rain a-started. I ain't gone nowhere. I swear it...I ain't done nothin' t' Doc."

Cole's hand slipped from the throat to the collar, but the intensity in his face remained. "Don't lie to me! No one but you lives on this side of Spring Holler. You're the only one who farms this hill. Your crops, your tractor tires, your entire house has that white powder all over it. It *has* to be you."

Ralph put his hands to his head in anguish as tears formed in his eyes. Cole let go of his hold on Ralph and the pitiful man sank slowly towards the floor. "No, Cole, you must believe me," Ralph tried denying in a soft voice. "I ain't hurt no one. I swear..."

Cole held in silence for a brief moment—the rain falling on the Chides' tin roof was the only discernable noise. "Then who Ralph? You do know, don't you?"

Ralph kept his head down. The tears were flowing faster. "It has t' stop…. This madness has gotta stop."

As Cole watched the broken man sob into his hands, he became conscious of another sound coming directly behind him—the unmistakable *clicking* sound of a weapon's hammer being locked back to fire. Cole made a slow turn—careful not to have his movements warrant any action from the person behind him.

Emma Chides stood there with her wobbly arm outstretched toward Cole—a .38 revolver held loosely in her grasp. She seemed out of it—like she hadn't slept in a week. Her hair was wildly unkempt and her eyes were ringed red—a disconnected blankness to them. Cole gave her nothing to react to, but she strengthened her arm anyway and raised the gun up to Cole's eye level.

"Emma…" Cole said dispassionately.

Ralph looked up from his crouched position. "Oh, Emma, no…" Pushing his back against the wall, he struggled to raise himself up. He stood—his eyes pleading. "No, Em…not Doc too?"

"He was going to tell Cole everything," Emma said in a faint voice. "I just couldn't let him, could I? I couldn't let him tell…"

Ralph closed his eyes fighting back more tears. "Oh, God, no…"

Emma refocused on Cole. "Doc called me this morning too. Said he was gonna tell ya. Said ya might could help. Help my boy, Tommie. But I just couldn't…"

"Tommie…" Cole said trying to comprehend.

Emma paused and breathed in a shaky breath. She tilted her head and drew the hair from in front of her face. "You don't remember me, do you, Cole?"

Cole gave her a puzzled look. His mind was racing—old pains began to flood his thoughts, but, still, he shook his head no.

"I remember you, Cole Millwood. It was long ago. I use to live near ya. Up on Roan," she said, her voice dispirited and faint.

Cole's heart began beating dangerously fast. He heard screams in the distance and then he heard himself mutter, "No…"

Emma continued to stare at him. Her face seemed to take on a different, darker look. "We was neighbors, Cole—you and me. I lived down the mountain road from ya'll. Don't ya remember?"

The .38 dropped from Cole's hand and landed with a thud on the wooden floor. He began to breathe harder—it was a struggle to think. It felt like a thousand needles were being pushed into his brain. And then it came to him, "Emily...Emily Platt."

Emma nodded. Her lips formed words but Cole could barely hear her. It was as if the whole world was now going in slow motion. "That was over twenty-one years ago, Cole." Tears began to roll down her cheeks and her voice was breaking. "Tommie's twenty-one now. Can't ya guess who Tommie's real daddy is?"

Cole saw his father lying on the floor. There was blood everywhere. "No!" he screamed. "This is not happening!" He heard his mother and his brother screaming, begging for their lives. "No!! Stop it!! Please...!" He bent over holding his sides.

"Cole..."

Cole looked back up at Emma—his body trembling—he was fighting it. "Don't tell me this..."

Emma continued on—baring her soul. "It's true, Cole. It happened. I was only fourteen. I was young like you. He grabbed me from my home— that monster did. He took me to an old barn near Silar's pond. He beat me and tied me up...he ripped my clothes off me...he...he did horrible things to me...my God...he wouldn't stop...he did *things*...to me..." Emma's voice faded away; she seemed to completely blank out.

Ralph wiped his face and moved over to her. He gently wrapped his arm around her and removed the gun from her hand. He then embraced her fully and hugged her—letting her collapse into his arms. "Enough blood on our hands, Em...enough." She went out completely and he held her tight as they both sank to the floor.

Cole fell to the floor as well—conscious but not—wrapped in his living, breathing nightmare. He heard his family continue to call out, *Help me...Please stop...I beg you....* His mind couldn't take it; and as it always did during this phase, it finally shut down. Like Emma, Cole had slipped away into a protective, merciful darkness.

The rain outside the house grew even heavier beating on the Chides' roof like a drum. Inside it was not unlike a morgue—cold, quiet and deathly still.

Cole finally awoke, again sucking the air in sharply as if emerging from an iced-over pond. He had no idea when and where he was. He looked around trying to get his bearings. Wooden floors...the tiny farmhouse...the white clay powder...*the Chides.* Cole saw Ralph on the floor holding his wife. She was completely passed out and he was stroking her hair humming a soft lullaby to her. Cole grabbed at his .38 and slid it back in his holster. He then struggled to his feet and went over to them only to go back down again on both knees. He looked at her for a long time trying to remember the girl from down the road. The life before...

"She's a good woman, Cole. She just ain't right in the head no more," Ralph said. "It really ain't her fault."

Cole nodded and reached out and touched her arm. "Can you tell me what happened? She said Tommie was..." Cole stopped—unable to force out the words.

Ralph nodded his understanding. "I met Em five years after Tommie was born. Her daddy had sent her away to live with an aunt up in Tennessee. She told me back then what happened. I didn't care—I loved her anyway. We moved back here eight years ago when my own daddy passed—took over this here farm. And we tried to make a go of it with her boy, Tommie...it just didn't work out."

"What do you mean?"

"Oh, he was a normal enough kid growing up, I guess. Had lotta learnin' problems. But a year after movin' here, when Tommie turned thirteen or fourteen, things got kinda outta hand..." Cole kept his eyes intently on the farmer needing more information. "He started actin' all weird-like...difficult. He stopped listenin' to us. Started hangin' out with some of them damn hooligans on the other side of the Holler there a piece."

"Who?"

"Them Conroy boys mainly. They live in them two trailers off Canyon Road. Got Cherokee in 'um. Ain't no damn good. They filled his head with crazy talk and dared him to do dangerous things."

"But Ralph...that doesn't explain what he did. It doesn't explain murder."

"No, I reckon it don't. I think he just had too much of that bastard's blood in him is all. I don't think he could help hisself. One day I come in from the fields and found our milk cow dead. It was butchered from the belly to the neck." Ralph rubbed his eyes. "I run in the house yelling 'Who a-done it!' And then I seen Tommie come out of his room—blood and all on his hands." Ralph momentarily closed his eyes. "He had it running down his mouth too." He made a pitiful face. "The walls in his room was covered with it." He looked up. "He done a lot of our animals that way. We just couldn't stop 'im."

"For God's sake, Ralph, why didn't you get him some help?" Cole asked realizing the same question could have been asked of him.

Ralph nodded. "Em…didn't want people to know. It was difficult enough for her. I talked her in t' seein' Doc Hatcher, but he had to swear to never tell nobody. He tried different kinds 'a medicines…but none weren't no good. Tommie stopped takin' them pills and then he stopped goin' to see the Doc at all."

"Did Doc know who Tommie's father was?"

"No, not at first. That was our little secret. He knew Tommie had hurt some a'our animals is all. But Doc's a smart man; he musta figured everything else out on his own. I reckon after that ranger friend of yours was kilt, that's when he really started to piece it together."

Cole silently agreed—Doctor Hatcher was a smart man. Cole often had to deflect Doc's probing questions about his own past. Sometimes he felt the old Doc had a sixth sense about such things. And now he's paid for it with his life.

"You could've stopped him, Ralph. You could've told the authorities," Cole said.

"You don't understand. We didn't really know at first. We was hopin' it weren't him. We was hopin' it'd all just go away."

"And when it didn't…? After Nic was killed?"

Ralph shook his head and swallowed his nervousness. "Em's love for her boy made her do crazy things herself."

Cole leaned back with the realization. "Macon Eldridge. That was Emma not Tommie."

Ralph shook his head again in silent agreement.

"To frame the Cherokee…. You knew, Ralph. You had to have known at that point."

"Maybe…maybe I just didn't want to admit it to myself. You of all people, Cole, should know how difficult a thing this has been for all of us."

Cole looked hard at the dirt farmer. He knew he was right. This was a shared tragedy and the Chides were no more to blame than anyone else. Tommie had committed unspeakable crimes like his father—a madness he had inherited and acted upon. Emma, on the other hand, had gone through her version of hell—twice. She just went too far to protect her son—maybe because no one had been there to protect her when she was young. And Cole was tragically unable to help his family in their time of need. The guilt had eaten away at him until it caused *his* madness.

But now he felt he was in a position to set matters right. Now it would be up to him to end it all. Cole stood back up. "Ralph, where is Tommie now?"

"He ain't showed back here for several days. Right soon after th' ranger feller was kilt."

"Ralph…I have to know. I've got to stop him."

"He ain't gonna listen to ya. We can't even approach him no more. He don't reason like a normal person no more."

"Where is he, Ralph?!"

"I swear to God, Cole, I don't know. He'd take off for long periods of time. He'd hike up the hill back toward the Pisgah forest or he'd get them Conroys to take 'im places. I never could track him down. He'd laugh at me. Said I'd never find 'im. He said no one could stop the Sul kaloo or whatever the hell it was he called hisself."

Cole's face tightened in amazement and the hairs on the back of his neck stood on end. "What?"

Ralph just shook his head. "Aw…it's just a name he started to call hisself. Sumptin' them injun boys started him in on no doubt. They was always makin' fun of 'im. Fillin' his head with all kinda nonsense. He thought hisself some kinda unstoppable giant monster. I know it all sounds like crazy talk, Cole."

Tsul-kalu. Judaculla. The monster.

Jesus Christ, Unilisi was right. It all made sense now. The seven-fingered goliath with the razor-sharp claws. The thirst for blood—the need to cause havoc. Smokemont. Graveyard Fields. Chimney Tops. The victims all fell in the realm of the old legend. The land given to the

Cherokees—the Judaculla had claimed for itself. Tommie had traced the giant's steps in its entire domain. It all made sense.

And Cole knew there would be only one possible place the monster would be hiding out now.

5:41 PM

Thurmond's patrol car sat idling outside Manny's—the lights flashing urgently on top and a plume of carbon monoxide shooting out the back. The rain continued to fall relentlessly, pelting blobs on the roof of the car and making a mud bath out of the parking lot.

The evidence from the doctor's office had been bagged and tagged, and the crime scene had been left in the capable hands of Krazenski and Jones. They were to secure the place for the coroner and his team which freed up Meyers and Thurmond to continue the search for Cole.

Meyers was still seated up front on the passenger side reading through his notebook. He periodically made left-handed checks in the margins and scribbled in comments via his own unique short-hand which he had developed over a lifetime as an FBI man. It was all right there in front of him now and yet….something was nagging at him about all this. Maybe it was the tidy way the case had been seemingly finalized. He wasn't use to having the puzzle feel this complete in so many ways and in so quick a time. Or maybe it was the fact that he actually had little to do with the solution. He wasn't ignorant to the reality that he always gained great pleasure in pronouncing verdicts in these matters—it was his job after all. But ego aside, there was still something else. A feeling that he had overlooked something. Something important. He just couldn't put a finger on it.

Meyers flipped back to the front of his notes and thought about beginning the process all over again. He then tossed the notebook aside. Perhaps it would be better if he just let it rest awhile—maybe just strike up a conversation with the attractive reporter sitting behind him—get her perspective on all this. She had seemed emotionally distressed to find Hatcher gunned down the way he was, but that would have been a typical reaction for any citizen. But then she also became strangely quiet throughout the ride from the doctor's office to this little, country store. She seemed to be trying to suppress her emotions about the case—perhaps about the suspect directly. And it made Meyers wonder just how far her relationship with the man had evolved. *What had that psychiatrist said about her? Something about having a connection with Cole?* Over the years Meyers had gotten good at picking up on the sexual connections of victims and suspects during cases—and he wondered about hers. After all, how did she come to suspect him in the first place? Was she that good of a reporter or was she just that good in bed?

"Are you okay?" Meyers asked as he turned to look over the seat. He caught a glimpse of her bare leg sticking out of her raincoat.

Amanda nodded but was rubbing her arms briskly. "Yeah, kind of cold though."

"Heater's on, but I think the sheriff might have left his door cracked," Meyers replied. He leaned over and pulled the door until it clicked tight.

"Thanks," Amanda said distantly.

Meyers smiled. "Strange weather you have up here in these mountains. Beautiful and sunny one minute, pouring and cold as hell the next."

Amanda just shook her head in agreement. She really didn't feel like making small talk of any kind. Not with him. Not now. To her, Meyers represented all that had gone wrong the past few days. He was another symbol of the madness, the hurt that had been brought to these mountains, these people. He was here for the end. He was like those buzzing flies on the carcass of that rotting deer—picking it clean and making it go away. He would finalize everything—including Cole. She was thankful that before he could say anything else to her, Thurmond popped the door back open and slid his massive frame into the driver's seat.

"Any word?" Meyers asked the sheriff.

Thurmond gave a disgusted shake of the head. "Nothing definite. But one of the locals said they think they saw his jeep speeding past here a little while ago. Headin' up the mountain towards the parkway." He jammed the transmission into drive and floored the gas. "He might be able to breach the gates. But don't worry—if he's out there, we'll catch up with 'im soon enough."

The patrol car squealed its way out of the Manny's and back onto Highway 19. Amanda just turned and stared out the window looking at the rain and the endlessly rolling black clouds. She, as well as the two lawmen, seemed acutely-unaware they were headed into the worst of the storm.

6:11 PM

As lightning *popped* and *cracked* all around the darkened Chides' farmhouse, a more distinctive sound *exploded* from within.

Ralph Chides had dressed his wife in her favorite white nightgown and had laid her on her side of their bed. Gently he had kissed her on her forehead and then covered her head with one of her pillows. He had placed the .38 against the pillow; and following a brief hesitation, pulled the trigger—effectively ending Emma's lifelong misery.

He now sat on the edge of the bed holding his dead wife's hand. Her blood had seeped through the pillow's fabric and was now rapidly staining the bed linen as well. "Not your fault," he said in a sweet voice. "You did what you thought was right." He squeezed her hand one final time.

Ralph got up and went to his side of the bed and sat down. He took off his work boots—all covered with the white clay—and dropped them to the floor. He then stuck the barrel of the revolver into his mouth and closed his eyes.

Dear God, forgive us....

The fire crackled through his mouth and then through the back of his skull. He fell against the bed having died instantly.

6:23 PM

Cole ran the jeep up over the curb of the parkway and across the flat bear grass until he reached the head of the Devil's Courthouse trail. He reached under the driver's seat and produced his heavy-duty emergency light. Flipping the switch, he hopped out into the driving rain and began his ascent up the steep ridge. The heavy conifers that lined the trail served as a natural umbrella from the onslaught of rain and wind, and Cole was able to make quick time up the mile and a quarter pathway.

Upon reaching the pinnacle, Cole left the trail and made his way through the laurel hells that entwined the otherwise barren head of the cliff. He knew that anyone or *anything* hiding out on the ridge would find plenty of protection behind the massive boulders and rock formations that were stacked on the eastern end of the ridge. He also knew there was a connector trail which led across the parkway and back over toward the balds of Black Balsam and could be used in case a quick escape was ever needed. He figured now that it must have been the route Tommie used after he killed that hiker in Graveyard Fields and then traveled so close to where he and Amanda had camped on his way back to the Courthouse.

Breaking out into the open, the storm whipped all about Cole in a wicked assault. The swirling wind continually knocked him around and the rain stung at him like thousands of angry wasps. He momentarily regretted not having any covering as he became soaked to the bone, but he surmised that a poncho or rain suit would have been useless at this point anyway. Despite his discomfort, he somehow managed to maintain his purpose and he scanned the ridge with the penetrating beam from his flashlight. He peered into the countless darkened cracks and fissures of the weathered rock face looking for any signs of the elusive Tommie.

For over thirty minutes he searched with no luck. But then as he was looking down between a series of wave-shaped monoliths, the flashlight slipped from Cole's hand and dropped several feet into one of the cracks. Cole stretched his arm into the tight opening but the light stayed just out of the reach of his fingertips. Approaching from another side, he was able to slide his whole body under the rock canopy and crawl sideways to its base. From here the rock formation opened up giving him plenty of room to maneuver. Cole was amazed at how much protection just three feet of rock provided him from the lashing storm above.

Now on his hands and knees, Cole made his way over to the fallen light. As he reached out for it, he thought he heard something move in the darkened recesses ahead of him. Cole fumbled for his .38 and locked it to fire. He centered the light and his weapon at chest level and focused in on an area in front of him. Only a blank rock wall stared back, and Cole breathed out a momentary sigh of relief. But as the light shown on the overhang above, he saw that there *was* something in the cave with him. *Something disturbing.*

On a jutted ledge underneath the rock, four severed bear paws with claws of varying length and sharpness were sticking out just inches from his head. He picked up one from the ledge and held it up to the light. Like the one they found near Nic's body, it had been molded to fit Tommie's hand.

A grotesque band of leathered hide used to hold it in place was strapped around its base. Cole gently drew the claws across the top of his hand raising blood trails everywhere the sharpened points met skin. Cole tried to imagine the horror the victims must have felt as the razor claws gouged and ripped away at them.

Suddenly, Cole began to again feel the swell of his psychosis bubbling up from within. The waves were coming more and more frequently now and he didn't know if he had the ability to quell them anymore. He was still mentally weakened as he barely had time to recover from his latest episode at the Chides' house. In defense of his sanity, he threw the claw against the rock wall and turned away trying to steady his mind—trying to suppress those slow-burning voices and images of his past. He felt swimmy and light-headed, his pulse continued to rise. He knew he had to get out of there.

As he scrambled back toward the base, however, he noticed that against the opposite rock wall there were mounds of raised dirt which had been recently dug. Cole paused, imagining what Tommie had so carefully buried there—animal remains perhaps or maybe even human body parts. But these thoughts also sickened him and continued to weaken his resolve.

Cole reemerged from the rock cave and out into the teeth of the storm. He stood for a moment allowing the wind and rain to clear his head. He then slowly ambled over the ridge making it to the observation deck on the farthest most western point of the Courthouse. There was no sign of Tommie anywhere and Cole was ready to give up the search. Although he had wanted to bring in Tommie himself, he began to second guess his motives for doing so. He considered returning to the station and reporting everything he had discovered so far. He figured now it might be better to engage the FBI and the rest of the team to help out with the search. They could return in the morning after the storm had blown through; and with all that manpower, the hunt for Tommie would go all that much faster.

He went to the edge of the platform to take one final scan of the multi-level ridges that tapered off below the rock face. There were five in all—each one protruding just a little further from the face of the ridge than the last. After the fifth ledge there was that twelve hundred foot drop to the rocky floor of the forest below. Cole hugged up against the brick wall that fronted the observation deck as the wind of the storm beat at him unmercifully. He steadied his light and saw the jutted ridges and the occasional odd rock formation, but there was no sign of Tommie. He was satisfied that he had done all that he could do at this point.

As he stood to leave, Cole was completely unaware that a solitary figure had appeared on a rise behind him.

7:23 PM

Amanda held fast in the back of the patrol car as it winded its way around the sharp curves of the closed parkway. She grabbed at her stomach as she started feeling queasy from the motion of the car and from a serious lack of food. She came to realize that the only thing she had eaten all day was that pack of peanuts she had had on the morning flight in from New York. And now nausea was just the latest addition to this never-ending day of misery.

Up front, Thurmond and Meyers kept a steady vigil—their eyes peeled and their senses attuned to any signs of Cole or his jeep.

"All highways leading out of Cherokee are blocked," Thurmond began. "The park is sealed and highway patrol has access to interstates 26 and 40 contained. If he's on to us and trying to run then his only escape route would be this way…up the parkway."

"But there are lots of these maintenance roads and scenic overlooks off this road—perfect areas to hide," Meyers said pointing to one as they flew past. "Let's make sure Pertand's men get a unit to cover each one."

Thurmond nodded. "Will do." He thought for a moment before adding, "Most of the roads lead to remote spots. But the forestry rangers can seal off each one and we can resume an air search in the morning if we need to."

Meyers just nodded focusing in on the upcoming mountain tunnel the parkway was about to run through when he caught sight of something out of the corner of his eye. "What's that?" he said turning and tapping his finger on his window.

"Oh, my God…" Amanda said leaning forward in her seat. She also pointed out toward the right window. "That's it! That's his jeep!"

Thurmond made a hard right and swerved the patrol car off the road tearing into the mud and grass of the shoulder. The patrol car fish-tailed for several yards and then quickly slammed to a halt.

"What the hell is he doing here?" Meyers wondered aloud as he threw open his door.

Thurmond ignored the question. "Stupid bastard…got 'im now." He hastily grabbed for his radio. "All units—respond! All units—respond! Suspect vehicle in sight—mile marker 422 on the Blue Ridge Parkway! The Devil's Courthouse! Officers proceeding on foot…" Thurmond threw the attached microphone on the car seat and hopped out. He quickly retrieved a flashlight and a Mossberg double-barrel shotgun from the trunk of the patrol car and followed after Meyers who had already made his way around Cole's jeep and was headed up the trail.

Amanda held in the back seat unsure of what to do. As she watched them head up the trail, she heard several responders calling back to Thurmond over the radio confirming their approach. Within minutes the entire area would be crawling with guardsmen and police. Amanda realized that she would soon have no chance to get the answers to the thousands of questions running through her head. And she needed those answers now. She wanted to look Cole Whitman in the face. She wanted to know how he could have possibly done such a thing. How he could have fooled so many people—*especially her*.

Amanda opened the car door and stood in the rain. She kicked off her heels, stripped out of her bulky raincoat and headed up the trail running as fast as she could.

7:27 PM

Tommie raised his hands high above his head and leaped from the rise onto Cole's back. He brought the claws down on the top of Cole's shoulders shredding the ranger's shirt and drawing out copious amounts of blood. Cole yelled out in agony—his flashlight falling to his feet. He pulled away from Tommie's grip and spilled over the top of the platform plunging twelve feet to the ridge below. He immediately winced in more pain as he had shattered his right knee cap and sprained his right wrist upon impact.

Cole collapsed from his unstable kneeling position and rolled over onto his injured back. He took a quick glance up at the platform. Although he knew it was Tommie, he wasn't prepared for the actual sight of his transformation as the Judaculla. His hair was blowing wildly in the wind and he was completely naked save blood-smeared tattoos over his entire body. And now with the savage claws extending from his arms, he no longer looked human at all. He was grotesque, horrifying—he had indeed become the Cherokee's monster of legend.

Tommie leaped from the platform wall and attacked. He brought the claws across Cole's face ripping open his cheek and gouging his left eye. Cole found the strength in his arms and managed to throw Tommie off of him and scramble to his feet. As Tommie swung his arms again, Cole blocked the move and was able to punch the madman hard on the side of his head. But Tommie lunged at Cole once again screaming manically in his ear.

This time both men fell intertwined to the next ledge. It was a shorter fall of eight feet but Cole landed on a rock half-earthed in the ledge and shattered several ribs. The air exploded out of his lungs and Cole had to struggle to force them back into action. Somehow he managed to get to his knees and to pull his .38 from its holster. But before he could fire, Tommie was all over him and the two made another roll off the tier falling fifteen more feet.

By the time Cole shook off the stun of the latest fall, the weapon was nowhere to be found. He was hugging the ground—his hands slapping at the rock—desperate in his search. And then he saw through his right eye that Tommie was coming at him once more. Cole struggled to his feet barely able to lift his arm to defend himself. A flash of lightning lit up the sky and Cole noticed fresh blood pouring from Tommie's mouth and nose, but it wasn't slowing him down at all. Tommie swung his claws across Cole's chest and drew more of his blood. Cole yelled again in pain and crumbled to his knees. He held up his shaking left hand. "Tommie...stop...please..." he begged.

Tommie held for a moment—perhaps confused by hearing his real name—but then his eyes rolled to white and following a high pitched, animal-like scream of his own, he went in for the kill.

7:32 PM

"Jesus Christ! What was that?" Meyers yelled as he came to a stop on the trail. He tried to peer past the wind-blown trees and the rocks of the ridge to see if he could find the source of the savage scream, but they were still too far away.

Amanda fell in behind him having easily moved up the trail past the out-of-shape sheriff. The mud from the worn path had caked up onto her feet and legs and the rain had drenched her from head to toe, and now she stood next to the

FBI agent shaking from the miserable conditions. But she was undaunted in her desire to be there, to be a part of the story's end. "What was it?" she asked through chattering teeth.

Meyers blew out a breath. "I dunno. Something...sounded like a scream—a man screaming."

Thurmond swinging the shotgun back and forth in his meaty arms and breathing heavily finally caught up with them as well. "What's happening? Why'd ya'll stop?" he managed.

"Agent Meyers thought he heard Cole screaming," Amanda said. She turned and pointed. "Somewhere near the top."

Thurmond nodded quickly. "That's out near the observation point. Could be harming himself again...maybe even a suicide. C'mon."

All three took off back up the trail with Amanda again starting out in the back. The reporter's face became grim and she bit down on her lip. It was the last thing she wanted to come upon, but she knew the sheriff was probably right. Her gut now told her that when they got to the top they would find Cole Whitman dead—just like the others. The same as Nic Turner and Macon Eldridge and Rayford Parker. The same as that Jacobs man from Tennessee, the young boy from Cherokee, Doc Hatcher and probably those missing hikers too. And, of course, the same as Cole's family. It was coming full circle, and Amanda saw it very clearly now. He had suffered terribly and everyone who came into contact with him eventually suffered as well—including Amanda. She realized now this would be a part of her suffering, her price for being involved—to be there at the end—to tell his story—to explain Cole Whitman to the world. And upon reaching the top of this ridge, to report on his last act—his own self-inflicted demise.

7:35 PM

Tommie brought his right arm under Cole's feeble block attempt and skewered his abdomen with the sharpened claws. Cole gave out a deep moan as he felt his blood pour from his body. His body buckled and he sensed his life ripping away. He grabbed Tommie's leg with his left arm in a desperate attempt to slow him down and dropped his right hand down near his foot. Despite the shock and pain of the attack, Cole remembered the knife that his father had given him all those years ago and unsheathed it from his boot.

As Tommie raised his arm for the final blow, Cole ran the knife behind Tommie and jabbed it deep into the small of the madman's back.

Tommie let out a scream of unholy terror as he arched his back and wildly threw up his hands. Cole reached out and twisted the knife until he felt the hot pour of blood on his fingers. Tommie collapsed on top of him kicking and scratching at the ground. Cole bent backwards towards the edge and the forced motion pulled them both from the precipice. They went crashing down another ten feet onto the fourth and next to last ledge of the Courthouse.

Cole struggled to one knee and saw that Tommie had landed beyond him and was now just a few feet directly in front of him. Tommie looked like a wild animal as he lashed at his back trying to remove the pinned knife. Blood ran down Cole's face and for a moment he felt himself losing consciousness. He gritted his teeth and forced his body to stand. The gale force winds from the storm continued to rock his stability but he knew he had only one chance left. Tommie managed to pull out the knife and stood there his face riddled with pain and confusion. Cole saw his opportunity—an opportunity to end it all.

Using what little strength he had left, Cole lunged at Tommie with all his might. He tackled him around the waist sending them both off the ledge. They fell straight backwards and then parted in mid-air. Tommie came down first—clawing at the rock face below him. But the momentum from the push was too great and caused him to bounce off the fifth and final ledge and tumble helplessly over the side. There was no other barrier. He fell through the clouds, the mist and rain for over a thousand feet to the rocks below. His body landed broken and smashed against the rocks. Tommie was dead. The Judaculla had been vanquished.

Cole had also landed hard on the last ridge, but he had managed to grab at a horn-shaped rock protruding from the outer shelf which prevented him from sliding off the side. His body had come to a sudden stop there on the rocky edge of the cliff. He now closed his eyes—his breathing sharp and labored. All he knew to do now was just to hold on to that rock.

Cole laid there for a minute trying to breathe, trying to stay awake. Every bone felt broken, every muscle felt torn. He thought he heard voices shouting at him, but he wasn't sure. They weren't the ones he normally heard, the ones from his past. It did not seem to matter now anyway. He felt himself blacking out. His body was beyond injury, beyond pain. He could not stay conscious any longer. The voices were getting louder, but he could not make them out. He could not understand. He was passing out; he was finally succumbing to the darkness.

It was over.

June 9, 1974

10:47 AM

Dressed in shorts, a black tee shirt and hiking boots, and with her auburn hair pulled back in a ponytail, Amanda walked slowly and self-assuredly up the pathway of the Devil's Courthouse. The sun shone brightly through the forest canopy allowing slivers of golden light everywhere along the trail. There was a slight mountain breeze wafting though the leaves; and with the temperature in the low 70's, nothing felt like it did two weeks ago when Amanda was last here.

It still all felt so surreal to her. All that had happened. The past few weeks had gone by in a blur and it was only now that she believed that she had finished processing it all. She had just completed her latest tie-in article to the case trying to explain the loose end's and follow-up's to a world still fascinated by the story. But she knew there would be some questions, some of the mystery, never fully answered.

Personally she had won great acclaim for her series of articles on the case. She had been inundated with job offers from media hubs all over— including a beef-upped position back at the *Post*. But she was still undecided on her next move—still undecided about so many things....

Amanda rounded the turn in the trail and headed underneath the cap of the ridge toward the observation platform. As she came out into the opening, she saw Dr. Jack Snyder leaning against a large rock—an orange nylon bag at his feet. He held a book of some sort in his hands and he seemed to be relaxing, taking in the beautiful weather. He caught the reporter's approach.

"Hello, Ms. Rivers," he began. "It's good to see you again."

Amanda stopped in front of him. "And you. I appreciate you giving me a call. It means a lot to me that you did."

Snyder smiled. "You're welcome. But it wasn't my idea. He wanted to see you before we left. And I just thought it was a good chance for you both to have some closure." He went to a more serious tone. "I realize this hasn't been easy for either one of you."

Amanda smiled at his concern. "Why here?"

The doctor pulled the book close to his chest. "Hmmm—I think there's a kind of symmetry involved in it. Don't you agree?"

Amanda nodded her agreement. "Where is he?"

Snyder looked over to the platform and then tilted his head in its direction. "Take as long as you like. I'll be right here."

Amanda acknowledged the doctor and continued on out the trail to the observation platform. It was simply gorgeous at the top as the sun was shining in the bright, blue Carolina sky. There were no others on the platform save one man standing next to its stone-block wall. Even from a distance Amanda could tell it was Cole. She thought it ironic that he was wearing the same jeans and wine-colored shirt from that night they had spent together. Amanda felt a little scared as she walked up behind him—no longer physically afraid of him, only of what he might think of her now.

Cole turned as he heard her approach. He instantly disarmed her by giving her a huge smile. She smiled back at him in return although a part of it had to be forced. She was taken aback somewhat by his altered appearance. His fight with Tommie had taken a toll on him and his looks had suffered as a result. The left side of his face was still swollen from the hundreds of stitches that had been used to tie his cheek back together. He also now wore a black patch over his left eye which had been ruptured by one of Tommie's claws. His right arm was in a cast and sling and he wore it sticking out of the inside of his shirt. A walking cane was propped up by his side. But even though he was in this weakened and infirmed condition, there was still a measure of strength to Cole for which Amanda couldn't account. Something in the way that he stood, the way that he smiled, and the way that he was looking at her now.

"You alright?" he asked.

Quick words—simple question—typical Cole, Amanda thought. "I'm fine. How are you feeling?" She reached out and brushed his wind-blown hair out of his face.

"Better," he stated. He looked over toward the direction of where Snyder was standing. "I hope to be much better soon."

Amanda smiled but tears welled in her eyes. "Oh, you will, Cole. You'll be just fine now. Everything's going to be okay."

Cole's head dropped slightly towards the ground.

"Cole," Amanda started again. "I'm sorry that it came to this." The tears rolled down her cheeks now. "I'm sorry that I didn't trust you."

Cole looked back up, his face also wet. He reached out with his right arm and grabbed her by the waist. "No, Amanda, it's okay. I'm the one who should be apologizing."

"But I should have come to you. I should have believed in you."

"My God, Amanda, you saved my life by doing what you did. I was the one with the problem. I was the one who couldn't trust...who *wouldn't* trust anyone. I put too many people's lives in danger over the years...including my own. Believe me when I tell you, you've helped put an end to all of this misery."

Amanda leaned in and gently hugged Cole putting her head on his chest. "Still..."

"No, Amanda, you saved my life and I'll never forget it. You've given me a second chance to heal. A second chance to put all this behind me."

Amanda looked up at him. She leaned up on her toes and kissed his forehead. "But this time...you won't have to do it alone."

Cole smiled back at her, nodded, and then kissed her on the cheek. "C'mon. You can start by helping this broken old man back down the hill." He breathed in deeply and took one final look out over the ridge before refocusing on her. "I think it's time to go."

Amanda put her arm inside of his and the two walked back toward the trail and together began the journey back down the ridge.

High up on a rise above the platform Unilisi secretly watched them as they disappeared down the wooded path. She was standing barefoot on square black cloth holding the book of parchments tight in her right hand—her pipe firmly clenched between her teeth. As they disappeared from her sight, she turned and refocused on her task. With her left hand, she sprinkled a white clayish powder on the rocks around her. She then held her hand above her head to allow the dusty remnants to scatter into the prevailing winds. She read from the parchments and chanted its secretive power in the ancient language—doing as she had been charged to do—keeping the Judaculla secure from her world forever.

Afterwards, she walked to the edge of the rise and gave witness to the Smoky Mountain skyline. Wisps of white clouds danced about the gentle sea of hills and forests below. All was as it should be: majestic, timeless, magical.

CPSIA information can be obtained at www.ICGtesting.com
Printed in the USA
LVOW13s0929140114

369251LV00001B/7/P